Marrying it All

For you, and the feminine
spirit in all of us,

best wishes

Diana Button
15th November 2003
Luxembourg

Marrying it All

Diana Button

iUniverse, Inc.
New York Lincoln Shanghai

Marrying it All

iUniverse, Inc.

For information address:
iUniverse, Inc.
2021 Pine Lake Road, Suite 100
Lincoln, NE 68512
www.iuniverse.com

This book is a work of fiction. Names, characters and places are products of the author's imagination. Any resemblance to actual persons is entirely coincidental.

Cover picture: original oil painting entitled 'Flying on Joy' by Diana Button.

ISBN: 0-595-29156-2

Printed in the United States of America

I dedicate this novel to all the women in my life
– especially –

Karen, Corinna, Nicola, Julia

and
Sophie

She
by Charles Aznavour

She may be the face I can't forget
A trace of pleasure or regret
May be my treasure or the price I have to pay
She may be the song that summer sings
May be the chill that autumn brings
May be a hundred different things
Within the measure of a day
She may be the beauty or the beast
May be the famine or the feast
May turn each day into a heaven or hell
She may be the mirror of my dream
A smile reflected in a stream
She may not be what she may seem
Inside her shell
She who seems so happy in a crowd
Whose eyes can be so private and so proud
No one is allowed to see them
When they cry
She may be the love that cannot hope to last
May come to me from shadows of the past
That I remember till the day I die
She may be the reason I survive
The why and wherefore I'm alive
The one I'll care for through rough and rainy years
Me, I'll take her laughter and her tears
And make them all my souvenirs
For where she goes I've got to be
The meaning of my life is 'She'
She, she, mmm…mmm, she.

Contents

BOOK THREE

THE ONE BEFORE AND AFTER
CHAPTER I

Sabina sensed before coming to live in Luxembourg that it was a significant move in her life; yet she only knew it as she typed the individual letters L-e-t-s-e-r-b-e-e-r-g-i-s-h into the word-processing document on the computer.

"*Lët-ze-bur-gesch*," she wrote, "is the name given to the national language of Luxembourg...

"It lives under the motto: *mir wölle bleiwe wat mir sin* (we want to be who we are), yet does not have a way of saying, 'I love you.' The closest you can get is, 'I am pleased with you.'...

"Though this has nothing to do with the political, judicial or administrative difficulties caused by the language, statistics have shown that it is frequently mistaken for English and vice versa.

"So far, there is no explanation for this bizarre phenomenon but there does seem to be one common denominator: most false identifications have occured when half hearing the language from a distance; words from a conversation in a shop, cafe, or on the streets drifting through the air like radio waves to where the person is standing, sitting or passing by.

"It is only when the person tunes in to the sound and really listens to it, that the language can be correctly identified...."

This phenomenon had fascinated Sabina for the seventeen years she had been living in the country but it was only now that she was beginning to understand why.

"In *Lëtzebuergesch*, the word *féiss* sounds like 'face' but means feet; the word *ei* sounds like 'eye' but means egg; the word *mi* sounds like 'me' but means more;

and the word *Pit* is pronounced and written as the English word 'pit', but actually means Peter.

"These words are like an overlap—an integration of two circles called language. Socio-linguists would no doubt laugh at the idea of an investigation into a linguistic correlation between the English language and the mere dialect (by linguistic definition) of *Lëtzebuergesch.* It would probably be called a meaningless freak of language exacerbated by the polysemous nature of English. In short, this negligible overlap would be treated with as little acknowledgement and respect as *Lëtzeburgesch* is treated by non-speakers living in the language's country. Ignored. The same-sounding words wouldn't even earn the grand name of *faux amis* (false friends) like English-looking French words such as *attend* and *sensible* do. False friends they are indeed—the one telling you to attend when it means wait and the other calling you sensible when you are actually being sensitive! They could get you into a lot of trouble. But couldn't the English-sounding Lets-er-beer-gish words get you into just as much trouble and so warrant scientific attention? Washing your face instead of your feet may not pose too much of a problem. But what about gobbling up your eyeball instead of your egg? Or jumping into a pit instead of going to see Peter? Of course, this is just tomfoolery. I am merely letting language jump and shuffle like pegs in a one-player game of *Solitaire.* Only a fool could be entertained by such self-righteous, intellectual masturbation!..."

She was shocked (and, at the same time, pleased) by her own subversiveness and wondered whether to delete the lot. *Not yet,* she told herself. *Let yourself be as subversive as you like—it's only a computer!* And she carried merrily on.

"...False friends, my dear, implies two players, not one. It's not masturbation—but a coupling. No, more than that! Group sex—an orgy—all bonking each other; scrubbing backs, arses and exchanging bodily fluids. Try and muddle out which one is 'false' and which is the 'friend' in that! How would you find out? Look for the one who screams the loudest, has the biggest..., the largest..., the most desirable?...

"Or are they all false?"

She stopped. *This isn't what I want! I want something meaningful, true, believable—clever, not vulgar, farcical and...*her mind trailed off as her hand took command, bashing her fingers down onto the keys with more force than ever.

"Fool! Thinking it is a game you are playing. Thinking you have heard right, know the rules. It isn't the language that is important—false friends or not false friends—pah!...

"Who cares?...

"It's the *non-words* that count!—that which is not said—

"That is what you must listen out for, my dear False Friend. That is what conceals the lot—the truth!"

And after clapping her hands in delight and yelping, not in pain as usual, but in pure joy, she let her fingertips dance over the keys as if composing a piano concerto, feeling, as she did, that a flash of blue sky had just broken through the cloud-cover of her mind like a line of code looms out of a computer programme to crack a complex computation.

What landed next in her New Document was perhaps not as profound as 'The truth, the whole truth,' or 'To be or not to be,' but, as far as Sabina was concerned, it was the key to her whole story. And with great pride, she placed in bold type and central on the page, the words

Things are not
always
what they appear
to be

Keeping this newly discovered wisdom in a minimized window at the edge of the screen, she began.

New Document

'Once upon a time in the fairytale kingdom of Luxusberg, a disease started to spread called Luxusitis.

Top physicians from around the world came to Luxusberg in search of a cure for this insidious disease and hoped that in doing so, they would find fame and fortune. They tried out all kinds of pills, all kinds of therapy and all kinds of diets. They didn't become famous, but they did make their fortunes. Alas, most could not enjoy the riches they obtained because they had stayed too long in the kingdom and had themselves become infected with the disease.

One sunny winter day, a woman called Pinderess came to Luxusberg. She recognised the problem at once and knew there was no medical solution. The disease originated from a place called 'Sowless' where it was kept at the ideal temperature of 14 degrees Celsius ready to infect lands in which wealth stood above humanness. This is why the disease had infected Luxusberg—a kingdom in which the rich congregated, conferred and competed. The people of Luxusberg had so much money that they forgot about the simple pleasures in life but relied on wealth as their main source of happiness. The day they stopped feeling any joy whilst sipping a glass of Grand Premier Cru or eating a dozen wild oysters, was the day the disease attacked.

Many sufferers threw themselves from the highest bridge in the kingdom.

The king, in desperation to stop his subjects doing this and spoiling his good reputation with neighbouring lands, ordered his royal army to erect special concave shields along the bridge's entire length. When sufferers started to throw themselves out of high-rise buildings, he ordered his royal army to secure all windows of all buildings and passed a law forbidding constructions higher than three storeys. Anyone wishing to open a royal-secured window on a hot day could only do so with special permission from the king.

Poor Luxusburg: one of the richest kingdoms in the world; yet so impoverished—a mere secure setting for a soulless play.'

Sabina glanced at the digital clock on her computer screen: *12:00. My God, how time has flown. Where did it disappear to? Where did I disappear to?*

* * * *

She turned to face her document on the screen, pressed Ctrl, Page Up simultaneously to get to the beginning of her piece of writing and typed:

Curtain Up

BOOK ONE

Mirror Talk

'I want my Mummy,' shouted the little girl, picking herself up from the gravel pavement and running towards her house away from the boys who had pushed her. 'Mummy, Mummy,' she screamed as she ran round to the back of the house and into the garden. The graze covered the entire knee and blood was running in thin stripes down her leg, into her favourite lacy white ankle socks. 'Poor darling,' her mother sympathised as she bent down to examine the injury. 'That looks sore!' Sabina sobbed and sank into her mother's open arms, resting her head on her soft breasts, tears rolling down her cheeks and into her mother's cleavage. Her mother gently dabbed the wound clean with damp cotton wool, smeared some antiseptic cream all over and covered the whole lot with a giant plaster. 'Some chocolate?' Sabina nodded whilst her body convulsed uncontrollably with violent sobs. She cuddled up under her mother's large bathrobe on the sun-lounger in the garden, popped the piece of chocolate into her mouth and closed her eyes. That was the second time those boys had chased her, trying to lift up her mini skirt to see her knickers. *I hate them, hate them, hate them! Snips and snails just like in the nursery rhyme.* 'Here's some refreshing water, my little bee,' her mother said and lovingly placed an orange-coloured glass into Sabina's trembling hands. This particular glass turned every drink, even water, into an exotic-looking cocktail. Outside, in the sunshine, it turned her water to gold.

Sabina was ten. Not a bad thing had ever happened to her and she believed it never would. Her family was not just safe and sound—it was invincible. She had it fathomed: bad things only happened to the neighbours or people in strange countries.

* * * *

What? Sabina asks. *Where did I disappear to?* Though her rational mind knows full well that a bathroom mirror can't transport someone thirty years into the past, respond to questions, or smack you in the face, hers had done all these things in the space of a week. Today Sabina feels a further development is in the making: her mirror seems to be thoroughly enjoying itself. It is feasting on her as if she were a turkey with all the trimmings and still steaming from hours in the hot oven. Travelling into the past and being hit in the chops was just the starter. Now it was tugging at the meat, ripping it off the bone, grinding it fiercely with it's teeth and rudely regurgitating food at her every utterance of a question. The only morsel she caught was in response to, *When are you going to give me some answers?* Though edible, Sabina found her mirror's 'what is an answer if not a question?' far from the palatable reply she had hoped to get.

It all began on the Millennium night when her mirror first struck a blow to her most sensitive facial feature (nose) and then launched into a full attack. Without so much as a sip of Champagne to dull the pain, it had simply lashed out with the unrelenting observation that her life was deficient in one basic ingredient: *life*—and sent her crashing to the bathroom floor.

A few moments before the final gong of the Millennium midnight hour had sounded, and her mirror miraculously transformed into a beast, she had innocently asked: *what have I got to take with me into the New Millennium?* She had expected to hear one of her standard replies like *a bag full of cheap make-up*, or *a house full of your husband's sweaty socks*. But no! She wasn't given a chance. The mirror butted in, gave her a full whack on the conk and said, *Nothing. There is no 'life' in your life.*

So, on that very special New Year's Eve in which people world-wide were yelling for joy as soon as the 99 changed to 00, Sabina was being broken into by her bathroom mirror like one breaks into a fortune cookie, the wise slip of paper yanked from her centre and the results reflected like two vacant eyes in the large looking glass: 00.

Exactly when her life had became devoid of its main ingredient, she's not certain (her mirror answered that question with *which life?*) but she thinks that one day as she was floating through the pipe she called life like one ambles along a nondescript road in a nondescript town, her identity, vitality, and *joie de vivre* ran off her face and down the plug hole together with her foundation cream, mascara and blusher (when all she had wanted to do was wash them off before going to bed!).

One hour into the Millennium and she vowed not to wash her face at night anymore—mildly hoping that 'life' might miraculously crawl back into her body through her ever-widening pores whilst she lay asleep in bed.

Two hours into the Millennium and she took down the following dictation:

New year's Resolution
1. Drive over the Red Bridge
2. _ _ _

It was going to be a list of vows to make up for her life deficiency; but she was so overcome with emotion at the thought of completing number one on the list that she scrunched the paper into a tight ball and hurled it with great force into her toiletry bag before her mirror could say (or do) anything to stop her.

A week into the Millennium and her mirror is asking her for the trillionth time why she doesn't take some constructive action for a change. Now that her urge to smash it into as many pieces as it smashed her is gradually subsiding, she is beginning to give it some serious thought: *Surely there is a simple way of salvaging that which has accidentally gone down the drain*...she muses.

...*Yes, why not call up a plumber to open up the pipes and fish out your lost earrings, wedding ring, milk teeth, and all the other precious things that have been swallowed by your sink, toilet, washing machine and dish washer?* her mirror sarcastically replies and maliciously flashes the white ball of paper at her from the bulging toiletry bag. Sabina retrieves it, smoothes it flat with her palm and, feigning a sigh of defeat for the sake of getting out of the bathroom before nightfall, takes an eye-liner pen and scribbles under item number 1:

2. Call Madame Anastasia

Then she folds the piece of paper into a neat rectangle, slides it into her back pocket and peers into the mirror. What comes back is far from the acknowledgement she hoped for. Her crow's feet pertinently grow legs and stomp madly around, leaving a trail of ugly little four-pronged footprints. Soon, there is not one square-millimetre trace of wrinkle-free skin in the eye area. Her fetching sand-speckled skin covering her cheeks (a remnant of childhood freckles) starts rapidly fading and the once distinguished-looking female nose erupts into a long, pointed protrusion even Pinocchio would be ashamed of.

I really will do it! she shouts and then, a little calmer, *How come you knew?* The mirror stares and, in its habitual, irritating manner, answers her question with another one: *Is it I or you who knew?* Before she has a chance to think of a reply, it is babbling all sorts of nonsense about growing up and genes and problems and passing on unsolved questions to the children…

Sabina doesn't let the mirror finish. She launches into a counter attack with strings of sentences she hopes will knit themselves into an effective web of defence. *It's nothing to do with me! You're just giving me more to worry about. Answer all the questions my family didn't manage to! So much for the growing up—going round and round—that's what we're doing. You mean I have to contend with my mother's greying hair because she didn't realise you're not supposed to pluck them out when they first sprout? Will my split nails fail to mend because father refused to eat gelatine? Will my varicose veins spread all the way up to my belly button because auntie Ethel couldn't afford support tights? Will all of uncle Bill's bulbous knuckles sprout overnight if I don't stop scrubbing the toilet bowl?* Then with a dramatic swipe at the mirror's ogling eyes, she finishes triumphantly with, *What about my auntie Vera's blue rinse and false teeth?*

The mirror simply hides its clenched teeth and resists the temptation to kick her perfect ones in. It would save that for later. It knew that her teeth had always been her most prided feature. Her teeth were so perfect, in fact, that when giving birth, the doctor had held a dish in front of her face and said she could drop them in there. 'Drop what?' she had asked in dismay. 'Your dentures, of course!' he had retorted. 'But, they're real!' she had protested, pulling at the front two to prove it. She needn't have bothered; he had sulked off to fetch forceps to pull baby through the birth canal and get home in time for tea.

Her imperfections (i.e. all of her face except the teeth) is covered laboriously and thoroughly in cosmetics: anti-blemish cream, foundation, eye-liner, mascara, eye-shadow, cheek and nose decreasing blusher, feature enhancer, and last but not least, highlighter for those days she's feeling more confident about her eyes. The make-up bag has become such an essential part of Sabina's daily life that she would rather burn in the house than leave without it. She fancies that her lips would not curve upwards as they do when she applies lipstick (forming a lovely delta shape), but slip down towards her full chest and point embarrassingly at her overly large boobs. That would completely annul all painstaking endeavours at concealing them using specially selected baggy shirts and jumpers. The rest of her wardrobe, (ten pairs of dark-coloured synthetic trousers) cover her other disaster zones: varicose legs and fatty thighs. Even when the thermometer climbs to 40 degrees Celsius, she would rather sweat than reveal an inch of her body. And the hair, though of exceptional quality, does tend to get drab-looking in winter. Once, a well-meaning hairdresser tried to persuade her that a 'few highlights would add extra vitality and colour.' She refused and never went back. No one was allowed to criticise her except herself; she would rather hack at her own hair, thank you very much!

The face in the mirror sneers; it knows why the skin around her mouth is cracking: *Did you smile too much in your youth, huh?* it provokes.

Well, even if I did, there's no danger of that now! she promptly retorts and pretends to swat a fly in front of her face (how she would love to crack it's shiny surface). Her voice makes a slight lisping noise as she continues complaining about her inability to smile, sounding like a pouting child with a cold, and giving the general impression that she is a soft and fragile person—perhaps even a little self-pitying. And then, as if she were an actor who had just received contradictory instructions, her arms start flailing at her reflection: *All this,* she shouts as the windmill arms spin wildly round, *is because I'm going to be forty!*

The dysfunctional old mill in the mirror says nothing and Sabina grabs the hot tap and twists.

I wonder how my mother felt when she was forty?

When Sabina's mother was forty, she spent most afternoons in the utility room, ironing and telling amusing stories. Sabina was thirteen then and spent hours in there with her, watching and listening. The mesmerising power lasted from the first T-shirt to the last crumpled tea towel. All the incidents of the past were told with a cheerful enthusiasm, which made her mother's face crease and eyes glisten with teardrops: she was ebullient on those afternoons.

"You know, Sabina, before you were born, your sister Jennifer wished for a puppy more than anything in the world. I always used to say that we were having a baby, not a dog, and we can't have both. You were only a few months old when she looked at me seriously and said: 'Mummy, you have to give Sabina back to the doctor in the hospital.' 'Why's that, darling?' I asked. 'Well,' she replied, 'we've had the baby for a long time and now I'd really like to have a dog.'"

Sabina forgot about her teenage troubles, exams, peer pressure, and the bullying at school as she let herself be whisked away to a land of tales far away from life's problems: her mother eschewed them with more skill than she knew she possessed, desperate to abscond to the safety of the utility room and the children's innocent past. Sabina never tried to discuss her feelings, worries and fears, but kept them to herself. And in a kind of unspoken solidarity, her mother did the same.

Most of Sabina's adolescence was spent in the cosy, industrious room. It was amazing how the washer, dryer, ironing board and boiler all fitted in—crammed in snugly together.

Her mother's long, black hair swished forwards and backwards in time to her arm pushing the iron. A hair flew out, floated down and disintegrated on the hot metal plate. Sabina wrinkled her neatly freckled nose at the smell and her mother laughed and rejoiced. 'Well, that's one less in the Sunday dinner!' Steam rose from the shirts, tea towels, and sheets, engulfing them in a cloud of hot vapour.

* * * *

Sabina plunges cupped hands into the sink and repeatedly draws them out, splashing warm water into her face. It feels good. The mirror mists over and, after patting her face dry, she uses the towel to wipe clear a melon-sized area. It's a futile exercise, she concedes, because all she has done is draw a fuzzy circle, which insists on reminding her of the round window in her mother's utility room. That window used to paint a hazy picture of the two women in there all blended and blurred. On winter days like this one, Sabina remembers, it was permanently covered with condensation.

* * * *

Water inside the iron sloshed, the ironing board legs creaked, her mother's bracelet chimed and the electric cord melodically tap-danced on the side of the dryer. In no time at all she had completed another shirt and glanced up to see if Sabina was still there. She was mesmerised.

"I used to put you into the carry cot, place it on top of the washing machine and press the spin button. You would be asleep before the drum had turned ten times!"

Sabina smiled and decided to stay in the room until the last article had been ironed. Today it was a large bed sheet. Her mother pulled it out, sighed deeply and dedicatedly proceeded to fold it in half, spray starch on it and glide over it with the iron. She winked at Sabina and confessed her secret:

"I cheat, you know," she said, looking over her shoulder to check that no-one else was listening. Sabina looked at her questioningly.

"I only iron the top side," she admitted with guilt. "When it's on the bed, you would never know."

Sabina looked at the huge pile of ironed clothes threatening to topple over and wondered what on earth her mother was talking about. Surely she didn't believe she was cheating.

"He's very particular about his shirts!" she insisted as she spent longer smoothing one shirt of his than she'd spent on every other item from the ironing basket. "I'm only glad he doesn't wear those old-fashioned cotton ones anymore. They were a pig to iron!"

And her arm carried on moving to and fro; the machines carried on washing; and the rain carried on tapping at the windowpane, driven by the wind.

Sabina leant on the tumble dryer and let the vibrations massage her lower back. The dull droning sound of the machine was soothing; the warm air it exhaled made her face glow summery red; and the fragrance of damp clothes drying left a delicious sweet taste in her mouth.

* * * *

A smile is about to form on Sabina's face as she sniffs the air like a dog after a scent. As soon as the pungent mixture of soap, make-up and toothpaste enters her nostrils, her eyes jerk open and the smile disappears. Her entire face also disappears as she clicks open the mirrored cabinet door to look at the digital clock inside: 9:30.

Nine-thirty, she mumbles to herself.

It was 9:30 on a Saturday morning and Bobtail, her pet hamster, was not in its cage. She had come to coax him out by calling his name as she had been doing every day for an entire year, smooth the fur on his back, feel the bumpiness of his spine and fill up on love and responsibility for the tiny, fragile creature. But as she crouched down next to the cage, she saw to her horror that the cage door was agape and Bobtail was no longer there.

Maybe he thought there would be a gorgeous female hamster out there. Maybe that was why he had been so enthusiastic about her innovation of the sleeve tunnel. He had been practicing for his great escape! With tears streaming down the metal bars of the empty cage, she promised there and then to never again let him venture down her sleeve. She would give up the wonderful Goosebumps she had enjoyed each time his cool, shivery hamster feet tickled their way along her bare arm under her sweatshirt. If only she could have him back and be forgiven for not securing the cage door properly. Sabina spent all Saturday looking for Bobtail. Saturday came to an end and there was no sign of him. He was still missing the next morning. Monday arrived and she miserably went to school.

When she returned, there he was sitting back in his cage—all fluffy and clean. Sabina leaped over to the cage and joyfully called his name. He cowered in the corner of the cage where he remained for the rest of his life. Sabina's mother consoled her by saying that he would need time to get over his traumatic experience under the floorboards where she'd found him. Despite Sabina's patience and imaginative attempts at re-taming him, her relationship with Bobtail was never the same. Instead of going up her sleeve (she'd decided to break her promise, just in case this was the reason why he was behaving so strangely), he bit her fingers and made her sad and angry. She decided that her mother must be right about the 'traumatic experience' and gave up trying to handle him. A couple of weeks later he curled up and died and she buried him in the garden under the tulips.

* * * *

Why am I back with Bobtail all these years later?

Is it the smell of piss coming from the toilet seat?

She ignores her mirror's provocation and continues filling in the crevices and cracks of her ageing skin. Over two hours have passed since she started her facial and she is nowhere near ready. She's annoyed with herself for letting her mirror steal her time again. Why did she let herself be taken back time and again to these scenes, and her mother, the smiling, humming, bright-faced pretty woman in the utility room?

After massaging a good walnut-sized dollop of expensive anti-wrinkle cream into her face, she slams the lid on and reprimands herself for buying it: *Such a waste of time and money, just like the fancy gels for my sagging breasts and vein-infested legs!* She pulls the jumper over her head, smudging her laboured complexion and shoves one leg after the other into some dark-brown synthetic trousers. Cold air pounces in through the open window making Sabina's body shudder. She shuts it and stands in front of the Venetian blind for a long time before carefully separating a couple of slats to peep out. She greets Luxembourg's dull face with a customary shake of her head and wishes the tidy street with genteel facades would protest, rather than stare miserably back. No protest comes and her disdainful looks don't prompt one either. As she stands there motionless, her gaze shifts from the street to her front lawn: a sodden Golden Retriever is sniffing wildly at what look like fresh Hyacinth shoots. The animal seems to be on one of those extendible leads that enable pets to venture ahead whilst still under the owner's control. The owner is nowhere to be seen and the dog, finding Sabina's delectable clump of winter green, is squatting down and dropping large steaming lumps on it. Sabina bangs angrily on the windowpane. The dog glances up at her and, without so much as a sorry-for-shitting-on-your-garden look on his face, trots proudly off. Now, if she were the woman from across the way, she would march outside, yank on the dog's lead, reel in the owner and order her to clear the shit away with her bare hands. But she's not the woman from across the way: she's Sabina Waldsmere—and Sabina Waldsmere just moves away from the window with a defeated look on her face and pretends she hasn't seen anything at all.

How she wishes she could behave differently.

Inside, alone, she can give anyone a piece of her mind. She politely, but forcefully tells the photo shop assistant, who has ruined her precious Christmas photos, that she will have the next five months' of films developed for free. She gives the clumsy postman who has dropped all her letters in a huge puddle a sympathetic smile and tells him that the size of his Christmas bonus will depend on how her letters are treated in future. She tells all the men who only inquire about her husband's job, interests and opinions that she is a psychologist studying the link between impotence and men's inability to acknowledge and respect housewives.

In her fantasies, she's Superwoman. Outside, in the real world, in front of real people, Shrinking Violet takes over: a limp woman identical in size and intelligence to a newly born mouse. And afterwards she runs through the scene again and again like a movie director determined to get it right, only for her it is too late. She can't take two, three, four…a hundred. The only good her soliloquies do is help her forget, if only for a short while, how pathetic she is.

For weeks before her husband's annual work function, Superwoman introduced herself to her husband's colleagues with a debonair: *'Good evening, I'm Sabina Waldsmere, Research Manager in the field of Child Development and Human Relations!'* or, *'Pleased to meet you. I'm in the Domestic Management business, what do you do?'*

So what happened on the actual night? Where were the original one-liners then?—locked inside with Superwoman whilst Violet went on the rampage with her ridiculous, self-recriminating line: '*I'm just a housewife!*'

She may as well have announced to the whole champagne-sipping, hors-d'oeuvres-eating lot of them that she was a frumpy bore!

Her mouthwash reminds her of the acrid taste that has been squatting in her mouth for fifteen years and she makes a mental note not to buy it again. *That taste is the reason why I eat hoards of sweet things and put on too much weight,* she confesses to her mirror. *Are you absolutely sure about that my dear?* comes the provocative reply.

"Mum! Are you still up there?"

Her son Dominic is calling from downstairs and Sabina is startled into looking at the digital clock again. It says 10:30—and she hasn't put the final coating of make-up on her face. How can she leave the house without it? She can't—it would be like parading naked in the streets without her 'face on', as her mother used to say.

Sabina peers through the blinds again. The mist has hardly lifted higher than a metre and looks as though it will stay for the entire day. She opens her tube of expensive 'full-face-cover-up' cream, which promises to conceal all shadows and flaws, and dabs it thickly on her face with the aid of a small sponge. 'The sponge is the key, Sabina, it makes the make-up nice and even,' her mother's voice tells her inside her head.

Is there nothing she can do without being reminded of her mother these days? Even the way she drives makes her think of her mother and will surely be the cause of an accident. *All this day-dreaming and reminiscing can't be healthy. Why not just forget?*

She ignores the mirror's comment this time and opens her eyes nice and wide, looks up to the ceiling (*must do something about those cobwebs*) and carefully draws a thin grey line above and below neat rows of lashes with the eyeliner pencil. Grey is a good colour for blue eyes, she remembers reading once, it accentuates their blueness.

So you think they'll twinkle today, do you?

"Mum!" comes the voice again.

Dominic is shouting from the hallway. She hates it when he does that. She can imagine the scowl he has on his face, harmonising with his looks: a lumbering, pimply, 21st century Punk Rocker with spiked up green hair striking off in several directions, and studs riveted in his ear lobes, nostrils and bottom lip. Adornment and hair dye apart, he looked just like her—with large blue eyes, coarse blond hair, and a pale complexion. The only mismatch is his father's temperament which seemed to just happen about a year ago together with the piercings. He arrived home from a weekend sleepover, walked into the kitchen and caused Sabina to drop a pan full of chicken soup. From that day on he was a changed person: he was no longer helpful and considerate, but an angry teenager with a frightening attitude. He became too preoccupied with his own life, his own interests and his own friends to consider his mother a human being at all.

Sabina has learned to remain composed whenever he enters the room these days. Just yesterday a whole gang of them came in to the kitchen demanding food. They were all replicas of Dominic with the same uninvolved stare, revealing nothing about their character or mood. One friend surprised her by posing a question. 'Mrs Waldsmere,' he asked, 'Why do your trousers always ride up your legs?' Part of her was shocked at such a question and another part was pleased he had noticed she had legs at all. 'It's the static electricity,' she had replied with poise. There was a pause in which whispers were heard before they chorused:

'So, what makes them come down, then?'

The gang howled in amusement and then stomped up the wooden stairs in their Doc Martens, slammed Dominic's bedroom door and put on a golden oldie by the Sex Pistols. Sabina sulkily finished wiping the sideboard in the kitchen, thinking up ways she could have replied and then fled to the bathroom. The mirror became witness to why she wore synthetic trousers in the same way as it was witness over the last fifteen years to why she crashed the car; why she used scourer to clean dead flies off the windscreen; why she broke an entire 36 piece dinner service; why she was known to the local police as the record holder for losing purses, keys and handbags; and why her weekly shop frequently landed on the supermarket car park.

She clears her throat and recites one of her favourite recipes from her mental archives:

Shopping on Supermarket Car park:

Ingredients:

1 child of approx. 2 years
1 supermarket trolley
A handful of negative comments
1 car
1 stressed Mum (preferably pregnant, but not essential)

Method:

Take the two-year-old, place it in a supermarket trolley and push it around. Keep on giving it negative comments like: 'Don't pull that off the shelf! Put that back! Leave that alone! Stop throwing the rice at the old lady! Eat some chocolate and be good! Don't wipe your hands on my sleeve.'

After approximately one hour, return to your vehicle. Try and get the shopping in the car before your blue, screaming child jumps out of the trolley and throws himself in front of a moving car. If you don't succeed, balance the shopping in one arm and the child in the other. You will now notice that you don't have a hand free to open the car door. Put the shopping on the roof of the car and then open the door. Throw screaming specimen into car and strap it down. Hurry into the driver's seat and set off to stop the screaming.

You have done it!

Shopping is successfully on the roof of the car whilst you drive off and the entire contents of the bag will fly across the car park remarkably well!

The edge of Sabina's delta mouth twitches in amusement and she quickly smears her lips with mauve-coloured lipstick, to preserve their cold-and-bruised look whilst keeping the triangle pointing up to her hair rather than down at her tits. If only she had thought of such a recipe at the time, her husband might have forgiven her. He still hadn't forgiven her for all her mishaps during pregnancy and afterwards whilst the hormones continued to rush through her bloodstream.

Sabina opens the bathroom window once again, hoping to clear the condensation that has spread all over the walls and door. She is tutting, irritated that she still ruminates on past events.

"Mum! How much longer do you need in there?" Dominic screams, banging his fist on the bathroom door.

"Soon, soon," she replies and her stomach tightens as a sudden attack of anger gushes into it.

Anger wasn't an emotion she frequently felt; yet it had been showing its head at ever-shorter intervals over the past few months. Now her mirror is asking whether the anger she feels is directed at her mother—*for giving you such a wonderful childhood?* She shakes her head at her reflection. *How could I be angry with someone who's main goal in life was to give me a childhood most could only dream of—full of tenderness and love? It is hardly my mother's fault that, as a grown woman of thirty-nine and three quarters, I am struggling to get a grip on my life.*

Sabina unlocks the bathroom door and comes out. Dominic looks at her blankly before ushering her down the stairs. At seventeen, he doesn't begin to pay any thought to his life beyond the next mealtime and mostly not even as far ahead as that. She has been watching him shoot up over the last eighteen months and now either has to stare at his Adam's apple moving up and down during a conversation, or else suffer a cricked neck. Her head nods up and down as he bellows his accusations.

"You've spent more than two hours in there. You promised to take me to Mike's house for eleven. Now I'm going to be late and it's all your fault! What were you doing in there so long anyway?"

Sabina agrees that he has every right to be cross and impatient with her and continues to explain how she has striven to salvage something of her original self.

"Hmm," he replies, scrutinising her face. "Was it worth it then?"

She doesn't bother to reply this time. She could have had a confrontation, a full-blown argument, berated him for his petulance. But that's her husband's department.

Before heading out of the house to the garage, Sabina digs in a kitchen drawer for her car keys. A sweet wrapper is stuck to them and she pulls it off in disgust. As she rips it into shreds and deposits it into the bin, she is reminded of a similar scenario when she was eleven.

It wasn't a sweet wrapper back then, but a receipt for a hamster from 'Peter Rabbit Pet Store'. That particular receipt had brought her pain—more than she would like to remember.

Thirty years ago, Sabina's mother must have spat out a sweet she didn't like and, for want of a better solution whilst driving along in her car, wrapped it in the receipt and threw it into her handbag. The stickiness must have seeped through the thin paper and stuck to her house keys. When she arrived home, she must have transferred the keys from her handbag to the kitchen cutlery drawer—as she always did—not knowing that the receipt was stuck on. This is where eleven-year-old Sabina found it. Being an inquisitive child, she prised it off, opened it up and read it. In this way she discovered that the hamster she had just buried, the one she thought to be her beloved Bobtail, hadn't been Bobtail at all, but a replacement hamster. Her mother had never found the escaped hamster behind the skirting boards like she said but had bought a new one and placed it in the cage, hoping that Sabina wouldn't notice the difference. Well, Sabina *had* noticed the difference; she had put it down to him having a 'traumatic experience' under the floorboards. She never in a million years thought of questioning whether her mother was telling the truth. *Why should I?*

The Crossing

Two weeks into the Millennium and she is sitting in the car, resolution vows safely in her handbag, determined to tackle number one on her list. Having completed number two last week, she feels (for the sake of continuity rather than order), that she had better tackle 1 before moving on to 3. Not that there is a 3 yet. Somehow she is sure one will pop up like the others—in a question-answering session with her bathroom mirror perhaps.

It's only a fifteen-minute drive into the capital city of Luxembourg from the suburbs where Sabina lives; yet she has been underway for over an hour. She has taken a detour—to drop Dominic off at a friend's ten kilometres north—and now she is doubling back on herself, southbound, to the centre. She told her son that she was going shopping nearby so that neither he, nor the other members of her family, would know what she was up to. The day has been chosen with care: Dominic is now away till six, and her husband is on a cycling trip with youngest son Carl. This was her safety net—just in case she decided to U-turn out of the whole idea.

Over the past week she has been tempted to postpone any action for a few decades, but failing to convince her mirror that this was a noble thing to do, has resigned to 'getting on with it'—as her mother used to say. And so she bullied herself out of the house, into the car and onto the motorway—more to ease the horrible guilt and shame she felt for having got herself into such a mess than to be 'noble'. She never does anything 'noble'. Her mirror does. In a moment of knightly exuberance, it had forced her to write, '*I shall love and treat you like a precious object from now until forever*' using a glittery blue eye-liner pencil and then ordered her to read the statement out loud ten times. She managed five times and then had to cancel play until the heavy tear-shower was over. When she finally left the bathroom, she rushed into her bedroom, opened the bedside drawer and stuffed the paper into the secret compartment of her jewellery box together with two other things she didn't want her husband to find—a past love letter from him and a heart pendant from the first boy to give her a French kiss.

When she had told her husband that she would be staying at home for the Millennium, he had been disgusted. How could she be so boring on the most important night of the century? What he couldn't possibly have known (and it took her a while to find this out as well) was that making this resolution turned it into *her* most important night of the century. So, whilst her husband hovered over New York on a turn-of-the-century celebration flight getting as drunk as possible on first class champagne together with work colleagues, she was crouching over a pile of broken pieces called 'life' trying to make sense of it all.

She has stopped at the traffic light at the junction with the motorway and fills the waiting time by taking the rectangular piece of paper out of her handbag, unfolding it and reading:

1. *Drive over the Red Bridge.*
2. *Call Madame Anastasia.*

The second item has a satisfyingly thick red tick next to it (lipstick) which gives Sabina's heart an unexpected jolt and she nearly forgets that the completion of that task has created another—actually meeting with Madame Anastasia. She immediately takes her 'reserve' make-up bag out of her handbag, digs out a black eye-liner pen and writes:

3. *Keep appointment with Madame Anastasia*

Only then does she realise she will be tackling two of her vows—1 and 3 today and the impact of this concept causes her car to stall. The horn of the car behind blasts her into action and her car literally hops like an injured rabbit onto the motorway.

Driving over the Red Bridge (the highest in Luxembourg) will be her first attempt at curing vertigo—a condition she has suffered from for fifteen years. The third task—keeping her appointment with Madame Anastasia—will introduce her to Luxembourg's most controversial seamstress and beautician.

Not being able to drive over bridges has made Sabina's life in Luxembourg highly complicated over the years. The centre of the city sits atop a plateau known as *Ville Haute,* or 'High Town'. At its feet lie the valleys of the rivers Pétrusse and Alzette which curl around the high rock they have sculpted like possessive cats, rendering it near-to inaccessible without a bridge crossing or two. How much time, patience and petrol she has wasted driving up and down alternative roads, weaving her way through the valleys to the centre, she would rather not know. She often wished she could simply wiggle her nose like someone bewitched and arrive there by magic. Her husband had suggested she use public transport and close her eyes when the time came to go over the bridge. She had tried—once by train, once by bus. Both times she had lost her nerve at the last minute, pulled the emergency stop lever (much to the disapproval of the other passengers and driver), and got off. No-one in her family understood her strange phobia; they cajoled rather than helped whenever the subject was brought up. And now, the subject is simply not brought up. All this has made her desperate to keep today a secret—at least until she felt she was getting somewhere.

If she manages to make it across the bridge, she tells herself, it will be a good omen for the meeting with the seamstress. Why she thinks this, she's not sure: she's not a superstitious person. Perhaps her views are already being affected by the seamstress who claims in her advert that the garments she creates not only transform the wearer's outward appearance, but also their whole attitude to life. Sabina feels a bit foolish believing something that is obviously just a marketing strategy, but does still hope that Madame Anastasia will indeed be the fairy godmother she has wished for—one who will help her shine on her fortieth birthday. Even though having a party is the last thing she feels like doing to celebrate her fortieth, in no less than ten weeks, she will be on her way to a posh hall, where she will listen to a jazz band playing 'Happy Birthday to You' and greet over a hundred guests! The party (and all the fuss) is her husband's work and she is trying not to think about it too much. A small part of her is looking forward to it because it will bring family and friends together for the first time since her marriage eighteen years ago, but a much greater part wishes she had gone against her nature and protested wildly and forcefully.

Having a celebration just because she's hitting that dreaded fortieth year seems so insignificant next to her other plans. Even so, she knows that whether she ticks off that number one task or not, today's achievement will only mark the first step towards a cure. You see, she's not just scared of bridges. Her fear extends to rims, curbs, edges…In fact, anything you could fall off or into! That is why she hasn't visited the Pétrusse Valley, her favourite part of Luxembourg, for many years. A long time ago (long before Sabina arrived in Luxembourg), part of the valley was turned into a park for residents and visitors to stroll in, play in—or simply retreat to when the noise of city life became unbearable. Sabina used to spend hours down there. No matter how busy she was, she would always find time to descend the uneven sandstone steps to its lush green depths and walk over to the slender waterway that used to be the mighty Pétrusse river. The river could hardly be called a river now—it's more like a purpose-built stone gully down which an aesthetically pleasing line of water flows—tamely and calmly. It's hard to imagine that this river's water was once powerful enough to carve the chunk of sandstone rock laying the foundation for *Lucilinburhuc*, the very first Luxembourg to be built a thousand years ago. The only time Sabina had glimpsed the river's original force was when she had been in the valley during a heavy downpour. So much rain fell in such a short space of time that the trickle became a torrent—rushing up the sides of the gully, disobeying the confines of its narrow, man-made riverbed and threatening to flood the neat grassy lawns. But that was a rare and thrilling occasion: most days, the river behaved itself like the tame creature it had been forced to become. Even the weeping willows didn't manage to fool you into thinking it was really a river. Sabina used to grab the willow's reaching arms, give them a hearty handshake and then let them plop back into the water, fancying they might one day weep for the river, fill it up and help it burst it's banks to freedom.

It was also in the spring, shortly after her arrival in Luxembourg, that Sabina had learned about the existence of a vast network of underground passageways inside the giant piece of sandstone rock, beneath the *Ville Haute*, original site of the fortress. It was the crumbly nature of the rock which enabled the tunnels to be hand-hewn by occupying forces and, when complete, allowed soldiers to move unseen from the fortress, down through the steep valley walls, beneath the river and up the other side of the valley. It made the fortification an absolute perfect place for would-be rulers to feel almighty and victorious. And it transformed the rock from a peaceful natural plateau into an unconquerable, man-made force.

Sabina had hardly been able to contain her excitement as she queued up with other tourists for a guided tour of the passageways. The one-kilometre stretch of tunnel she was ultimately shown left her feeling far from satisfied. The general public wasn't allowed to access the rest of the 20 km network—many tunnels were unsafe, the guide explained; some had been destroyed due to construction work in the city, and the rest served as cellar to the only remaining villa perched on the valley side.

The section of valley which is now a park has an altogether sport-and-leisure feel about it. In the summer months, the air becomes saturated with scents from the lush and exotic vegetation creating a perfume that could be sold under the name of 'Ripening Energy' or 'Budding Vitality'. Sabina used to be addicted to it and would miss it if she didn't manage to go for a sniff every day. It was the only place in Luxembourg where she felt happy and alive. Even the people were friendlier in the valley than in the 'High Town' atop the plateau: strangers would greet, stop for a chat. She didn't understand or communicate well in French, German or Luxembourgish but it didn't matter; the valley was a permanent haven, offering refuge from the noisy life at the rim. She had felt this way about it on the very first day she saw it from the passenger seat of the car as she was driven over the Red Bridge seventeen years ago by her husband. She had been three months pregnant at the time and wasn't convinced they were doing the right thing. They were leaving behind an adequate semi on the outskirts of London, friends, family, and well-paid jobs. When she caught sight of the valley with its welcome array of bright autumn colours, she had felt such a boost that she was instantaneously reassured that she was going to love living there. Adrian never seemed to have an unsettling thought about the whole move: he was more than eager to leave his job as programmer for a no-name computer company behind. It had always bothered him that he earned less than her, despite having more professional experience. So, when a colleague pointed out an advert for a high-paid job in Luxembourg addressed to graduates with 2-year's experience in the computer branch, he applied. He was successful and the idea of having a more central European position and greater affluence thrilled him. Before Sabina had time to think, she had resigned, sold her house, married, got pregnant, said goodbye to friends and family, and was on the ferry to Calais. Six hours later she was crossing the Red Bridge into the capital of Luxembourg.

As she approaches that very same bridge today, her biceps react spontaneously, balling up in an attempt to pull her hands off the steering wheel. All they do is kick-start her hands into a machine-like grip of the steering wheel welding them on like solder. Her upper body becomes so rigid that her mind warns her brain that the use of the gear stick may be difficult, hand brake impossible, should she have do an emergency stop. Blood pulsates noisily behind her ears, drumming her onward, even though her body is making all signs of seizing up and letting her down. Before her accelerator foot is affected by the same fate as her hands, she shifts it to the brake pedal. The car stops abruptly and she tries to calm herself by doing some breathing exercises she remembers from the time she gave birth. She sucks in as much air as she can and forces it down her throat and into her stomach. The first two attempts make her cough and splutter the lot out, popping as noisy little burps in front of her face. The third attempt traps the air inside long enough for some to get into her belly. The oxygen unclamps her muscles and brings a tingling feeling to the rest of her body as she slowly releases it again through her open mouth. An onlooker may have thought her car was filled with water and she, the fish in it, was drowning in its own tank.

When she finally looks up, she sees that her car has come to a halt in front of a weathered placard at the beginning of the bridge. She reads:

Protection Contre Le Suicide

Sabina swigs another carful of air and forces it down. The bridge looks longer from this angle. It has recently received another coat of paint and is the only bright object to be seen for miles (except for the traffic lights at the far end, which are also red). The bridge has also changed: concave constructions have been attached to the metal railings, right and left along the bridge's entire length. Even with these so-called protection shields, Sabina still thinks it must be an attractive jump-off point for suicidals like it's larger brother, the Golden Gate bridge. The difference with the Luxembourg version is that, instead of spanning an expanse of water, taking you from one side of a bay to another, this bridge takes you from one plateau to another: the one on which the 'High Town' sits and begs visitors to squander their money and time in its countless restaurants and boutiques; and the one known as *Kirchberg,* 'Church Hill', where the international banks live counting their profits.

Though Sabina knows that the protection shields have probably made the Red Bridge one of the safest in the country (traffic accidents caused by crosswinds, and the high suicide rate have both been greatly reduced), she still doesn't feel as confident in front of it now as she had told her mirror she was earlier that morning. Thoughts from her past keep jumping into her mind uninvited and she is finding them very interfering with her ability to concentrate.

Despite the country's offer of over 90 bridges, the Red Bridge was favourite in suicidal circles until the day the protection shields were attached. Unlike the people living in the houses beneath who celebrated their erection—neither bodies nor vehicles would ever again land in their back gardens—the suicidals were at a loss for where to go. Most sloped off across the border to neighbouring Germany, France or Belgium.

Quite out of the blue, and without needing confidence at all, something triggers Sabina's foot into action and it slams down hard on the accelerator. Sabina grabs the steering wheel as though grabbing hold of a bucking bronko and, seeing the traffic light turn green at the far end of the bridge, pushes her foot firmly into the rubber mat on the floor. As her car charges at the green light, the stiffness she had previously felt disappears as if by magic and her hand begins to nimbly shift up the gears; to third, forth, and then fifth. She is in full flight when a car with foreign registration plates veers in front of her without indicating. *Bloody tourist*, she shouts and scowls at the owner of the offending car. He waves politely back and points to a mini trailer attached to the back of his vehicle—as if this were an adequate excuse for his inconsiderate driving. In the meantime, the light has turned red and her bronco skids to a reluctant halt behind the tourist. Whilst she waits, she is entertained by the children's less polite, but internationally comprehensible sign language, and her thoughts are diverted away from the bridge, suicidals and the long drop beneath her.

Green—and it's off, overtaking the tourist and bounding to the other side. Her excitement nearly throws her out of the car seat, her bronco onto an oncoming lamppost, and all the air she has held in her stomach gushes out in one huge outward breath. What comes out isn't a familiar belch but an unfamiliar shriek of delight.

Soon the bridge is a miniature picture in her rear-view mirror and Sabina is breathing normally again, concentrating on her next task—meeting the seamstress. Thoughts about this conjure up all kinds of emotions and when she sees an ambulance loom up in the mirror, she nearly jumps out of her skin. Her mind tells her that it is a bad sign, counteracting the good omen of the bridge crossing. *How stupid*, she tells herself, *this is only a seamstress I am visiting—not a witch!* and tries to make light of the unbearable tension she is feeling.

She starts thinking about the birthday party and can't stop herself from wondering whether Adrian missed the pomp and grandness of a church wedding with large reception and, for that reason, is trying to make up for it on her fortieth. How she wishes now that she had rejected his idea from the start, nipped it in the bud. Now it's too late. The party ball is rolling, adding to the pressure that has already built up around her resolution, and pumping the ball up into a giant balloon. She only hopes it won't burst open and spill her all over her party guests on the actual night. It maddens her to think that, by organising this grand do for her, her husband is selfishly forcing her to delight and be delighted on her birthday. If only she hadn't been her usual complaisant self: ensnared by other people's opinions whilst hers gurgled beneath an ever-thinning skin threatening to boil over like a pan of overheated milk.

Sabina is now very close to the street where the seamstress lives and suddenly decides to turn right into a side road and park.

Her ever-busy mind rattles through mental catalogues of ideas, things she would prefer to do on her birthday. It chooses a romantic candle-lit supper at an exclusive French restaurant, classical music in the background, handsome waiters...

Her lips twitch, attempting to smile.

A knock on the window nearly makes her choke on her imaginary *pâté de foie gras* and she strains through her coughing and the closed window to hear the man's voice:

"*Excusez-moi Madame, est-ce que vous savez ou se trouve?...*"

Before he can finish his sentence, she holds up her hand as though ordering traffic to halt and shakes her head.

"*Non!*" she replies and turns the key in the ignition. Pleased with her resoluteness, she drives further down the road and sneers at the reflection of the tourist in her rear-view mirror. He is turning his map round and round trying to puzzle out his route and Sabina is thrilled to finally see an example of a man who cannot read a map. Adrian is always criticising her for her inability to read them. He says it is another example of men's superiority to women. And she, fool as she was, believed him. After watching the man struggle like she normally does, she feels triumphant and quickly gets back to her thoughts on an alternative way of celebrating her birthday. The restaurant idea is being attacked by her reminiscing mind: they had a dinner for two—which she had enjoyed—on her birthday last year. Despite Adrian's visual enjoyment of the *haute cuisine*, he had, in his well-practised, humiliating way, fussed about the bill presented on a silver platter with mint chocolates at the end of the evening. He had said that you could feed a house full of people for the same amount of money. Without conferring or asking for her assent, he'd made up his mind about her next birthday celebrations.

She wishes she could call the whole thing off but her mind freezes as she imagines the faces of relatives and friends. She can't—it would be as bad as calling off a wedding!

The only comforting thought is that she will get a hand-sewn dress out of it. Of course, she hasn't mentioned Madame Anastasia to Adrian. The controversy about her methods of dressmaking would surely make him boycott the whole idea just when she had mustered up enough courage to go. She hoped he wouldn't find her collection of newspaper articles, cut out of Luxembourg's

English-speaking news magazine with headings such as: 'Controversial Seamstress Adds a New Dimension to the Party Dress' and 'Clandestine Happenings at Villa' which tattled about suspicious incidents in the vicinity of her home. Apparently, the freshly pregnant wife of a European Civil Servant collapsed two streets down. A man clad in one of her dresses and a bank director were caught in flagrante on a grassy bank only a few metres away.

Last autumn Sabina had been at the exhibition centre, visiting a friend who had a stand, when she learned that there was a spectacular fashion show in the annexed hall by the 'Enigmatic Madame Anastasia'. This was the first time Sabina had heard of her but from then on, kept hearing the name spoken everywhere she went. Most intriguing, yet unsettling was a conversation she overheard between two young English women (fashion designers, Sabina thought) in a café the day after she called to make an appointment.

A tall blonde (who was probably also a model), and a stumpy brunette (who probably wasn't), were digging long spoons into a mountain of cream on top of large *chocolat chauds* as they spoke.

"Madame Anastasia isn't really in her sixties," said the blonde.

"Fifties then," retorted the brunette.

"No, not even as old as that. Apparently she just makes herself look older."

"Why on earth would she do that?"

"The mature look."

"But that's ridiculous!"

"I'm only telling you what I've heard."

"Well, I don't believe it. She can't make herself look old *and* attractive. It'd show."

Sabina had nodded in agreement with the brunette.

"So how old is she supposed to be?" the brunette finally asked.

"No older than me or you. She's found a way to attract customers—mostly bored housewives wanting to please their husbands, or lovers…"

Sabina had flinched.

"…and when they see how good she looks at sixty, think that she can work wonders for them too! If they saw her real face, they'd know that she was fresh out of dressmaking school. Even housewives wouldn't be stupid enough to go to a beginner and spend thousands of Francs on a dress."

"But that's criminal!" exclaimed the brunette.

"Call it what you like. I'm all for it. Fuck the system. Been thinking of setting up a similar business."

"Geraldine!"

"Ideas—all you need is ideas and know how to implement them. It helps if you're a millionaire's daughter, of course."

"Is she?"

"How should I know? But she must have had some savings to buy that villa."

"I thought she was renting it."

"Apparently not."

"She must have inherited then."

"Or earned the money from other 'criminal' jobs. I reckon she's come straight from the drug scene. You know—synthetic drugs—like Ecstasy."

"Really?"

"Yes! She takes them herself apparently. It's probably her key to the mature look!"

"No!"

"It's true."

"But surely if she was on drugs, her clients would notice."

"They're housewives, remember. They've no idea."

The air in the cafe was thick with smoke making it difficult for sound waves to be received.

"Well, at least they get an original dress for their money."

"I've heard reports to the contrary. You know the story about the emperor's new clothes?"

"Yes."

"Well, that's what she does. Makes dresses with the cheapest material, a few frills and fancy stitching and convinces the housewives that it's priceless."

"And they believe her?"

"Yeah. Just like you believe every word I say."

Geraldine began laughing in a malicious way. "You're so gullible," she cried, pointing at the brunette's sullen face. "It's so funny watching you."

The brunette pouted, revealing a third chin, swigged down the last of her drink, pointed to the white till receipt, said "You get it!" and left.

Sabina had left at the same time pretending that she had known all along it was a lie.

The front windscreen has misted over and she rummages in the glove compartment for the cloth to wipe it. She peers out. The air is still thick with mist and the cleared patch of glass reveals nothing but greyness. The sound of bells can be heard: probably from the cathedral on the opposite side of the valley. As she listens, her mind can see the large bell swinging and the pendulum oscillating as the midday hour is called into the air in a foreboding way. When all is silent again, she opens the car door, steps out and walks nervously over to the impressive villa belonging to Madame Anastasia.

Dipping In

The gate swings open without the accompanying whine Sabina expects. Balanced on a bed of sandstone rock overlooking the Pétrusse valley, the house looks like a brooding hen struggling to stay on her nest long enough for the eggs to hatch. It not only looks precarious—it feels it. As Sabina approaches she is made further ill at ease by the apparent absence of a front door. Entering via the roadside gate, the villa does appear to be doorless. There is a front door of course, but it is at the back, forcing visitors to walk around the house and into the garden that slopes towards the edge of the gorge. Sabina walks cautiously down the path, her eyes searching for an object to focus on and keep her balance. At first, they cling to the cathedral's spires on the opposite rim but a tree blocks her view as she enters deeper into the garden and she is forced to search for something else to take her mind off the drop. Her mind obliges, conjuring up pictures: memories of the Pétrusse valley park. She hears water running down the man-made river gully; sees herself sunbathing on the long sloping lawn; smells spice from exotic trees; feels the smoothness of tarmac pathways under her bare feet; sees a cyclist speeding silently along; a lonely jogger; a man walking his dog; and a group of children throwing stones into the water. She hears the children's shrieks, the dog's bark, the pounding of the jogger's shoes and, in that brief, distracted moment, she very nearly smiles.

These pictures disappear as a dizzy spell overcomes her. *Pull yourself together, Sabina,* she mumbles under her breath and hopes she won't relapse into another attack of vertigo after such a positive start. She wishes she were inside the house already, out of danger. No matter how much she wills her legs to go faster, her careful feet make slow progress along the path. She wonders whether there is a fence or a wall at the end of the garden to prevent an accident, but doesn't dare look. How could she have known when reading Madame Anastasia's advertisement, that she would be venturing as far as the valley's edge on her way to the front door? She snatches at air like she had done in the car to combat the nausea, but it enters too fast, making her stomach knot and fold with pain. In a hunched position, she shuffles down the paving-stone path and, when she finally looks up, is greeted by bold letters:

Residence Avoir

Sabina commands her cold fingers to press the doorbell and the clicking sound of footsteps on a stone floor announces that her call is being answered. When the door is swung open by an exceptionally tall and robust woman, she is shocked into attention.

"I'm Sabina Waldsmere," she fires.

There is no affirmative reaction.

"I—um—spoke to you on the telephone last week…for a dress?"

"*Ah oui, oui, oui.* Please come in, Madame Waldsmere. *S'il vous plaît,*" she replies in a throaty, but appealing voice, which sounds and smells like menthol cigarettes. Sabina brings her nausea in with her despite attempts at rubbing it off on the doormat.

There she stands, Madame Anastasia in the flesh. Sabina's inspecting eyes conclude that she is not a twenty-year-old in disguise. Her make-up has been professionally applied, giving her the refreshing, youthful look the girls had mentioned, but the wrinkles were still visible to the naked eye. A shade of lipstick, more burgundy than strawberry, paints fleshy lips and an ochre shadow creates prominent cheek bones and soft eyelids which radiate underneath two bushy, but shapely eyebrows. Her face is vibrant, her eyes cheerful and optimistic. She is unique; made by an artist's brush on sanguine skin.

Sabina watches in silence as confidence and assertiveness ooze through Madame Anastasia's pores.

If only I could have a fraction of her self-esteem!

It's hopeless. She nervously asks where the bathroom is and scuttles away like a disobedient schoolchild who has asked to go to the toilet during lesson time. A spider with skinny legs stares accusingly at her from its corner web on the ceiling whilst she sits half naked on the cold seat. Without really knowing why, she sticks her tongue out at it.

When she hastily swings the door open to get back to her host, it knocks into a pedestal on which sits a priceless-looking vase filled with tall red tulips. The vase rocks to and fro, threatening to fall. Sabina grabs it, tries to steady it with her shaky hands but instead knocks it causing water to slop out and onto the floor. She is about to tear off some of the pink recycled toilet paper, get on her hands and knees and mop up the spillage when Madame Anastasia's beckoning voice interrupts her.

"Oh, there you are, Madame Waldsmere. *S'il vous plait,*" she says, ushering her towards another door. "Please step this way. Come in, come in."

Sabina is hesitant, tearful. She wants to tell her about the accident and imagines a possible conversation in her head: 'M*y handbag knocked the vase slightly—and, well, it kind of rocked. No, it didn't fall. Water? No, it didn't spill—well, yes it did actually. Yes, a little bit of water spilled. Just a small splash—yes, on the floor. Oh, they're irreplaceable tiles, are they? Hmm, yes, I understand. It'll be expensive to have them cleaned. Yes, I understand. Water is the worst thing that could spill on them. Okay, I will ask my husband to re-mortgage the house.*

"Madame Waldsmere?"

Sabina jumps half a metre into the air.

"Please do not worry about the spilled water. I will just tell my *femme de ménage* to clean it up before the cat slips on it."

Sabina nods in embarrassment and enters the living room. It's a spacious room that the winter light struggles to illuminate despite two broad windows on the valley side. Square floor tiles sparkle an unclouded black, displaying perfect reflections of modern furniture and *objets d'art.* Sabina feels disconcerted by the small amount of seating available and remains standing, her right hand holding onto her left as though trying to squeeze something out. Madame Anastasia points at a chair. Sabina obediently sits down and starts rubbing her blood-drained hands that feel painfully prickly inside. For a few seconds, the wide-armed chair, one of two in the room, invites her to sink down, nuzzling, cuddling. Her eyes are just closing when a noise from the adjacent room makes her open them again. A loud gasp escapes from her mouth at a woman slumped in a chair opposite her, about two metres away. As the stranger comes into focus, she can be identified: it is her own reflection in a three-metre by three-metre mirror on the opposite wall. A significant amount of shuffling and fidgeting ensues as Sabina re-positions her chair to avoid both looking at her own image, and the valley through the window behind her. Scraping is still audible when Madame Anastasia reappears through an ebony door and tip-taps her route to the empty chair. Manicured fingernails carry a tea tray and harmonise in colour with a wine-red skirt and shoes. Sabina's magnet eyes try to draw in details of Madame Anastasia's glamour but only attract unwanted attention. Their eyes meet. Sabina lowers hers and clears her throat as though preparing to speak; she doesn't, but feels bound and gagged by debilitating shame.

"Would you like a cup of tea? Help yourself to one of the chocolates; they are my favourite—Belgian," Mme Anastasia says, setting the tray down on a round table between them.

"Thank you," Sabina croaks and, leaning forward to receive the hot drink, inspects the hands. Compared with her own they are huge—hands which could grab the largest watermelon on a market stall, lift it up to be smelled for ripeness, and discard it. Sabina carefully counts five dark hairs at the base of her forefinger and joyfully follows the course of two fat veins running towards the wrist. The tea soothes Sabina's dry throat and warms her. She hadn't realised how deeply the cold had penetrated her skin. "These chocolates are my favourite too," she admits politely, "but I haven't actually had one for a long time."

In truth, she hasn't eaten chocolate since the summer: a punishment for putting on too much weight. Even over the Christmas period she strictly denied herself the pleasure of eating sweet things and miserably obeyed her bad conscience. Her family went against her instructions by continuing to offer her chocolate on a regular basis. None of them were overweight and found it hilarious to see her fighting her daily battle. Up to now, she has been determined not to give in to her weakness, if only for the sake of her fortieth birthday.

Today she doesn't care—she craves comfort and hungrily grabs the largest one, stuffing it into her mouth before a mood change can stop her. Her mouth, heated by the hot tea, welcomes the chocolate and melts it rapturously. It is a bright feeling flavoured with the fragrance of Madame Anastasia's potpourri: a honey-lemon mixture. The scent rises up from her taste-buds into her nose, passes through her head into her mind and leaves in its wake a numbness with a pinch of dizziness and a dash of sensuality.

The scent becomes more intense: the stronger it becomes, the more it soothes her and draws her on, commanding her to travel to its source. She feels like she is gliding on powerful wings, moving steadily forwards—however the mood takes her. She becomes light: a serene body suspended from helium balloons, dancing in the sky with the agility and grace of a feather in a playful wind. On and on, higher and higher, brighter and brighter. She is getting closer to the centre of the source, she is there now and…

…she can hardly focus. A blur of red, a ruby-red smear. Tulips. Yes, they *are* tulips. Hundreds of them standing tall, straight and proud. Shades ranging from crimson to deep orange. A glorious sight. A delicious smell. Her eyes move on, beyond the tulips, focusing wider. More red, brick-red. A house, standing alone on a quiet street with bay windows and a smoked glass front door. She sees herself running past the tulips towards a figure in the garden. It is a woman with lips that reflect as many shades of red as the tulips. Beautiful lips. Perfect teeth. Together they form a unique smile. Her eyes are still fixed on the smile when it detaches itself from the woman and floats towards her like a Dali painting come to life. The lips form words of praise, pride, joy. A piece of paper floats down as if just released like a snowflake from the sky. The lips dance around it. Uninhibited, carefree, happy lips. 'Ice cream and strawberries for tea,' they say.

Dong, dong, dong...the deafening sound interrupts, getting louder. Sabina struggles to hold on to the picture, but the ringing sound snatches it all away: the tulips, the house, the lips—swallows it whole and pushes her to the ground.

When Sabina's bottom smacks the floor, her eyelids spring open and her eyes, blinded at first, strain to focus on something. They finally settle on a colossal *Art Nouveau* clock on the mantelpiece. Beneath the clock, she sees herself on the floor in Madame Anastasia's living room, legs ungainly straddled, hair a knotted mess around a smudged face. The clock is still chiming: *dong, dong...*

Disoriented and confused, Sabina pulls herself up and into the chair. She stares at the mirror. The clock in the mirror stares back, impertinently continuing to chime.

Seven o'clock?

Seven o'clock in the evening?

Sabina looks at her mirror image. She tries to brush her hair with fingers that feel like raw sausages and stuffs it into a loose ponytail. The clock. The time.

Seven o'clock. Adrian, Carl, Dominic. Oh my God!

She imagines the scene at home. Adrian will be back from his trip with Carl wondering where she is, what they are going to eat for tea, a message on the answering machine from Dominic accusing her of forgetting to pick him up. She looks into the mirror again. A reflection! She turns to the real clock:

Five o'clock!

Whilst she tries to remember what she has done and said since she arrived at midday, Madame Anastasia enters with her coat and gloves.

"It was a great pleasure making acquaintance with you," she remarks, handing over the clothes. "We shall discuss more detail on the dress next time. I have enough information to make a start. How is next Wednesday morning? All right, Madame? At half past ten?"

Sabina is still bewildered. "Um yes—err, certainly," she replies absently.

"*D'accord. Au revoir*, Madame Waldsmere. *A la prochaine.*"

The door to the dark, drizzly outside opens. Sabina steps down onto the path and walks dreamily to the gate.

Lost…

Sabina can hear the phone ringing as she approaches her house. She leaps up the front door steps, rams the key into the lock, bangs the door into the newly decorated wall and darts over to the phone. She can't ignore a ringing phone—it's like a crying baby to her. Even when she is already out of the house and late for an appointment, she always runs back in to get it. In the worst case, it is a wrong number. And when not, it isn't usually worth running back for. Adrian never does. 'Just let it ring,' he says. 'If it's important, they'll leave a message on the machine.'

She seizes the receiver. "Hello?"

"Oh, hi Sabina," replies the familiar voice. "Are you okay?"

"Of course I am. Why shouldn't I be?"

"You sound out of breath."

"Oh, no, not really. I mean I had to run back and forth to bring the shopping in," she lies. Her sister might otherwise think that she was in the habit of running to the phone, desperate to talk to someone, lonely.

"Oh, I see. Sorry for interrupting. Well, I'll be brief then…"

"No, there's no need. I've finished now," Sabina assures her.

All the same, Jennifer feels awkward, unwanted—as though she's intruding. "I am actually just calling to see how things are and to ask whether I can come a week earlier than planned?" Her tone of voice goes up at the end, full of hope and expectation.

"Can you get away from work for such a long time?"

Sabina wishes she had said that she is pleased, that it is a great idea and it will be fantastic to see her. She had truly felt this way, but her brain had decided to tackle the conversation differently. Jennifer pretends not to notice.

"Well," she continues merrily, "my boss isn't pleased with the idea of me taking five days off at a time when, he says, he needs me most. But this is your big day—a bit like the wedding party you didn't have—so, well, I thought I should support you a little more."

"Wedding? What gave you that idea?"

"I don't know. It's the impression I got," Jennifer replies and wishes she hadn't begged her boss for the days off and then agreed to take unpaid leave, 'jeopardising your position within the company', as he'd put it. She grits her teeth.

"Anyway, it's beside the point. Shall I come earlier or not?"

"I don't want you to feel obliged. You don't have to make a big deal out of this party. It's not. It's just a normal birthday party that Adrian has decided to throw for me."

"You don't sound very pleased about it. Maybe it'd be better if I didn't come at all."

"I didn't say that. It would be great if you could come earlier. But don't expect it to be an amazing do like you're probably used to because you'll be disappointed."

Jennifer doesn't bother putting her sister straight on that score. "Okay, so I'll come."

"Good. It'll be just like old times."

Why she said it, she doesn't know. It slipped out. Her sister pauses for too long for it to be accidental and Sabina feels compelled to say something constructive.

"When were you thinking of coming?"

"On Friday 18th, on an evening flight."

"Great. I'll jot it down. The flight gets in at around 8 p.m. doesn't it?"

"Yes, how do you know?" Jennifer asks, astounded that her sister might know the timetable off by heart.

"It'll be the one Adrian always flies back on. Besides, I think there is only one flight out of London in the evening to Luxembourg. We're living in the back and beyond here, you know."

Jennifer laughs.

"Does Adrian go to London a lot?"

"Not really. Not these days. There was a time when he was away more regularly. Brussels mostly," Sabina says and Jennifer detects sadness in her voice.

"You don't like him going on business trips, do you?"

"What makes you say that? I don't mind. It's not always convenient. But I can't complain. How about you? Are you getting around these days?"

"No, not lately. Well, I do get to visit Birmingham and Manchester sometimes to see what the other branches of the company are up to. It's not real travelling, though..." She pauses, not wishing to elaborate. "Listen, I've been meaning to tell Adrian that he can always look me up whenever he's in town. I'd be glad to put him up."

"How kind of you, Jennifer. But, well, you know how these conferences are. Zoom in, zoom out. No time for a friendly chat or family visit."

"Yes, I know. But if he's in town and stuck for a place to stay, please tell him that he's welcome here."

"Okay. He'll have to pick an evening when you're free though," Sabina adds and Jennifer detects maliciousness in her voice this time.

"What do you mean? You'd be surprised how often I am free these days, Sabina."

Jennifer doesn't want to say how often she sits alone in her apartment wishing someone would call: an old friend, her sister. Sabina rarely calls from Luxembourg. Jennifer rarely feels in the mood to call her either.

"You mean you've given men up? Come on, Jennifer, you don't need to lie to me. Every letter from you is plastered with the name of another new date! There must have been over a dozen in the last two years."

Over the last two years Jennifer had been out on more dates than she had drunk cups of coffee, and she likes coffee which is more than she could say about her excessive dating. How much she longed to settle down with a man and have a family. She is tired of all the one-night stands, the dead-end relationships, the rigmarole of starting one up, building it up, putting effort into it and it leading nowhere. She felt a deeper loneliness than she thinks her sister can imagine.

"Okay, so I get invited out quite regularly," Jennifer confessed, "But..."

"So, who is it at the moment? David, Stephen, Jerry?" Sabina teases.

Jennifer is reluctant to talk about it and hates her sister's tone of voice. Now she knows why she hardly ever feels like phoning.

"I can't believe you haven't got a date. Jennifer without a date? Now that earns an entry in The Guinness Book of Records!"

"Okay, so I am dating someone. He's called Rick. Satisfied?"

Sabina is speechless for a second. Rick, short for Richard, her father's name. She hasn't heard it for years and she feels uncomfortable about it.

"How serious is it?"

"I don't know. We've only been dating for three months."

"Three months? Sounds pretty serious to me!"

Sabina would hate to have a Rick as her brother-in-law. It would make her sad; remind her that she no longer had a father.

"How old is he?" she asks, but she doesn't listen to the answer. She has turned into a fifteen year old, watching an American series on the television in the living room. Her father is in the kitchen and her mother is reading a book upstairs in her bedroom. Fifteen-year-old Sabina has just been rejected by a blind date her sister had dragged her out on and is feeling lonely. She wished she could go to her mother and tell her how wretched she feels. Sabina knows her mother would listen, but she still can't go to her. If only her mother would come and ask her why she was sighing so heavily this evening. Hundreds of piled-up computer printouts have rendered her father inaccessible and blind to her female troubles. How could she talk to him about the fact she hadn't sprouted breasts yet, and was as much interested in boys as a cod in a chip?

"Is it important?" Jennifer says curtly.

"What?" Sabina is snapped out of her daydreaming.

"His age!"

"No. Oh no. I just thought…It doesn't matter, forget it. I'm glad you're still enjoying your single life. Look at me! I've been put on the shelf already," Sabina adds adds, trying her best to make it sound light-hearted.

"So, how are the boys?"

"Oh, they're fine. No sign of a girlfriend. They're both too busy at school." She laughs. "Actually, they're doing well. Carl got A's in History, Geography, German and French. Dominic struggles a bit in those subjects, but has excelled in Maths and Physics. He'll probably study one of the two subjects. He's been looking through prospectuses already and he's short-listed Manchester and Bristol."

Jennifer fights to suppress a yawn. She is genuinely tired after being out Friday night. She only goes out on a Friday and Saturday so she can have a lie-in. She kicked Rick out of her bed before dawn, reluctant to have him around for breakfast, clanking his spoon in the cereal bowl, slurping his tea, smacking his lips and speaking with his mouth full. That would have ruined it. She loved having a man in her bed, strong arms wrapped around her, warm breath on the nape of her neck. Sex didn't matter—it just came with the package. She was always glad when it was over and they could concentrate on the cuddling.

Sabina was still going on about her boys. "…I would prefer Dominic to go to Manchester myself. People are friendlier. He'd get quite a shock after Luxembourg—would get to see some poverty. Strange how the people are still friendly, though. You'd think they didn't have a care in the world. The faces don't match. It's the same here. You'd think the entire population of Luxembourg had had their houses repossessed and their children were begging on the streets going by their sullen faces. Didn't you notice that when you were here?"

Jennifer suddenly realises that Sabina has asked a question and is waiting for a reply. All Jennifer can hear is the sound of her own breath as it bounces off the mobile phone.

"So, the boys will be fleeing the nest soon then?" she volunteers, remembering the main topic of conversation.

Sabina feels rebuffed, her opinion annulled. Just like Adrian makes her feel.

"Yes," comes the laconic reply.

"How exciting! You'll be childless again. A bit like me, only a couple. I bet you're full of plans for your childless life? Just think. No more troublesome teenagers around the house. You'll have the place to yourself. So, what are your plans then? You have made plans, haven't you?"

There is a moment's silence as Sabina fumbles with a pad of paper and pen which she drops on the floor whilst doodling large, pointed zigzags.

"Oh yes, of course and I'm—I mean, we're looking forward to it." She bites her lips.

Sabina hasn't made any plans. She knows what Adrian will do as soon as the boys leave: knock their bedrooms into one and turn it into a multi gym. Sabina was horrified when he first suggested it. "Where will they sleep when they come home in the holidays?" she'd asked. "Come home?" Adrian had mocked. "After the first semester maybe. After that, they'll only stop by in passing to say their dutiful hello."

Sabina had given him one of her I-don't-believe-you looks and just-wait-and-see smiles. Surely they would want to come home to see her, tell her all about university life, chat about old times, bring a girlfriend to stay? It would be awful if they didn't have a room in the house they could call their own, where they could put their old things, the stuff they didn't need at university? They would feel like strangers in their own home if they didn't have a room. Where would they sleep anyway? On the living room floor? In the local hotel? "They could sleep on a mat on the gymnasium floor," he had retorted. "Harden them up. They have it too easy. They're spoilt." She had insisted that they weren't spoilt, that things were different in Luxembourg compared with Britain, that it wasn't her fault that it was one of the richest countries in the world.

How was she supposed to bring up kids thinking that they weren't privileged and rich when they were? Their expectations were automatically higher than theirs had been as children. But it had been to no avail—she had been talking to herself and ended up going off in a sulky huff to the privacy of the downstairs toilet.

Her grip on the receiver tightens, turning her knuckles paler than plucked chicken's skin.

"We're bubbling over with plans for our future together. We can't wait, in fact. It's amazing what pressure children put on a couple. Never would have wanted it any different though. I'm surprised you haven't wanted to settle down."

Jennifer wishes Sabina could see the tears streaming down her face, smudging her make-up; tears she had successfully suppressed for a week dribbling down her cheeks, neck and cleavage into her special breast-enlarger bra.

"Well, mustn't spend too long on the phone. I'll be able to talk to you face to face soon," she says bravely and hangs up.

Jennifer has no time to ruminate over the conversation she has just had with her sister: she is eager to get back to the kitchen. Her boyfriend Rick and four colleagues will be arriving shortly for an evening meal she invited them to and she has no time to lose. It all started last Friday, the day of her promotion. She invited her close colleagues, including Rick, to some celebratory bubbly and ended up drinking most of it herself. The subject of good food and wine had come up (because her colleagues were pleased to have Rick, the French expert, in their midst) and Jennifer, feeling radiant and completely under the influence of alcohol, impulsively invited them all to dinner at her apartment: the words had just spilled out of her like the champagne bubbles out of their bottle. 'What shall I cook for you, then?' she had asked, not really expecting a reply. Rick had jumped up straight away shouting '*Asperge Argenteuil*' and promptly dropped a French cookbook into her lap as if he had been waiting for that moment all his life.

'Asperge Argenteuil,' Jennifer reads, 'is a vegetable dish which takes its name from Argenteuil, near Paris, famous for its asparagus.' She closes the cookery book and glances at the asparagus spears lying in their paper wrapping on the draining board. All fifty point pertinently at her white kitchen tiles which are still speckled like a bird's egg from her last culinary disaster. It happened when she attempted Seville marmalade to show off in front of Alberto, her Spanish boyfriend. The marmalade reached temperature in the pressure cooker and then spewed it's entire contents over the walls. The speckles (now four months old) have defied every brand of detergent available on the market and cruelly remind her that she can't cook. She had tried to blame the catastrophe on Alberto, seeing as he was the only other person in the kitchen at the time of the disaster and she was desperate to save herself. She knew her talents were more evident in the reading of account sheets than recipes. He enjoyed joking about it in front of her friends, making her relive again and again her awful sense of failure. It became so bad that she no longer felt worthy of being his girlfriend and left him. Now she is dating Rick. He has French parents and was raised on gourmet meals prepared by a mother whose family fortune came from restaurants with Michelin stars.

Jennifer sighs as she collects the necessary utensils and ingredients for her work. Most are 'poor-me' sighs, a few are sighs of frustration and the rest are sighs of anger at her current predicament.

She re-opens the cookery book at the right page (Rick has earmarked it) and slams the metal colander down. 'I shall make this dish, and fantastically, if it's the last thing I do,' she resolves.

'Clean the asparagus!' the book dictates. She runs the tap and pushes the asparagus into the sink like lemmings into a raging sea. The water splashes her face and the spears make a sound on the bottom like distant drums. She pulls out one spear at a time, rubs it from tip to end and back up again and places it into the colander, pleased that she rejected Rick's offer of help: he would have loved how she handled the asparagus, attaching sexual innuendo to her every move.

When the asparagus is finally standing upright in the pan of boiling water, she heaves a sigh of relief. Fifty tips peer over the pan at her accusingly and she wonders what her colleagues would have said about it; they had joked about the phallic nature of the food all last week, laughing more than they had laughed about anything in a long time. Jennifer didn't think it was funny at all.

She pushes the point of a knife into a spear as she recalls one of the numerous pieces of advice Rick had given her throughout the week. Each helpful hint had been offered in a half-serious, half-jovial manner, making it impossible to tell whether he was teasing or genuinely wanting to be helpful. By Friday she wasn't only exasperated from all the information he had fed her with, but completely confused. And, whenever she wanted to get angry with him, his French lips had pursed in an irresistible way making her feel bad for having a cross word about him at all. As far as she was concerned, he was the only gourmet meal she needed.

But it seemed that 'Asperge Argenteuil' was what he needed and, if she wanted him, she would have to serve it to him.

'Cut off the woody ends and discard.' She lines them up ten at a time and swipes off the fattest part at the bottom (about 2 cms). Some still look longer than others, so she trims them to the size of the shortest ones. Occasionally one slips her grasp and she cuts it even shorter. She throws all this waste in the bin reserved for 'compostable' rubbish.

She's a bit worried that the she has cut off too much, but loves their uniformity and hopes her friends will appreciate the work she has put into the cutting.

Now for the top end, she says to herself, reluctant to do anything with the phallic tips. She decides to trim them—just a little and tentatively snips at them. The knife slices through with ease; quite a sensuous feeling and, before she knows it, she's gone through the whole pile and stands back to inspect them. Not quite right, she thinks,—still too vulgar looking. She puts the knife down for a second and then goes into the attack. She manages twenty-five at a time—one long swipe and they're off. If only Rick could have seen her professional knife strokes. Before she realises what she has done, the once long asparagus stems have become a mass of rods rolling about the cutting board amidst a lot of mush which was once asparagus tips. Whilst pondering what to do, she re-reads the instructions in the recipe book. She has already cut them and discarded the woody ends. But all she has left now are some maimed bits. Rick had told her at least twenty times that the length of the asparagus was extremely important: no shorter than 2.5 cm. 'Don't forget that, Jennifer!' he had said with urgency. 'It makes all the difference.'

What to do? The only bits long enough for the dish were the so-called woody ends which she had already added to the 'compostables'. She feels she has no choice but to fish them out again. She empties the entire contents on the kitchen floor and pulls each rod-like part out—one by one. After rinsing off all the slippery, smelly decomposing bits accrued from other organic waste, she places them tenderly into the casserole dish and arranges them as prettily as she can.

As she does, a burst of creativity comes over her and, for a brief moment, she understands how Rick must feel every day of his life when he rustles a three-star meal from leftovers in his fridge. She prefers to plan, organise and manage and, up to now, thought that he liked their contrasting qualities. He called them 'complémentaire'. Or was it 'contradictoire'? She's no longer sure.

She opens the wine Rick has given her, pours herself a glass and nods her head with approval. The twenty-year-old *Grand Premier Cru* from his grand-mother's cellar which Rick had said must 'breathe' for an hour or two to let its full-bodied flavour develop before they drank it, tastes all right to her without all the waiting and she gulps it down. It is then she remembers that she was supposed to have bought a selection of wine (Rick had written a detailed list) and cheese for desert from the delicatessen. No doubt the guests will bring a bottle or two, she thinks and pours herself another glass. She is soon in full swing, submerged in the smells and sounds around the hob, enjoying the wine. Cooking can be pleasurable she muses and resolves to do it more often. Not for him—for herself.

That is the only problem in their relationship, she surmises. She fell in love and started doing things to please him: French lessons, visits to Paris, museums, weekends in Brittany, French wine courses. It was thrilling, romantic, delicious. But where was the relationship going? A proposal. Is that what she was begging for?

The bottle is nearly empty by the time she gets to the trickiest part of the recipe—the thickening of the sauce. 'Stir rapidly to prevent lumps from forming,' she reads. Jennifer's sauce already has lumps and she hasn't done any stirring yet. When she does begin, the lumps seem to multiply even more rapidly than when she left it to boil by itself. A wave of indignation which has undoubtedly been whipped up by the wine, rises and breaks over her and she finds herself encouraging larger lumps to form by adding spoonfuls of flour to the boiling liquid. It's child's play.

The doorbell rings. It is Rick and her other guests. She shoos him out of the kitchen, ordering him to wait with the other guests in the lounge where the table has been laid. When he asks her what to serve as *apéritif*, she shoves a bottle of mineral water in his hand and tells him to leave her in peace. No-one has brought any wine and, failing to find the bottle from his grandmother's cellar, he reluctantly does as he is told and then sits at the edge of his chair sipping furiously at the water.

Half an hour later, Jennifer staggers in, plonks the casserole onto the table, places a ladle next to it and invites her guests to help themselves.

'*Bon Appétit*' they chorus and tentatively lift spoonfuls onto their plates. Rick pokes about at his portion with a fork—shoving certain pieces to one side—and finding it hard to conceal his disgust on discovering that most are neither the right length, nor actually parts of asparagus at all but lumps of sauce. Everyone except Rick manages to eat a forkful—chewing in silence whilst delicately pulling asparagus thread from between their teeth behind cupped hands. All eyes, except Rick's, are fixed on the plates.

A few moments later the door slams shut. Rick has left. Everybody is looking at everybody and guffaws of laughter turn into tears of laughter running down each one of their faces. It reaches a climax as they take turns to peer into the biological waste bin at all the discarded parts of asparagus: the succulent tips, the delicious centre. In fact, nearly all edible parts of the asparagus are mushed up in there among potato peelings and egg shells.

"Why didn't you say something?" her colleagues say in unison. "We would have helped."

Jennifer is trying too hard to take it lightly and hide the tears of sadness under the tears of laughter.

...And Forgotten?

Sabina sits staring at the piece of paper full of zigzags she has drawn during her conversation with Jennifer. 'You have to get some experience,' a voice tells her. 'You're nearly fifteen and haven't even kissed a boy!'

* * * *

She trailed behind Jennifer, pretending to be grown-up, interested in flirting and such nonsense, all the time feeling uncomfortably foolish.

"This is my sister Sabina," Jennifer announced with false enthusiasm to the poor victim.

He had been set up. He looked from one to the other, comparing, his face visibly clouding over as he realised that he had drawn the shortest straw: there was not just disappointment in the young man's eyes but raw, panicky horror. Jennifer stood beside Sabina, taller by a head and a half, well-developed, older, more sophisticated. From a distance, she could have been mistaken for Sabina's mother; and that was exactly what the young man had thought as he stood there, dumb struck and aghast, wishing he was playing darts with his mates down the local pub.

Sabina felt wretched, sick and wanted to run home. Jennifer would make humorous excuses for her appearance: 'She had a little too much birthday cake the other day which gave her a few spots. They'll go in a day or two'—or: 'The hairdresser that worked on her hair has been given the sack.' Jennifer had only made matters worse. The young man usually believed her and ran away. In her frustration she fumed at Sabina all the way home on the bus, telling her to grow up and take an interest in boys. "It's you that has to make an effort you know—they don't just fall off trees into your arms like ripe apples. Stuff your bra, put more make-up on, wear higher heels, flirt a little bit! For God's sake, Sabina, when are you finally going to act your age?"

Every one of those evenings ended in tears—Sabina's tears. She stormed up to her room and banged the door shut with house-shuddering force. She bit her Barbie dolls, singed their synthetic hair on the light bulb, and hammered her fists and feet against the door. She was furious—not with her older sister—with herself. She had failed, would always fail. Their mother didn't intervene—she was either listening to classical music in the lounge or having an early night, pretending not to notice the racket going on in Sabina's room. And Sabina didn't want to disturb her mother's few moments of hard-earned peace.

* * * *

The horn of Adrian's car sounds. It's eight o'clock and the rain has increased since the afternoon drizzle that accompanied Sabina home from Madame Anastasia's. She is rattled after the telephone conversation with her sister and still feels bewildered from her bizarre experience at the villa. What had caused her to black out, lose control, forget? She often catches herself daydreaming so intensely that she peels a second batch of potatoes when at least a kilo is turning flaccid and grey on the draining board, but that's normal. She's never found herself on a tiled floor staring at a mirror and looking as though she's been roughed up by a vacuum cleaner. She can't remember further than the cup of tea and chocolates. How delicious they were. She even stopped at the *Confiserie* on the way home (and was nearly caught out by the name again—hearing 'confession' more than 'confection') to buy a three-layered box full. *A special treat,* she told herself, *for those 'down' moments,* and tucked them safely away into the bottom drawer of her bedside table. She wouldn't want her family knowing about her failing willpower. Despite her unsettled mind, she has resisted so far: Dominic, her eldest son, has been pottering in and out of the kitchen and would have smelled them on her breath. So she has been strong and he hasn't suspected how tumultuous her mood is. Now that the rest of her family has arrived home after a holiday weekend, she doggedly puts the day's events to the back of her mind and greets the new arrivals.

Adrian looks well. Too well for his forty-one years. His dark, rain-soaked hair shines under the outside lamp as he leaps up the steps, three at a time and bounds through the doorway. Sabina is overcome with a strange giddiness and her heart races. His energetic eyes give her the positive feeling that the trip with Carl has been a success.

"Hi, Sabina," he says, out of breath and embraces her. She struggles against a sudden spark of excitement and lowers her head. She hadn't reckoned on what she is next confronted with and the shock makes her jump out of his arms as one who has just received an electric shock. He was wearing a pair of jeans she hadn't seen for exactly thirteen years—a pair she had thrown with great disgust to the back of the loft. She had found out where (and with whom) he had bought them. He must have found them whilst rummaging for the camping equipment needed for the trip. Thirteen years ago to the date and her resentment, anger and grief is suddenly as fresh as if plucked from the garden yesterday. He had come through customs at Luxembourg airport after a business trip to Brussels looking bronzed and ravishing in those pale stone-washed jeans. Her heart had leapt like it used to before they married and had kids. She still remembers that wonderful surge of hope she had felt—the strongest she had felt since Dominic was born. In that moment and afterwards as they had made love, she had felt that life was worth living after all. If only she had known the truth at the time, she would have made that pert bottom of his black and blue with bruises, instead of red with the colour of her lipstick. Her thoughts break off abruptly as Adrian suddenly exclaims:

"I had a great time!"

"Oh, good." Sabina finds herself replying whilst her mind is turning into a thousand knotted vipers. She turns to ask Carl about the trip but sees that he's not there.

"What about?—" she begins

"His Lordship?" Adrian interrupts, eyes rolling in the direction of the stairs. "He fled to his bedroom like a wounded animal as soon as I drew up to the house. Didn't you see him scamper past just now?"

No, she thinks, *I was too busy thinking about your bloody jeans and all that is associated with them.* She knows that he wouldn't even begin to appreciate the amount of distress he could cause her just by wearing an old pair of faded jeans, so it would be useless trying to explain.

"It's been disastrous, this whole trip. Stupid idea. I don't know why I let myself be talked into it."

And Sabina knows whom that criticism is directed at. She was the one to insist he take Carl on this trip even though she knew it could jeopardise what little there was left of the father-son relationship. She had placed all her hope in Carl who can be extremely obliging towards the man with whom he has very little in common except his looks. The last time Adrian took the boys on an excursion, he had returned vowing never to take them ever again. In a rare moment of compassion (following a successful week at work), he had agreed on a biking weekend with Carl. 'How very humble of you,' Sabina had told her bathroom mirror shortly after he had announced his plan and showed her the 250km route with its numerous long ascents. She should have known that Carl would not be up to the challenge. Adrian is a very keen mountain-biker; Carl is the museum and book type.

Father and son have been having great difficulties for over a year. When Carl turned thirteen, he became more resolute and headstrong compared with the passive, resigned boy of the preceding years. Adrian suddenly noticed that his authoritative tone no longer had the desired effect on him and blamed this phenomenon on the new teacher at school. 'He's teaching them to be disrespectful and disobedient!' he fumed after another one of their fights. 'Who gives him the right to change our innocent young boy into such a convoluted, self-centred and altogether problematic child?'

Sabina tried to protest; reason with him—tell him that all Carl needed was his support, approval and encouragement. Adrian didn't want to listen; he wanted to be right and did not believe that half the battle could be won by giving his son some attention, the feeling that he is loved.

Adrian finds that hard to give, not because he doesn't love his family but because he never experienced it in his own childhood. He was a male growing up with brothers and there was no room for a quick sob, an embrace or an understanding ear. He learned to grit his teeth and get on with it, eventually losing touch with his own sensitivity and the sensitivity of others. Faced with a pubescent male who moaned at the slightest physical exertion made him angry and unsympathetic. He couldn't relate to how his son felt and so he blamed him for it.

Sabina knocks on Carl's bedroom door.

"May I come in?" she asks

There's no answer so she slowly presses down the door handle to test the ground before entering. Hearing no protests, she opens the door just far enough to peek inside. Carl is lying on his back; shoulders propped up with pillows, headphones of his CD-walkman plugged deep into his ears. For a brief moment, his face turns towards the door to display a handsome profile and the expressive face which never failed to inform Sabina of his mood.

"So, it wasn't much fun then?" she ventures.

He remains silent whilst Sabina tiptoes further into the room, taking care to close the door quietly. Half a metre from his bed she stops. "Did you have bad weather?"

He continues to gaze absently into the middle of the room, ignoring her presence, and Sabina acknowledges his need for time and space. She pats his hand compassionately and leaves the room.

Adrian is in the kitchen, banging about with a cup, tea bag and the kettle.

"Adrian?"

"What?" he fires.

"Tell me about your weekend."

"There's nothing to tell."

"But, Carl..."

"What about Carl?"

"He's upset."

"He's always getting upset over the smallest things."

"Maybe you should talk..."

"We talked enough on our little trip. He won't listen to me. You talk to him—you know how to pamper him."

"I don't pamper him," she protests, cross that he has cornered her already. She remains silent—a statue amidst a raging sea. He does not bother with his usual 'yes-you-do-pamper-him' look but continues unabashed to place the blame on her.

"If you hadn't pampered him for all these years," he begins, arms swaying grandly at fourteen imaginary years, "he might have been able to take the pace. But he was always behind. I mean, *really* behind—like a couple of kilometres." Sabina's jaw drops. She stares at the balding patch on the back of Adrian's head and considers smashing one of his favourite whisky glasses on it. She restrains herself.

She can just imagine him, head down, thighs working madly, fingers nimbly moving up and down the gears, racing ahead of his amateur son. How can he enjoy treating him like that? He probably raced harder against him than his most competitive rival.

"He moaned that I was going too fast, that it was raining, that it was cold."

"But didn't you let him catch up?"

"Catch up? I wasn't exactly going fast. If I'd gone much slower I would have fallen off."

"You don't have to exaggerate."

"Exaggerate? You're always on his side. For your information, I did try to talk—after we had pitched the tent up."

"And?"

"He refused. Crept in and didn't come out again."

"But didn't you try to..."

"No. He was tired."

"He was upset!"

"Of course, the mother knows best. You would have begged him to come out and pour his little heart out to you and he would have done and you would have lapped it up."

"Adrian, he's an adolescent. He's having a hard time dealing with all the hormones in his body."

"You always have an excuse for him, don't you? It's the hormones now, is it? Last time it was the growing pains; before that it was the stress of school, and before that it was teething pains!"

Sabina is silent. He continues:

"I have just spent a whole weekend with him. That's a lot of time. Just the two of us. And it didn't work."

"Maybe you need to spend more time..." she ventures.

"Oh, really. And when, may I ask?"

"Another weekend may..."

"No. We don't share the same interests."

"Well, you could just chat, go for a walk, find something you both have in common."

"Listen, I'm in the office ten hours a day. When I come home, he's out or doing his homework. The weekend is the only time I have to do some sport, my hobbies. I gave up my time this weekend for him and look where it's got me!"

"But..."

"No buts. It's true. He's been mollycoddled too long."

Like a politician in front of a nagging reporter, he had made his final statement and scurried upstairs to the office with his cup of tea.

Sabina doesn't try to broach the subject with Adrian again that evening, but spends the rest of it watching a dull film on television, guiltily hoping that Carl is sorting out his problem alone in his room. She knows what Adrian is doing: hammering through the Internet as usual—enjoying the warmth coming off the monitor.

It has been an exhausting day and, though successful as far as her resolution is concerned, she finds herself unable to really acknowledge it. The shadow of the day has grown plump, consuming her achievements like a ravenous animal, devouring them and swallowing them down to the dark inside. She now feels that she has achieved nothing more than another argument with Adrian and feels that she is back where she started in the morning—with Shrinking Violet in the mirror who hasn't the courage to frighten a shitting dog away from her front garden.

Whilst the television flashes pictures, colour and sound at her, she lets her mind run through the blurred memories of her meeting with Madame Anastasia. No matter how hard she tries, she can't remember what she did or said during the five hours she spent there. Even the composure she felt on leaving could have been imagined. She hopes that her next appointment will shed light on the matter and continues watching the film. It ends happily ever after as she expected and she is disappointed that it didn't surprise her by ending tragically, or comically, or in any other way than happily. Excitement and romance lapsed; it was as banal as her existence. As she presses the off button on the remote control, she hears a noise in the hallway and turns to see Carl walking towards the living room. She always dreads these moments because she feels like a fraud. How can she help other people when she can't even sort herself out?

"Mum," Carl begins

Sabina listens.

"I wish father would just accept me for what I am."

"Oh, darling, he does try. You both have such diverse personalities that it's not always easy," she replies diplomatically.

"Well, do you think that this biking trip was easy for me?" Carl's voice is already shaky. "Do you realise how much I hate biking? But I went—because I couldn't just stand still and watch our relationship going down hill. I thought I could do something about it, change it."

Sabina shifts her weight.

Carl continues: "I've tried my best and no-one can deny that. But he's such an egoist..."

Sabina opens her mouth to protest but nothing comes out.

"He didn't even try to listen to me. He didn't want to hear what I like to do and what I want from life. He just expects me to be enthralled by everything he does. All the sporting things. Do you know what he said?"

"No," she says quietly.

"He said that I wasn't normal because I would rather read a book or walk around museums."

His eyes began to water. Sabina is speechless. She knows what he meant by his words and so does Carl. Adrian supports the old-fashioned notion that, to be a man, a boy must face the elements, show his strength of body and willpower by challenging them to their limits. In moments of fury and frustration at his younger son's disinterest in sport he had suggested that this 'abnormal behaviour' meant that he was gay.

The tears that Carl tried so hard to hold back begin to run in a stream towards his chin. Sabina puts her arms around him and holds him close.

"I love you," she says.

One hand stroking his hair, she continues: "Look, I know your father is a difficult man. He has his fixed ideas and it's very hard to convince him otherwise. He does love you, though."

Carl raises his head and looks at her, disbelieving.

"You're strong, Carl. You must ignore his attempts at pushing the emotional button. He only does it when he's feeling powerless against you—which happens a lot."

Then, with a smile, she adds: "Maybe you should invite him on a cultural weekend and give him a taste of his own medicine!"

He also braves a smile and gives his Mum a hug.

"I love you too, Mum."

Sabina is always amazed at how little discussion it takes to help him work things out. How did he manage to do it? He obviously didn't have that characteristic from her. She found it hard to let go of experiences, put them behind her and let them rest in the past.

Carl lies back down on the bed and plugs Beethoven's 5th into his ears. That is not 'normal' either—'listening to classical at your age!' his Dad once added as punctuation to an argument. Carl rarely takes his father's advice, holding on to his own interests and opinions. His self-esteem suffers in his father's presence and he is sad about that because it means that his father never sees what he is really like. He jumps to conclusions, knocks him down before he has a chance. The mountain-bike trip was an attempt at approaching his father and even that became a power struggle.

He often feels jealous of his brother Dominic who doesn't seem to provoke his father in the same way—probably because he shares similar interests. His appearance is brought up now and again because Adrian hates Dominic's green hair and punk-rocker image, but it never has real consequences for their relationship.

Carl doesn't consider himself the rebellious type—even though he has been accused of it. It was his teacher Mr Toking, his father said. He was putting ideas into his head. Maybe it was true. If it was, Carl couldn't help thinking that Mr Toking's ideas were enlightening and far more educational than anything his father had ever taught him. It was that same teacher who helped him kick the habit of saying and doing things just to please others.

*   *   *   *

The entire class of 32 kids were waiting for Mr Toking. He was late and the noise and activity in the room had been increasing at an exponential rate. One boy was jumping in and out of the window, smoking with fifth formers who were supposed to be in a Maths lesson. A girl and a boy compared nail length and colour and tried to put nail varnish on a third child's finger stumps. A further five pupils were playing Postman's Knock behind the row of lockers at the back of the room until Julie refused to kiss Harry on the lips and caused a fight to break out. Ben, the smallest and fattest boy in the class, was meticulously tearing strips of paper from his school book, modelling them into tiny bullets and firing them, one by one, into the waste-paper basket at the front of the classroom. Most of them successfully landed in the bin that was now overflowing with the ammunition. With every hit, he roared in delight and punched the stale, warm air with victorious fists.

When Mr Toking finally arrived and entered the classroom, Ben had just started firing a new round of paper bullets. One, badly aimed, brushed the side of the teacher's leg. The teacher felt a tap on his trouser leg, turned towards the front row of children and roared:

"Who the hell did that?"

There was a scurrying and shuffling, banging and scraping and everyone was shocked into attention. All thirty-two faced the front, guilty as hell. Carl was standing with his best friend in the second row of desks. He was gob-smacked at his teacher's angry tone. Mr Toking repeated the question with ear-bashing loudness.

"If the culprit doesn't own up to his deed, I shall have no other choice than to put the entire class in detention."

Silence.

"Well? I can't wait all day."

Silence.

"Right—det..."

Ben piped up:

"It w-was m-me, S-s-s-sir. I didn't..."

"You didn't what?" the teacher interrupted, approaching Ben and pointing a shaky finger at him. "You didn't hit me? Is that what you were going to say? Well, you're wrong. You did. And I'm sick of being Mr Let-Pupils-Walk-All-Over-Me. From now on, I'm going to have discipline, discipline, discipline!" And he underlined each word with a bang of his clenched fist on Ben's desk.

Ben looked as if he was going to have a heart attack at the age of thirteen.

"Do you usually go around hitting your teachers?" Mr Discipline asked.

"I-I didn't..."

"Don't you dare be so cheeky. What on earth got into you, boy?" he screamed. "Don't you have any respect at all?"

"N-no. I m-mean, y-yes. But..."

"No buts. I'll teach you what respect is and so will the headmaster, and so will your parents when I tell them about your abominable behaviour."

"Um...I," he paused "Sorry," he added forlornly.

"Sorry isn't going to be enough. What do you think the headmaster will say, when I tell him? Do you know what happens to boys like you?"

The boy was looking at the ground, trembling and pale.

"Do you?"

"N-no," he sobbed.

Carl was in shock. The whole year of teaching raced through his head. He did not understand what was going on. It was unheard of, criminal. All because of a small ball of paper. He turned to look at his friend, Dave. His face reflected the same expression of confusion. He shrugged.

"We have to do something," Carl whispered.

"What can we do?" replied Dave. "The teacher has totally flipped."

"I know. But we can't let Ben suffer like that. The teacher's gone mad. We'll have to intervene."

"I daren't. I mean. I thought I knew Mr Toking. I thought he was one of us. Now, I'm more confused than ever."

Carl agreed. But he couldn't let it go on. The poor boy was still quivering like a jellyfish at the front of the room and the teacher was threatening to expel him. The rest of the class was silent; a room full of dummies stuck to seats.

Carl stood up.

"Sit down!" his teacher blasted at him.

Carl remained standing, eyes steadily ahead, and fixed on his teacher's reddened face. The remaining sixty-two eyes turned towards him.

"Sit down I say!" Mr Toking repeated. "Or do you want to go to the headmaster as well?"

"No, Sir, I don't. And I won't sit down either."

"How dare you be so cheeky! You're well on your way to the headmaster's office, young man. And those who have to visit the headmaster are labelled misbehavers, trouble causers. The staff talk about boys like you in the staff room."

Carl remained composed, inching forward. Surely he wouldn't resort to physical violence? He held the teacher's stare.

"Why are you so angry, Mr Toking?" he asked calmly.

Mr Toking looked at him, visibly reflecting.

"You saw what Ben did, didn't you?"

"Yes, I did. He was misbehaving. But, don't you think you're overreacting?"

The teacher was actually calming down. Carl's best mate gave him a nod of encouragement. Ben's face turned from white to dough-coloured.

"Why not let Ben explain himself, instead of shouting at him."

Mr Toking's accusing finger went limp. His nostrils closed again.

Ben started to talk, quietly at first, and then louder so that next door could have heard.

Mr Toking smiled at Carl, at Ben, at the whole class. Extending his right arm, he said:

"Congratulations!" and shook Carl's hand.

Continuing to smile warmly at him, he added: "My friend Ben and I have held a veritable show here for you today. What do you think? Will we be taken on by the Royal Shakespeare Company?"

Ben beamed and bowed.

Everyone began to breathe. Everyone clapped, whistled, stamped their feet.

"I take that as a yes!" he chuckled. "This little scenario has shown you how a slight misunderstanding and the wrong temperament can develop into a threatening situation with a total communication breakdown. My reaction caused him to panic, bow to my authority and not attempt to explain himself. That's a situation that you can easily get yourself into and it's not easy to break the spell that holds both parties involved. Young Carl here found a solution. It worked. He pointed out what I was doing, that I was overreacting, that I was angry and that there was another way to deal with the situation. He did it calmly and confidently. Does anyone have other suggestions or comments?"

Every hand in the class went up and the rest of the lesson was spent discussing all sorts of situations, real and fictional that were related to the one in hand.

Another Encounter

Despite her inner nervousness, Sabina forces herself to appear calm as she enters the villa. Seeing as she has spent an entire week practising for this morning's meeting, it is the least she can expect. Madame Anastasia takes Sabina's coat, scarf and gloves, folds them carefully and places them in a neat pile on the arm of a red chaise-longue that guards the old-fashioned telephone in the entrance hall.

Today, Madame Anastasia is again dressed in wine red—a colour that features throughout the house. Her black hair is neatly rolled into a French pleat at the back of her head, making her appear even taller. With one hand she reaches into an oak cupboard and pulls out a large wicker basket crammed full of traditional sewing equipment: a pincushion, needles, tailor scissors, buttons, cotton reels and scraps of material. A tape measure dangles over the side and wriggles like a worm as she walks past Sabina towards the living room.

Sabina enters the room, pushes passed her host, races over to the chair she is familiar with, and plonks down. She has mentally rehearsed this move a thousand times; hoping it will give the impression that she is confident and resolute. Instead, she looks like a scared rabbit running away from the magician before he turns her into a puff of smoke. Madame Anastasia places her enormous hands on the back of the chair opposite, pushes it closer to Sabina's and finally perches on the edge, leaning forwards and gazing directly into her eyes. Sabina slumps back to avoid eye contact.

"You know that I design my dresses for each individual. No two are the same. But please look through this catalogue again and tell me of your preferences," says Madame Anastasia and hands her a large leather-bound catalogue that was lying on the glass coffee table.

Sabina is slightly disturbed by the word 'again' but reminds herself that Madame Anastasia is French and so her English will not be perfect.

"Thank you," she says, taking the catalogue and placing it cautiously on her lap. Her fingers glide over the gold-embossed script on the front cover, feeling the ins and outs of the low relief and enjoying the smooth bumpiness under her fingertips. She then reads out:

Avoir Robes de Distinction

Her own voice startles her and her cheeks redden. She lowers her head to hide her embarrassment and opens the book. Each picture has been hand painted in a rainbow of colours that are the rarest and most vibrant Sabina has ever seen.

These are far too beautiful for me, she thinks and snaps the book shut.

"Are you all right?" she hears and looks up to try and explain her rude behaviour to Madame Anastasia. When she looks up, Madame Anastasia is no longer in the room. The next voice she hears is Adrian's. She knows he's not in the room with her—he's inside her head; yet she feels utterly powerless at switching the voice off and preventing a repeat of the exchange she had with him thirteen years ago.

"Are you all right?"

"Yes. Why do you ask?" Adrian asked "You seem to be bothered by something."

"Hmmn."

"What does 'Hmmn' mean?"

"I don't want to talk about it."

They were lying in bed—he on his side, she on her side. There was no chance of hands, feet, or buttocks coming into contact without concerted effort. Adrian turned to face the wall as she spoke.

"Why don't you? Has it to do with us?"

"I don't want to talk about it, okay? It's late."

"But, I can sense that something isn't right. Do you know when you last said that you loved me?"

"No."

"Nor do I."

"Hmm."

"Do you love me?"

Long silence.

"Do you love me, Adrian?"

Still silence.

"Answer me, for God's sake!"

"I don't know."

"What do you mean—you don't know?"

"I don't think so—not at the moment."

"Not at this precise moment? Or not any more?"

"Sabina, please."

"Please what?"

"Don't make me say it—I'm a little confused at the moment."

"You're confused?"

"I need a little time."

"Well, I need to know right now!"

Sabina turned her head away. Tears had started to roll down her face. "Are you going to tell me?"

"Okay—if you insist."

"Well?"

"Sabina, I don't want to hurt you, but…"

"But what?"

"Well, I just don't feel the same for you anymore."

She knew it. She knew there had been something wrong. She had avoided bringing the subject up for a long time. She had felt too vulnerable. She had not wanted to hear what she feared she was going to hear. And as long as she didn't know—she was safe. But tonight it had just happened, without her really wanting it. Maybe she didn't think the conversation was going to lead where it did.

"What do you feel for me then?"

"I don't know."

"Do you like me?"

"Yes, of course!"

"A lot, a little bit?"

"Please!"

"Is there someone else?"

Silence.

"Is there?"

Telling silence.

"Yes, but that's not why I don't feel the same for you."

"What do you mean?"

"I mean—I don't love her either. She's just there. It's just a coincidence that it has happened at the same time as my changed feelings towards you."

"You mean, there's nothing to salvage?"

"I don't feel like doing anything about it at the moment."

"Shit, Adrian. This is not a game! This is serious. Who is she?"

"I don't want to bring her into it."

"Where did you meet her? At work? Is she a colleague? Do I know her?"

"Yes, I met her through work. No, she's not a colleague directly. No, you don't know her."

"I suppose everyone at work knows about you and this other woman."

"No-one knows."

"Oh, don't be so naive, Adrian. Of course they'll know."

"I assure you, we've been very discrete."

"How considerate!"

Silence.

Sabina bit her lips. What was she going to do? Her heart hurt.

"So, if this woman doesn't mean all that much to you, why are you still seeing her?"

"She does mean something to me. I don't want to give her up."

"How long has this been going on?"

Silence.

A few weeks? A few months?"

"I met her just over a year ago."

Oh my God—A year ago! Sabina—you have been Blind!

"So where does she live—near by?"

"No. In Belgium."

Sabina felt slightly relieved.

"Where? Brussels?"

"Yes."

Sabina's mind raced through all the times Adrian had been in Brussels. He was there quite often—at least once a month. She felt sick.

"How often do you see her?"

"Once every two months or so."

"And then every time she comes here."

"No! I really don't see her very often."

"Oh, you poor thing!"

Silence.

He was with her on Dominic's birthday! And I sympathised! 'Poor Daddy is away on business, but he'll be back in two more sleeps to wish you a happy birthday.' Two more sleeps. With her!

And I had put the kids to bed extra early and made Scampi in Garlic for 'Dear Daddy' and we celebrated with champagne. We celebrated his great bonk!

"Has she ever been to Luxembourg?"

"Yes."

"When?"

"Sabina!"

"When?"

"Four weeks ago. But..."

"I don't ever want her to step foot in this house. I don't want her anywhere near Dominic and Carl. Do you hear?"

"Yes. We never would."

We. God, that hurts!

"So, what are you going to do?"

"I don't know."

"What am I supposed to do?"

"I don't know!"

"I can't stand it."

Silence

"Sabina?"

Silence

"Let's talk about it again tomorrow. I have to sleep now."

Silence.

Sabina was no longer in the bedroom. She had slid out of the bed and crawled into the children's room. It smelled of the sweet calendula cream she had rubbed into their child-soft skin after their bath. Dominic was in the 'big' bed. His legs were dangling over the side, his arms wrapped tightly around his favourite cuddly toy, his mouth slightly open. Sabina placed her cheek on his and stroked his thick blond hair. His breath smelled of strawberry toothpaste. She gently lifted his legs back onto the bed and pulled the covers over them. He sighed, smacked his mouth like he was chewing bubble-gum and then fell back into his deep slumber. Sabina glanced over to her 'terrible two-year old'. He still slept in a cot. He had kicked off all his covers and his pyjama top had ridden up to expose his rounded belly. She could not resist kissing his tummy button and he smiled in his sleep as she did so. She wondered what he was dreaming about and whether that kiss had influenced it. She rescued his dummy which was squashed between the mattress and the side of the cot and placed it next to his head. She also rescued a tiny piece of fluffy material that used to be the ear of a cuddly dog named Woof. Carl used to take Woof with him wherever he went, carrying him by his floppy ears. One day, the ears fell off, so Sabina sewed them back on. They fell off again. She sewed them back on. This went on for a while until one day she could not be bothered to sew them on yet again and gave him the dog back without ears. He screamed. He was heart-broken. He hated Woof now. Sabina rushed to get the ears from the bin and was about to sew them back on when Carl snatched them out of her hands and held them to his cheek. He didn't care about Woof—he just wanted the ears. So that's how he had ended up with two fury nose-ticklers: one in his cot and one in the kitchen cupboard—in case of emergencies!

Sabina looked admiringly at her boys:

You're so beautiful!

I love you both.

Without reflecting for even a second, she climbed into Carl's cot and snuggled up next to him.

Oh my sweet boys—what am I supposed to do? I can't face it. I can't stand it. Let's run away together and start again. We'll find a new Daddy who loves us.

She stayed in the cot all night, not sleeping, just running through the last year and finding all the possible rendezvous between Adrian and his lover.

Until the sun shone into Sabina's eyes and colour started pouring into the room like a bottle filling up with orange squash, she thought she was back in her children's nursery with their bright curtains drawn across the window.

"Madame Waldsmere?"

No answer.

"Madame Waldsmere?"

"Wh-?"

"Don't worry, Madame. You are with me. You are all right," she says, holding a red piece of material up to Sabina's face and saying that she can use it to wipe the perspiration off her face.

Sabina slowly sits up, takes the cloth.

"But?" she begins and then flops back into her seat. "Oh God, my head hurts!"

Madame Anastasia carefully massages Sabina's scalp and when she has finished, Sabina sees the catalogue on the floor and places it back into her lap at the open page. She pinches herself just to make sure she's really there and then pretends that she has been looking at the book.

The first picture depicts an evening gown in dazzling greens and blues. The neckline curves its heart-shape over the model's firm breasts and continues in two straight lines up to the neck and behind it, outlining the shoulders and dainty protrusion of the collarbone. A tear-shaped emerald hangs on a fine silver chain just above the cleavage and the peacock colours of the silk glisten in the gem making it come alive with colour and energy. Sabina stares at the picture, mesmerised by its uniqueness and charm. The dress has a bodice and a full skirt that is gathered to form a V at the waist and ends just above the ankles in a curved hemline. Behind, the bodice has been fastened with laces running criss-cross all the way up to the back neckline and the skirt has been drawn to a sizeable mound over the buttocks, resembling a nineteenth-century bustle. Sabina squints to decipher the handwritten notes in the margin. She is surprised that they are in English:

Peacock's pride rewards wearer with regal colours and lustrous silk

She continues to leaf through the catalogue, looking excitedly for the handwriting next to each picture.

Black tempest of anger roams free through the grey cloth of wisdom

Assert and express yourself in revealing glory

The woman in intoxicating red will favour sweeping change

The dress described by the final piece of text is familiar but she can't recall where she has seen it.

"Ah, I see you are admiring my latest creation," Madame Anastasia interrupts, approaching her with a wide smile displaying impeccable ivory teeth. Sabina drops the precious leather book.

"I'm so sorry, I didn't wish to startle you," she remarks when she sees Sabina fumbling with the catalogue.

"Oh, no, you didn't. I was just—" Sabina searches for the rest of the sentence, fails to find it and remains dumb, hoping that Madame Anastasia will help her by continuing the conversation.

"This is the dress you so admired last time you were here."

Last time I was here! Sabina thinks, *I…, but can't remember.* Surely, she hadn't seen the catalogue—she would have remembered that. She drank tea and then…daydreamed, like today. Only last time, it was not a book, but she who had slipped off the chair and woken up in front of that ghastly, gigantic mirror of hers. Perhaps Madame Anastasia was confusing her with someone else.

But instead of voicing her concern about this, she merely croaks, "I did?" and opens the catalogue at the last page to examine the picture once more. There are no clues in the drawing. *It now only looks familiar because I saw it a few minutes ago*, she tells herself; she hadn't seen it last time. But not wanting to embarrass her host, offers.

"Oh, you mean after we drank the tea?"

"Yes, Mrs Waldsmere, you were in raptures about it—wished I could make exactly the same one for you!"

Oh my God. I must be going crazy. What the hell went on here last time?

She can't remember when she was last in raptures about anything. About the birth of her babies, maybe. But apart from those special experiences, her life had always resumed its banal, numb course. She showed emotions of enjoyment, excitement, happiness and pleasure without really feeling them.

Just then a prickling sensation zooms through her arm. She is beginning to worry about another attack of pins and needles when she suddenly finds herself sitting opposite Adrian—Adrian before the permanent frown and receding hairline.

He is smiling at her, gazing into her eyes, stroking her hand with his thumb, yearning. They are sitting in a noisy underground train in Paris on their way to a modest French *pension* near to the *Sacre Coeur*. Sabina has been away for a few months and today is the day they have both been waiting for. The last three months have been torturous. Every free moment has been spent writing love letters; every day has been ticked off in the calendar; every week there have been hours of phoning. But in the three months' separation they hadn't found a substitute for the physical proximity they desired so desperately. Sabina found it hard to sleep at night. She lay awake imagining Adrian's strong body next to hers, thinking about his silken skin, his voice, and his words. All his letters lay in a crumpled heap next to her bed; mauled and tear-stained. She had read each one more than a thousand times and they still managed to make her head spin and her heart leap.

Their embraces are now loaded with many months of desire and she begins gasping for air as sensation zooms through her body. They are like live wires: every touch, every glance, every word is buzzing with sexual electricity. They can hardly wait to get to the hotel. Hand in hand, they pelt through the crowds in the underground station, through the hotel lobby, up the stairs, two, three steps at a time, and into their room, banging the door shut behind them. They are laughing like school kids running away after a prank. As they turn to each other, the laughter subsides. At last they are alone. At last they can express their feelings through their bodies. They undress slowly. They face each other, naked. They lie down on the bed and remain there for a while, admiring their nakedness, not touching—just looking. It is intoxicating. Her breathing becomes more irregular and sexual desire gyrates, getting faster and faster, spreading from the centre of her heart through her stomach, her throat. It is wonderfully choking. Adrian reaches out and strokes her face, her neck, her breasts, her stomach, her hips, her thighs. All the time he watches her reaction and she watches his—they can read the yearning in each other's faces. Hot passion possesses her and she clambers onto it, grabbing, squeezing, lurching, lead by pure desire. She no longer knows where she ends and he begins; her body and mind blend with his and melt as his sex moves in and out, growing harder, stronger. He is deep inside her, caressing her inside. Deeper and deeper. Higher and higher they climb until they can't climb any further. They stay there. On the highest plateau. Holding on. They hold on, hold on and hold on. Then it comes: the gush and pull. It pulls them closer than they have been before. It pulls violently, deliciously.

"Mrs Waldsmere?"

Sabina squints as she tries to bring the person into focus. Madame Anastasia is leaning over her with a glass of water in one hand and a damp cloth in the other.

"I think you passed out," she remarks in a matter-of-fact way and holds the glass of water to Sabina's lips. Sabina drinks obediently and then tries to speak.

"What happened?"

"Ssh."

"But, I…"

"Ssh."

"I was dreaming. It was a dream about me and Adrian."

"I know, ssh. It's all right. You're beginning to feel again."

"What?" Sabina exclaims. "Feel what?"

"Feel what it is like to be alive and to be you."

"Oh!" is all that comes out this time.

Madame Anastasia places a hand on each of her shoulders, looks kindly into Sabina's eyes and says gently:

"Lets begin by making you a beautiful dress. I will see you next week. Okay?"

The Soaking

Sabina is glad that Adrian is still at work when she arrives home from her appointment with Madame Anastasia. An empty house is soothing when she feels emotionally drained and would like to re-live the closeness she once felt with Adrian without him disturbing it. She pours herself a large glass of red wine, goes up to her bedroom, and pulls out the crumpled letter she has hidden in the secret compartment of her jewellery box. She reads:

Dearest darling lover,

When I read your letters, I feel so close to you—I feel as if I'm inside you again, where I belong. It's such a wonderful feeling that I don't ever want it to go away. Thoughts about being inside you make me feel on edge, like every nerve is exposed. Everything—all sensations—are so much clearer, sharper.

Do you remember when we were lying next to each other in that Paris hotel, caressing each other's bodies for the first time in weeks and we came together with such intensity? I can't help thinking about that when you're away and it turns me on.

Am I turning you on with these words? I hope so. I often try to imagine what you're feeling, what you're thinking. I want to be near to you all the time and feel everything you feel, think everything you think—be one with you. I feel like that when I'm inside you and it feels right. I want to spend the rest of my life with you! God, I don't believe I wrote that. It makes me go weak at the knees just thinking about it. Shit, Sabina, I want to give you all the pleasure and happiness you'd ever dreamed of—just for the sake of giving. (I'm really sweating now). I love you so much that I couldn't bear to be without you for another 6 weeks. I NEED you and I WANT you. Please don't ever forget that.

Hugs and kisses in all the right places
Your ever-loving Ade

He used to sign all his letters with the name Ade. She doesn't call him that these days. He finds it ill fitting—belonging to his childhood, student days. It also sounds just like 'Aids' and he hates to be reminded of anything bad—especially life-threatening diseases. A noise from downstairs disturbs her and, thinking it might be Adrian returning from work, she hurries to put the letter back into the box. Her haste punishes her like it did at Madame Anastasia's the first time, knocking over the glass of wine and spilling it over the letter. She considers drying it on the radiator but quickly decides against it—it would take too long and she wouldn't want to risk Adrian seeing it and humiliating her. He had no idea of its existence—probably wouldn't even remember sending it to her. It meant so much to her that she frequently tapped it for warmth and comfort whenever she felt unloved and lonely. She quickly picks the soggy thing up, rushes it like an emergency patient to the bathroom and shakes off the excess fluid into the sink. There was a period of time when she didn't rely on the letter so much—that was when the children were small. They made her feel loved and needed all the time. They accompanied her to the supermarket, they rode with her on the bus, they walked with her through the park and travelled with her in the car. All the time they helped her to laugh and love. She thrived on their company, their uncomplicated love, their spontaneity and carefree way. But as they grew older and more independent, that faithful feeling of loneliness came back and now it pounced on her every morning like a stalking cat. She miserably plugs her hairdryer into the socket, unfolds the limp and wet paper and, holding the appliance at a distance so as not to blow rips into the drenched paper, gently blows the letter dry. The ink has run and smudged all but the first couple of lines, rendering it illegible. Whether she could read it or not, she didn't care. She knew the words off by heart anyway. Throw it away? No, she wasn't ready to do that yet. She was just superstitious enough to want to hang onto it for a while longer. At least until her fortieth Birthday party. And she folded it tenderly and placed it back in her jewellery box.

By the time it's my birthday, she muses, *I might have the courage to talk to him, tell him how I feel.* The problem was—where to start? So much had remained unsaid that it seemed an insurmountable task. Adrian would probably refute it all, start up more endless arguments and she would go off in one of her huffs, slam the bathroom door and complain to the mirror about how sorry she was for herself. And he would go back to his computer screen, not working, just staring so that he wouldn't have to look at her and puzzle out her silent sulks.

Sabina goes back into the bathroom and switches the tap on to fill the bath. As she undresses, and the room fills with hot vapour, the resolution list, which was now safely back in her toiletry bag, peeks accusingly at her between the blusher and eyeliner. She turns her back and continues to prepare for her bath.

She knew what she was doing by keeping silent about her feelings and wasn't exactly proud of herself for doing it. Her main excuse was that he didn't understand her and that the marriage was still functioning all right—ticking over quite nicely—compared to many of their friends who had divorced! In their marriage, no one shouts, no one has arguments. There is just a lot of door-slamming and silences, that is all. Every family has those. It's normal. Anger and arguments are a sign of unhappy families. Theirs was not unhappy. She was unhappy. And who was she to ruin the harmony in the home? She doesn't want her children thinking that she is a marriage-breaker. *I'm not! I'm just a lonely, miserable, depressed specimen of a human being that is struggling to be a good housewife without arguing about it.*

And when things bothered her, she tried to ignore them. Adrian would only be angry with her for being so fussy if she mentioned her trivial problems: he was far too busy working hard at a serious job, earning serious money and providing serious support for the entire family.

During her three-year university course and her short career in the computer business, she thought she would only be happy in full-time paid work. She pitied the women she saw pushing prams up the street, tugging at a toddler, nagging them, hurrying them along. She never wondered whether they had been to university, had a career, or even a brain. Women who became housewives were taking the cushy option. Only dropouts did it. Educated, intelligent women either didn't marry and have babies, or employed a nanny. No woman in her right mind would jump straight off the podium after collecting a Bachelor of Science and straight into a pair of baggy dungarees to breast-feed, rock and burp baby, scrub floors and hang out washing. But that is exactly what she found herself doing. And then, a while later, she felt she was just there—a function, a nobody. She forgot who she was before she became Sabina Waldsmere, wife and mother of two boys.

Is that how her own mother had felt? She never asked her. The last time she saw her was fifteen years ago when Dominic was a toddler and she was expecting Carl.

*   *   *   *

Her mother stayed for a week, helping her with housework and Dominic so that she, being pregnant with number two, could rest as much as possible. The doctor had given her strict instructions not to overstrain herself during this pregnancy because she had already suffered two miscarriages. Baby was not due until February but she was having mild contractions and feeling exhausted. After talking to her mother on the phone about it, she had persuaded her to fly over. Her mother cancelled her plans to go walking in the Lake District, insisting that she didn't mind in the least. Sabina knew by the tone of her voice that she did mind a great deal. Picking her mother up from the airport, Sabina was struck by how much she had aged since their last meeting the previous Christmas.

She is haggard and worn. She's so pale. Her complexion is grey. God, she doesn't look at all well!

"Sabina, my little Bee, how wonderful to see you!" her mother exclaimed, hurrying over to embrace her. "You look so well. No, radiant, is a better word," she continued and smiled one of her deep, warm smiles.

The two embraced for an exceptionally long time, neither of them wanting to end the softness and cosiness of it. Dominic squeezed his little body between their legs until they finally let go. Sabina took a step back. Her mother's smile wiped away her momentary concern and she chose not to spoil the visit by mentioning it.

"And you, Dominic? What a grown up boy you are! Come and give Gransie a hug."

Dominic gave Sabina one of those do-I-have-to glances and Sabina nodded and whispered, "Go on." He gave his grandmother a quick hug and then squirmed free of her tight hold.

"Let go. I don't like it!" he shouted and retreated back behind Sabina's legs.

Gransie's eyes lowered, her mouth drooped.

When Sabina came back from paying the parking ticket, Gransie's smile was fixed into place again and she patted her daughter's bump.

"Let's have a better look at you!"

Sabina stood still and let her bump be inspected by her mother's hands.

"Could be another boy—by the size and shape," she stated and shot an endearing glance at little Dominic who still had a firm hold of his mother's legs.

"But I told you in my letter that I already know what sex it is!" said Sabina, surprised that her mother could have forgotten, seeing as she usually had a talent for retaining that kind of information.

"Well?"

"It *is* another boy!"

"Have you thought of a name then?" she asked absently, apparently unperturbed that she had failed to remember.

"No."

"Oh, well. I'm sure you'll find something suitable. I'm only good with girl's names," she said and sounded rather sad.

"I've always liked the name Maurice," continued Sabina, "but Adrian isn't shifting from his choice of Carl."

"That reminds me of when your father and I were looking for a name for you—we just couldn't agree on one."

Her eyes began to sparkle as she saw an amusing side of the story she was about to tell. Sabina who had heard it countless times. Each time she told it, it was as if a bit more of the anger her mother had felt all those years ago, broke away. Listening to the story today gave Sabina the impression that her mother had been absolutely delighted about the choice of names for both daughters. She had, in truth, been disgusted that her daughters were being named after two past flames of his. Her mother was not supposed to know about it but she had probably known all along. That was why she had fought so vehemently against her husband's decision; she had refused to go to the town hall to register the child and they very nearly missed the deadline. In the end, she gave in and that is how Sabina became Sabina.

Her mother had immediately found a suitable sobriquet— 'Bee'—partly because Sabina used to buzz busily around the house and garden as a child, but mostly because she was making a point of not using the name she disagreed about. Jennifer was nicknamed Guin, short for Guinevere.

"You used to turn a hundred perfect cartwheels down the lawn and never get dizzy."

"I know. I sometimes get the urge to do one."

Her mother laughed. "You won't, though, will you?"

"Of course not. But it's a good sign to feel that way, isn't it?"

"Yes, of course. This one's solid. It's not going to shift. Don't you worry."

"No."

"You do look radiant, my love. I wish I could have looked half as well as you during pregnancy."

"Oh, Mum, you probably looked ten times as good. Don't you remember that old photograph—the one of you in the maternity dress you sewed? You looked great!"

"Did I?" she said with the thankfulness of a child.

"Didn't your Mum say so?"

"My mother? I don't think she ever saw me pregnant," she stated and quickly looked the other way so that Sabina could not see the expression on her face. Pretending that she had been searching for a trolley, she pointed to one and exclaimed cheerfully, "Look, we can load my bags onto that trolley over there!"

"Come here, let me get that for you," said Sabina, tugging at the heavy suitcase.

"Not on your life—or your baby's—I should say. I can manage. I'm not as old and frail as I look."

Sabina could not prevent the corners of her mouth from sagging in a telling way and her mother read the meaning of it.

"You're looking great Mum," she said to her mother's back as she loaded the suitcases and hand luggage onto the airport trolley.

Sabina started to push it before her mother could protest and steered it towards the car.

"Want a ride?" she called to Dominic.

He nodded.

"Come on then, hop on."

As she held his hands high above his head to help him step onto the trolley and manoeuvre himself into place in front of Gransie's heavy suitcase, he asked, "Why has Gransie got a baby in her tummy?"

"Gransie hasn't got a baby in her tummy, Mummy has."

"But Gransie has!" he insisted

"No."

"Yes."

"No, darling." she repeated softly, not daring to look behind her, hoping that Gransie had not heard their little discussion.

"She eats too many chocolates," he stated.

"Chocolate? Did I hear chocolate?" her mother interrupted.

Sabina blushed

"Gransie," Dominic began, "have you got chocolates in your tummy?"

"Of course I have, little man—and some more in my bag—just for you," she replied and her eyes twinkled briefly as he screeched with joy.

*   *   *   *

Sabina grabs a bottle of lavender oil from the bathroom shelf and pours it into the bathtub and the bathwater greets the blue-coloured liquid by instantaneously turning it into a sky-blue lagoon. In she dips, letting the water pull her down deep, away from the January dankness, and into a healing pool of thick, scented bubbles. Her eyelids close as she sinks in, the foam concealing her body like fluffy clouds hide the sun on a clear summer's day. All that is now protruding is a pair of breasts that float like huge jellyfish on the surface.

She lies there motionless so as not to disturb the white lavender clouds and reveal the rest of her body. She is not particularly proud of it and is pleased when she can forget it for a little while each day. In this warm place, she thinks about her heart that is behind the large breasts, hidden from view and human scrutiny.

It's not like her to be philosophical. Maybe it was the lavender reaching her; maybe it was the warm water, Adrian's letter or the experience at Madame Anastasia's. She was not at all sure what was happening, but in a sudden wind-like gust, she realised that her husband had been the keeper of her most prized possession for the better part of seventeen years. Next to him, she had put herself up for sale and let herself become who he wanted her to be. By his side, she had become a vulnerable little mouse and forgotten her secret inside: her heart, key to the truth. The truth that is at the same time life.

Can you have both, she reflects, life and Adrian?

Sabina wipes her hands on the towel lying on the floor next to the bath, reaches over for her toiletry bag, pulls out the paper and the first pen-like thing she can get her fingers on (a red strawberry-flavoured lipstick liner), and writes under item 3:

4. Open mother's trunk

When she is dressed and back in her bedroom, she fishes the noble mirror statement out of its hiding place, reads it ten times, and before placing it back into the secret compartment of her jewellery box, draws a plump heart with the lipstick liner to punctuate the sentence.

Going Back

"So, let's get back to the matter in hand," says Madame Anastasia resolutely.

"Yes," replies Sabina even though she isn't at all sure what the matter in hand is. Among the reminiscing and philosophising, she has been having strong doubts about the true intentions of the seamstress. Was she really going to design a dress for her, or was she simply milking her of her money, with no intention of helping her look great on her fortieth at all? Anyone in their right mind could see that the dresses in the catalogue were far too exquisite for someone like her. She neither had the figure, the youthfulness or confidence to wear one. Perhaps Madame Anastasia was a hoax after all—a money-grabbing businesswoman who takes advantage of insecure housewives and their rich husbands. In the foreground of her mind was the niggling thought that this was her third meeting with the seamstress and she hadn't so much as seen a piece of material yet—unless she counted the red scrap of cloth she was given to wipe her sweaty brow!

Sabina thinks that the sensible thing to do would be to cancel the whole dress project. She would resolutely inform Madame Anastasia that it was nice of her to let her look at the designs, but she has decided against having a dress. The words refuse to come out. They form in her heart, nearly choke her on the way up towards her throat and then seem to burst before they find a voice.

Sitting in her usual chair opposite Madame Anastasia who she'd called 'Miss Glamour Features' and 'Madame Model-of-self-control' that morning in front of her mirror, Sabina finds that her only weapon is a harsh glare. She fancies she may yet discover a way of putting the message across without having to say anything. The more she glares at the woman, the more appealing she finds her and the less resentful she feels. Her make-up gives her an artificially-applied youthfulness that would make other women of her age (and she counts herself among them) appear cheap. When Madame Anastasia smiles in a warm and encouraging way, Sabina feels guilty and starts coughing to conceal the fact that she is inwardly choking on her own bad thoughts.

"As you said last time," Madame Anastasia offers, "the colour would be very flattering—especially for your tone of skin."

"Pardon?"

Madame Anastasia repeats her words, pointing to the colour.

"So, if you agree, I shall make something using the same tones of red as in the picture here."

Sabina can't concentrate on the conversation and Madame Anastasia, ignorant of her malaise, isn't helping by treating her like someone worthy of wearing one of the dresses. Sabina feels flattered and, at the same time, furious that she is being treated with such respect and consideration. She isn't used to being treated like this by someone close to her—like her own husband—let alone a stranger.

Madame Anastasia's voice becomes audible again as Sabina's thoughts draw to an end. *Has she been talking all this time?—what has she been saying?* Madame Anastasia is still smiling at Sabina and Sabina avoids looking directly at her.

No wonder I can never remember what she says during my visits. I'm always too busy day-dreaming. When I'm deep in thought, I probably just nod in agreement to everything she says and that's why I can't remember a thing about it.

Relieved that she has found the reason for her mysterious memory lapses, she looks up again. Madame Anastasia has become animated and is talking excitedly about the dress she hopes to create. Like an artist with a paintbrush in her hand, she gesticulates the size and shape of it whilst she speaks.

"Of course, I wouldn't dream of creating something with a tight waist like the dress this model is wearing—that would merely enhance the fact that you are thick around the middle," she says, unashamed of the honesty of her remark.

Sabina is feeling hot and can't decide whether it is due to the woman's audacity; the truth of her words; or simply a flush that her doctor said could be menopausal even at the age of thirty-nine.

"P-pardon?" Sabina stutters, even though she doesn't want to hear the remark about her flabbiness again.

"I was simply pointing out that the shape of the dress must be considered with care in order to accentuate the fullness of your figure in a flattering and striking way. Do you agree?"

"Y-yes. I think so," she says calmly although she wants to get cross with this woman, disagree with her, give her a piece of her mind and, once and for all, find out the truth behind her facade. But she can't. Every time she feels insulted or annoyed, Madame Anastasia manages to stroke it away with her words, her voice, her composure. Instead of being cross, Sabina becomes dazed and confused about what she should think.

"Mrs Waldsmere," the seamstress begins in an earnest tone, "I need to know whether you prefer a full chest in the dress or a flatter one. I could either give your breasts a lift up by inserting an under-wired bra-like arrangement, or else have a tight-fitting top piece that would flatten you."

Sabina tries not to flinch and contrives an uninvolved look.

"I have allowed myself to make the observation that you have full breasts, and I would like to highlight this natural phenomenon in my design—I would, nevertheless, need to have your approval."

Sabina doesn't react, she wants to just hear this one out and then say something. At the moment she is too put out by Madame Anastasia's openness to say anything.

"I have noticed that you like to hide your breasts under your clothing and, I must say, you very nearly did fool me into thinking that you were flat-chested. But, whilst you were absorbed by the pictures in the catalogue I managed to sneak a closer look from the side. You are well endowed, aren't you?"

Sabina feels sick.

Who does this woman think she is? Interfering old cow! So what if I don't like to show the world that I have got overly large tits. I hate them, always have. My god, she wants me to flaunt them. No way!

Sabina nonchalantly erects herself from her slumped posture, easing her shoulders back a millimetre at a time, hoping that Madame Anastasia wouldn't notice what she was doing. Instead of protesting to Madame Anastasia's suggestion, she stammers a list of implausible medical reasons for her stooping walk, rounded back and baggy shirt, and finally adds that she had never actually found the right clothes to give her the opportunity to show off her full figure.

"Good. So you agree," she says to Sabina's horror.

She has trapped herself.

"Don't worry," the reassuring voice says. "I know that the matter is an extremely delicate one. I wouldn't want you to look cumbersome or top-heavy. That is why I said that we must give it great thought. But I am dedicated to my work and it has become a forte of mine to create something that will suit the wearer in a way no other dress has done before. Everyone dislikes one part of their body or other and hides it because of this. But that doesn't mean that this disliked part is, in fact, unattractive. I usually find that a woman's opinion of her own body has been tampered with by other people's opinions, and by the standards the fashion world so selfishly dictates. All it takes is for that person to reconsider himself or herself in a different light, without the cruel influence of fashion's wagging tongue and perfectionist image. They soon discover that they can wear their own body and all that is placed over it with great pride."

Sabina doesn't dare look at Madame Anastasia. Inside, her heart is sobbing. Outside, the tears are splashing onto the leather catalogue her hands have in a tight grip. She is crying at the simple truth, honesty and wisdom of this stranger's words. She is crying for all the years she has suffered under the pressure to please everyone else. She is crying because a person who hasn't known her for long has shown great openness and concern towards her. One tear follows another and plops into the wet patch on the catalogue. Madame Anastasia doesn't say a word but simply moves closer and, taking Sabina's hands into her own mammoth ones, cradles them, rocks them, and comforts them. The large hands are like a swaddling. They warm her, soothe her and protect her in this moment of need. The two women sit there for a long time in consolatory silence.

* * * *

Sabina feels secure. She's a little girl again, holding on to her mother's large, comforting hand as she breezes from market stall to market stall at a brisk pace, lifting her free arm now and again to greet the 'Fruitcake Man' from the fruit and veg stall, 'Mr Sausage Fingers' from the meat market and the 'Very-Lovely-Material-Indeed' lady from the fabric stall. Her mother had a pet name for every single market seller in the entire complex. They all knew her and were always more than pleased to offer a bargain or two. When Sabina and Jennifer went along with her on a Saturday morning, they would be given so many different foods to taste that they had no appetite left for lunch. They were endearingly called *'luvely lasses'* in the northern accent of the merchants in the market. Her mother would smile and blush all morning, returning from her morning shop in the same mood as the neighbours did after the morning service at the local church.

Sabina's mother followed all the stories the market people had to tell and would often be caught with a tear in her eye as she moved from stall to stall, gathering real-life souvenirs as she went. She was friends with every one. Always cheerful, always with an open ear and mind. It was taken for granted that she would come along on a Saturday morning and let them unload their stories, good or bad, on her. No-one asked whether she had a problem. She didn't give the impression that she was the kind of person to have any. Not to Sabina, not to Jennifer, not to the market people, not to the neighbours, not to her closest friends, even her husband. When Sabina's father died of cancer, she didn't mention it to anyone at the market.

"*How's thee doin', duck?*" asked Mrs Nice-Frock.

"Fine, thanks," she answered without a hint of sadness or tragedy in her voice.

"*Dun't thee look reet bonnie in thee new frock what I selled thee?*"

"Thanks. I'm pleased with it too"

"*Bet tha hubby's reet chuffed wi' it too, eh?*"

"Yes, he is."

Sabina had passed a sideways glance which, though inaudible, asked: *why don't you tell her?* Her mother later said how sorry she felt for Mrs Nice Frock and the pain she was going through with that terrible teenage son of hers who kept running away from home and getting into trouble with drugs and the police. 'I think it helps her to talk about it to me,' she had stated without actually hearing, or understanding what wisdom she had just uttered. She would have never accepted such a thing herself—help from a stranger. Not even help from close family, friends or the neighbours could be accepted. She pretended that it was a relief now that he had gone, that she hadn't wanted him to suffer any longer, that it was better for him that way. She wouldn't admit to feeling tired, sad, grieved, exhausted. The day after the funeral she rushed round to a friend of hers whose second cousin had recently died in a car accident. Sabina's mother spent the entire day there comforting her friend with her compassionate hands.

* * * *

"It's important you know what you are feeling on the inside to be able to clothe the outside," Madame Anastasia's voice interrupts. "I want you to find out who you are. I can help you to do this by tapping into things you may not be aware of. I've had experience in the world of psychology, Mrs Waldsmere; I am a person who goes deeper than the surface," she pauses, sits back into the chair opposite, lowers her voice and states (as if revealing a great secret):

"That's is my way of doing business—my method of dressmaking, if you like, and the reason why every dress is unique."

Sabina listens.

"I don't know you well enough yet, but I will and I can help you if you let me. For 60,000 Francs, I will provide you, not only with a dress, but also with a complete mind and body lifting treatment. I intend to help you find out who you really are and learn to love every inch of yourself by fitting the dress for you, stitch by stitch."

Sabina nods and continues to stare at her feet.

"Once the design has been decided on, the dress will be created over a five-week period. It will be hand sewn by ten seamstresses—the pleats, hems and buttonholes minutely worked on. If you want to have this dress ready for your fortieth birthday party, we must move quickly. We have much work to do. I have to start with the foundation: what you are trying to achieve, what your spirit is. So, to begin with, I must know what your main goal is. Why you came here?"

Sabina lowers her head, closes her eyes, and speaks with such clarity of voice and mind that a listener could get the impression that she had rehearsed.

"Since I married and had children, it is as though my vitality, sensibility and sensuality have been deflating like tyres with a slow puncture. I now feel devoid of my own ambitions, desires and feelings. I continue from day to day, living my life by halves: half knowing where I'm going, half knowing what I want, half knowing who I am. For years, I've not wanted to see how flat it is. For years I've been living for other people: for my husband, for my children; not for myself."

"I understand," Madame Anastasia says and moves closer. "And now you want to change."

"Yes," she replies and nearly chokes on her own words. "It's become a habit and I don't know where to begin to stop it."

"You have already begun. Your next step is to recognise yourself and your achievements. No-one else's recognition matters. You wouldn't accept it anyway. So, just pat yourself on the back and thank yourself for getting on so well, so far. Stop comparing your life to the lives of other people. This is *your* life. You are unique. There is no other person in the world with your credentials. You have become who you are because of who you are. All the choices you made were the right choices at the time you made them. You can be pleased that you were gifted with the power of judgement and decision. There is nothing in this life that can chop you down except yourself. Love yourself and you shall grow. In autumn you lose your leaves, in winter, you freeze and feel the north wind. In spring life returns and in the summer you will blossom. That is your life cycle—every year—if you let it, if you choose it. Let life take you along its exciting energy-filled path full of new opportunities. No-one has the full answers to life. They are picked up along the way. You just have to watch out for them—be alert, listen, watch. As long as you stay awake, you will notice them. You may miss a few. That's normal. Don't go back. Move on. They will be there again waiting for you when the time is right. Trust your instincts, your power of judgement. Listen to your heart and your inner feelings. There is always light at the end of the tunnel. The laws of physics don't allow there not to be. Hold on to such facts. They are your tools. They are the walking sticks of life's adventure. Use them and you will be able to find your way. Follow it. The path beckons because it has something to tell you. Find that experience. Don't be afraid. The path can't bite. It is not alive. *You* are. The path will go on with or without you—that is what it is there for. You can choose it, or not choose it. Either way, it is about you and not about the path. Trust yourself. Love yourself. Love life."

Sabina suddenly feels the burning desire to get out of the villa; away from everything to somewhere she can be alone and think. She's too scared of her own reaction right now. It is as if Mme Anastasia understands her without her having to explain anything. This is confirmed when she looks up and sees Mme Anastasia coming towards her holding her hat and coat ready for her to slip into them. She then gently guides Sabina to the front door and, without a word, opens it and lets Sabina out; a simple act and yet so meaningful. Sabina nods her head at Mme Anastasia in acknowledgement and walks with quiet confidence down the path and out of the gate.

The water is cool and her eyes welcome the blue balsamic fluid as it caresses her head, breasts and buttocks. Sabina glides gracefully along, enjoying being completely weightless. Swimming used to be a passion of hers: how could she have forgotten? The sweet smell of the chlorine, the sedating sounds of voices, the splashing, the laughter. As a student, she used to swim every day; up and down, length after length, not counting them, just letting her mind unwind. She would analyse all her conversations, her thoughts and significant happenings of the day, staying for as long as she deemed necessary. By the time she left the pool, she was cleansed, content and able to leave resolutely with a flush of vitality and a stride that set her toward life with confidence.

Today she rediscovers the same revivifying effect the water used to have on her body and mind; with each stroke, her body tingles and her mind begins to unravel its woolly inside, throwing out knots and debris. The pool is unoccupied except for one swimmer—an elderly gentleman—who is agile for his years. The fifty-metre pool has been split into sections; lanes, for those who want to swim lengths, and a section for easy swimming. Sabina chooses the lanes and shares it with the old man. He crawls, Sabina swims breaststroke; she on the right, he on the left: two souls swimming and unravelling. Madame Anastasia's words about inner growth and truth reach her and she reflects, wondering what truth she needs to wring from things. Religious scriptures come to mind, but she shuns them with a powerful feeling that she will find it without them: it is within, part of the deep instinctual life. Like a sharp gust of wind on a hot summer's day, a refreshing thought hits her from behind and gives her stroke an extra metre: she has grown since the morning and there is no way back. She thinks and sees differently now. Again, Madame Anastasia's words accompany her down the pool: 'It will feel uncomfortable at first, like the ball gown I will create. You will feel odd, perhaps sad, with people you used to feel happy and familiar with. They will tell you that they want you to be happy; yet it is their own happiness that depends upon it.'

A further twenty lengths of breaststroke, head down, face in the water, and she feels ready to leave the pool and enter the sauna area to relax in its desert-like heat. Lying in the quiet room in a reclined position to recover from the sauna as you are advised to, she notices how peaceful she feels. She thinks about times she has felt most loved. There was the first time Adrian and she made love. She remembers words of warmth from her father, mother and sister Jennifer. Then her mind strays away from thoughts of love to times she felt in need of a helping hand. Each time her mind searches for something, it comes back empty: when the doctor butchered her to open up the birth canal in her first labour, when Adrian threatened to abandon her for his Belgian lover, when she miscarried two babies, when her mother…She stops herself thinking anymore. Of course there had been people around to help her—perhaps not the ones she wanted, but they were there. She wonders how much she wills onto herself and how much comes from others. *Is it all within? Does it all have to do with your inner feelings, hurts, anger, love, as Madame Anastasia said? Do I only let in that which I choose? If I choose no support, I don't get any? If I choose it, I do. Is it that simple?*

The light above her clicks and Sabina turns to see who is responsible for this rude intrusion in her thoughts. An old woman is leaning against the wall where the switch is and quickly manoeuvres away to switch it back off gasping, 'Excusez-moi Madame!' Sabina nods, smiles and whispers to herself, 'I needed to be woken up anyway.' And it is in that moment that she realises that by refusing to confront problems, by failing to acknowledge her feelings and communicate her needs, she had filled up, over the years, with as much regret, remorse and bitterness as her mother had. By suppressing her inner life, it had abducted and garrotted her: it had become her captor, turning her into a wretched, dejected human being who scurried through her years on earth.

A myriad of questions is released, spouting red lava from the locked volcano that is her heart. She doesn't find many answers just yet; nor does she know how she will feel when she leaves this renewing place and returns to her home and family. She has no idea whether she will find the strength to deal with her past. What she does know, though, is that she has taken a stride today; one that will help her pull herself out of her prison of passivity. And she knows, too, that she has the determination to continue pulling no matter how much strength she needs or how much pain she must endure. She no longer wants to be living in the dark dungeon alongside the putrid stench of stagnation. Her path is towards the small, bright opening above her that is the entry to freedom—even if it takes for the rest of her life to get there.

BOOK TWO

Falling...

"Sabina...Sabina?"

There's no answer. Peering into the living-room window, as he approaches the house, Adrian can see her body opposite the sofa. She's staring at the sofa, motionless. For a brief moment he wonders whether the person in there is his wife at all.

"Sabina?" he asks softly, squinting at the window.

There's still no answer. Adrian unlocks the front door and goes straight into the kitchen to get a beer. It's been an exhausting day and he's horrified to see a stack of dirty dishes on the draining board, cereal packets and crumbs on the table, a half-eaten sandwich next to the bread bin. *Sabina, what on earth is going on?* He jerks the metal lid off the beer bottle, sending it spinning menacingly across the Formica, turns his back on the untidy kitchen, and enters the living room. A surge of anger floods his stomach.

"Sabina. Anyone at home?" he shouts at the dummy and feels like knocking on her head with his knuckles.

Still no answer.

"Ani? For Christ's sake..."

Sabina begins to stir. Still facing the window, she yawns, stretches her arms high above her head and licks her lips.

Ani. I haven't heard that name in years.

She's surprised to hear the name again. It was given to her by her classmates. As soon as she left school and went to university she was pleased to shed it and return to the name she was christened with. (She had told Adrian about it once and he used to tease her about it.) When she was growing up in Yorkshire, she found the name Sabina the worst she could possibly have. People used to say: *You what, duck? What's thee name?* The kids at school found anything foreign-sounding highly suspicious and tried to steer clear of it. So, one day, when everyone was having fun writing and reading their names backwards, she was re-christened *Ani*, short for Anibas which sounded just like 'Annie' from the musical and everyone was familiar with that. Sabina had accepted it too. She had no choice.

She lifts her head, rubs her eyes, groans and, without reacting to Adrian's attempt at annoying her, says sleepily:

"You're home early!"

"Yes, and what a state the kitchen is in!"

Sabina switches back into stare mode.

Adrian walks round to face her. She looks frightening with her large eyes open as wide as saucers and her hair straggly and wet from swimming.

"Are you all right?" his voice quavers. The anger ebbs. What he now feels is genuine concern and he approaches the sofa, stooping, frowning. Half a metre in front of her he stops and stares. It's such an intense stare that Sabina feels exposed and vulnerable, as if she doesn't have a stitch on. Instead of bashfully turning her head as she would usually do and telling Adrian that she is all right and then scuttle away to the bathroom, she begins to stare back.

Do I look any different?

She feels different. This morning she kissed him good-bye as usual and now he is standing opposite her—a mere ten hours later. It feels like several decades. She's no longer the Sabina of that morning. She's a different Sabina. How different she's not yet sure. She feels stronger, that is certain. Adrian's silent stare holds steady and she continues to stare back. They haven't looked at one another like this for years. Without knowing it, he's looking at her for the first time—the new Sabina, the one who has vowed to stop ambling through life wishing things were different. His eyes are scrutinising, his expression vaguely questioning, with a hint of confusion; hers are smiling, happy and definitely challenging. His eyes dive down, searching for answers to unasked questions and hers surface confidently, eagerly awaiting the acknowledgement of her new self.

"Is everything okay?" he inquires.

Sabina detects urgency in his voice.

"Of course! Why shouldn't everything be okay?"

How can he ask such a banal question on one of the most significant days in my life? Why can't he see that my entire outlook on life has changed?

She beams at him:

"I have never felt better in my entire life!...well, once, maybe," she admits and then explains: "We were sitting at the edge of your bed in your room. I was alleviated and elated. I felt tremendously good about myself, about you and about life. So good, I wanted to run to the top of a mountain and shout it out to the world. For the first time in my life I had made love to a man and it was the most beautiful experience I had ever had. I finally realised why such a fuss was made about love, why it was so highly rated and why people spent their lifetime in search of it. On that day, I was profoundly happy and relieved that my search had ended. If it hadn't been for you, I would probably still be searching. You knew how to handle me. You were patient. You communicated your love in words before showing me with your body. You respected me and earned my respect for you. When you knew that I was ready, you made love to me—gently, tenderly, exquisitely. On that day, I grew taller than I had ever been before. Our love made me strong, confident and gave me a feeling of self-worth. I could have conquered the entire world that day." She pauses, letting her words sink in and then, as she raises her eyes to meet his, she adds: "And today, I feel exactly the same way."

Sabina's words are a surprise. She has complimented him and that feels good. But at the same time, she has confused him. How come she has never told him that before? Why now? And what does she mean about feeling the same way today? They haven't made love for months.

Seeing Adrian's frown forming, Sabina decides to go into the kitchen and begin tidying up.

He remains speechless, motionless, fighting emotions that are rising to the surface, emotions that have lived in a separate room—a room he doesn't frequently visit. For a long time now he has been worried about her, about them, but has found it impossible to approach her, communicate his fears. Communication is a strain and something he can't seem to do well anymore. Now he has forgotten who she is, how to handle her. Not like when they were students; when he was a student that was all he had ever thought about. He spent hours reflecting how best to approach her, win her over, get her to spend the rest of her life with him. His hard work and expertise paid off; he won her heart, her body, her mind. Through his love and care he gave her the strength and confidence she needed to flaunt herself, her femininity, her intelligence, her self-esteem. She blossomed under his care and attention. When had he stopped giving her that?

He thinks back to their wedding day. He was so excited about the new job and the move to Luxembourg—and then there was that awfully bland wedding; a quick and nasty job in a registry office, totally lacking in the qualities he would have liked. But it wasn't just the way in which they became man and wife that caused him to stop caring for her. He wanted to make a new start in life on leaving London and, for the first time ever, decided to take what life offered him without giving anything back. He had his wife, he had his family, he had the high-powered job, he had the money and he was ruthlessly and egoistically going to reap the rewards of the years of hard work that had got him there. He no longer had the time, patience or desire to woo his wife. He resented her for not being assertive like him and, instead of coaxing her out of the depression she was slipping into, he chose to ignore the fact that they were moving farther and farther apart.

"Sabina, I..." he starts and then sees that she's no longer in the room. He hears the familiar sound of a glass smashing into a thousand pieces on the kitchen floor and decides not to go and look. It'll only make him angry with her again. That was a shame because he had just had a spontaneous desire to tell her something important—that he is sorry, sorry for everything. Before he heard the sound of breaking glass he truly felt sorry. How simple it had been for Sabina to evoke that feeling in him. *How had she done it? What made her different today?*

A large lump, like a big chunk of gristle, starts growing in his throat, causing his eyes to water. Visions loom up before his eyes—the most vivid of which is one of Sabina with another man. *How come it has never crossed my mind before?* Now the thought stares him pertinently in the face and calls him an idiot. Of course—that must be it, he thinks, gathering saliva in his mouth and forcing it down his throat, hoping to shift the lump.

He's surprised by his own reaction to the thought of Sabina having an affair. She's his property—like one of the many used and battered books on the shelves of his office (which he has not looked at for years). They used to be his pride and joy, and he periodically took one from the shelf, handled it, gently leafed through its pages, read a line or two and then replaced it, taking the utmost care to return it to the correct place. He has always been meticulous about the order of his books and even wrote a computer programme to spew out coded numbers for them so that he could locate any one at the touch of a button.

What if she is having an affair?

It was possible, of course. Now that the children are grown, she has all the time in the world to go out and find herself a lover. She has the house to herself during the day and I never come home earlier from the office without prior warning.

Adrian feels woozy and has a strange dryness in his mouth like the morning after a dinner party. He runs his tongue over his teeth and lips until everything is moist again. He wants to speak to Sabina, find out about her, interrogate her. *She could walk out on me—and then what would I do?* He instantly thinks of the huge pile of crumpled clothes that has been mounting up on the chest of drawers in their bedroom. It's unusual for her to neglect the ironing. It's habitually done before the pile gets higher than the tall vase next to it and it is already double its height.

Is she planning to leave me with all that ironing to do?

Sabina has finished in the kitchen and glides gracefully into the living room. Without realising what she is doing, she sings a tune that has been turning round and round her head like an old-fashioned record with a scratch ever since she left Madame Anastasia's to go swimming: 'Falling in love again."

How could she do this to me? She is having an affair then—the deceptive... and he stomps upstairs to the computer.

He opens the e-mail and double clicks on the message. It's from Jennifer:

> Hi Adrian,
>
> Yes it would be okay for you to stay from 12th to 14th February. If you want I'll take you to a show in the West End—or to the Millennium Dome. That's if my sister wouldn't mind. I'm sure she's rushed off her feet because of the party preparations. It would give her the chance to put her feet up.
>
> Let me know what you decide. You're very welcome to stay.
>
> Jennifer

Put her feet up? I am the one who should be putting my feet up! She's not doing a thing for the party. If it weren't for me, there wouldn't even be one. She should think herself lucky that she's got me to organise her life for her!

In the Forest

The laughter became more menacing the closer she moved towards the house. Sabina tried to see inside the window before ringing the doorbell but it was covered in heavy condensation. It was suddenly quiet again and she strained to hear through the thick stone walls. All she could hear were the cries of crows high above her in the trees. The commotion was preventing her from listening to the goings on inside. She looked up. A dark feathered blanket was coming towards her. It fell on top of her, knocking her over, pinning her down, blotting out all light, smothering her, choking her. She grabbed at it and a handful of black feathers came out, throwing her back. She cast them away and tried to struggle to her feet, but the feathers started to tumble down like soot, thicker and thicker until she was choking and unable to see any light. In desperation she squeezed out a cry. It wouldn't leave her mouth. It was being held back by the thick layer of crow's feathers.

Sabina wakes up and puts her hand to her throat. It feels thick and sore. Her nightdress is soaking, her bedclothes are soaking, and her forehead is burning with temperature. She first wonders whether the doctor was right about the menopause coming to her at such an early age, but then realises she has been having a nightmare. She has been having a similar nightmare every night since her first visit to Madame Anastasia's—but it has never been quite as vivid as this.

Outside, the dustbin lorry winces, wails and bangs methodically down the street. She squints at the electronic alarm clock: 6:00. Apart from the noise of the dustbins being emptied, everything is still. Sabina fetches a couple of soluble aspirin from the medicine cabinet, drops them into a glass of water on her bedside table and gargles with the liquid before swallowing it down. Adrian is fast asleep beside her. In desperate search of warmth and comfort after the terrifying dream, she snuggles up next to him and closes her eyes.

Sleep comes again fast and she's shocked out of it when the alarm rings at 7:30. It's Wednesday—midweek already. In approximately 54 days is her birthday. Thoughts of that and the accompanying party have become permanent squatters in her mind.

This morning, after the upsetting dream, the resolution is also on her mind again. Thoughts of it are spurning her inner nervousness and spoiling the excitement she had felt about seeing Madame Anastasia again tomorrow, hearing her soothing voice.

Restlessness gets her up and takes her on a walk in the forest. It's a dull day at the beginning of February, the trees are dark and shadowy and the forest has nothing green, lush or enticing about it. She feels subdued, aimless, unsure of why she's going on a walk in the first place, her mind rattling on, getting on her nerves, whining and creaking like a swing that needs oiling. The occasional knocking sound as two tops of trees hit each other snatch her mind away from it's chatter and she continues, listening out for anything else they might offer as a way of distraction. Was that whispering she heard? *Oh, if they could tell me what they know. Wise old trees—keepers of the truth.* The trees—lives standing tall despite the wind and rain lashing at them, hitting them, beating them, trying to knock them down. Despite Fungi's cancerous warts and Ivy's twisting hair creeping up the stem to strangle the life out of them. Silent souls who only speak to those who listen. They know. They have lived and seen many a soul walk amongst them. *Can you tell me who I am?* And an answer was whispered gracefully through the wind as though carried on one of the leaves that had been picked up by the wind and sent floating towards her. *If you can stand to hear the truth*, it sang. *There you will find your story, your truth, your life.*

As if in a corny movie, her attention is suddenly caught by a tiny ray of sunshine bursting through a black cloud. From where she is standing, it looks as if a mere millimetre of sun is up there; yet it has managed to travel all the way to the forest floor to shine on the dead beech leaves lying limp and useless on the ground around her. It turns them all shiny and copper-coloured. Her step becomes more dance-like as she carries on her way, through the scorching leaves, enjoying the give in the peat earth underneath her step. *It's like walking on a sponge cake,* she thinks and hops merrily along. When she turns her attention away from the bright forest floor and looks up, she sees a group of rocks looking down at her from the top of the hilly part of forest on her left. *Funny, in all the years I have been coming to this forest, I've never noticed those rocks.* Her feet urge her to head off the path in their direction and she scrambles up the hill towards them. A noise startles her and she looks back—it's only a fallen branch. *Good, no one is watching. They would think me abnormal—going off the path and up the slippery steep slope.* She can't rationally explain it, but she feels a strong need to touch them, welcome them into her life, lay her head on the cool surface and feel the feeble warmth of the sun on her face. And without thinking, finds herself doing just this. In the instant she does, she feels liberated and free, close to nature and loved by the forest. When she opens her eyes again, a craggy rock shelf beckons her with it's provocative, jutting jaw and she climbs higher to greet it, too. Her breath becomes shorter and her heart begins to race with the strain as adrenaline rushes though her veins. Imagination tells her that there could be a madman in the woods, watching from behind the rock, waiting to pounce on her. Fear makes her stop for a second—like a startled deer listening out for hunters, but then she quickens her step, alert and agile. When she finally reaches the piece of jutting out rock, she strips her gloved hand and rubs over its sandstone lips, chin and neck. It is rough and gritty—damp in places. There are little dents, dimples and cracks to explore with her fingers. One crack is wide enough to fit her whole hand in. She retrieves it as her mind draws a picture of a cloaked figure with fangs of a vampire. Her fingers move away from the mouth and up to a tuft of moss, the moustache, where they linger for a while, enjoying the furriness of it. She fantasises about a secret world of mini creatures living in and around this rock face—Daddy Rock, the good wizard looking after the inhabitants with tenderness and love—just like they do in fairy tales. What a beautiful spot they have found, she reflects, on top of the hill in the forest, looking down on the valley of giant trees. They must feel very powerful.

Rat droppings and used candles catch her eye. Someone has been there—at night—probably teenagers for want of a better place to drink and smoke.

How I would love to come into the forest at night, alone. Just me and the moon: a fly on the wall in nature's abode.

She creeps into a hollowed crevice, just large enough for her to crawl into and she crouches, knee-deep in leaves. Words pop into her head *peace* and *quiet, beauty* and *light. How simple this pleasure—how unexpected,* she muses and, as she turns her head toward the weak sunshine once more, finds herself talking thoughts out loud to herself: *The forest is my inspiration. The trees whisper and say who you are. If you can stand to hear the truth, they will tell you.*

In her little cove, kept warm and protected by the leaves and sheltered from the wind, the sun is remarkably warming and she sits there still and pensive until it disappears completely. Then she crawls out with a promise tucked under her breath: *I will open my mother's trunk this afternoon,* and sets off home.

Sabina runs the last few metres out of the forest and down the road to her house. There's a large patch of blue sky and the sun is dousing the valley in glorious winter sunshine. Funny that she rarely sees a glimmer of blue sky when she looks out of her window. If she hadn't gone out this morning she would still be in the dark mood of the nightmare and swear at her mirror that every day in Luxembourg was a dull day. It wasn't true.

Just as she has hung up her coat and put the kettle on for a cup of tea, the doorbell rings. And, as if the forest was desperate to prove a point, the postman at her door hands her a parcel, some letters, and says with a smile whilst pointing at the valley, "*Regardez—le soleil. C'est manifique!*" (Look—the sun. It's magnificent!) "*Oui,*" she agrees and takes the pile of post from his outstretched hands. "*Il faut en profiter,*" he says (take advantage of it!), and waves goodbye to a nodding, beaming Sabina.

The parcel is addressed to her and she recognises the handwriting at once. It's from her auntie Vera, her mother's sister. On the back, next to the 'from:' and the sender's address is a note in block capitals: PLEASE OPEN BEFORE YOUR BIRTHDAY! Sabina tears the brown paper, yanks out a large squashy package covered in multicoloured gift-wrap and rips it open. Inside is a patent gold leather toiletry bag (*yeuch!*) and an envelope. She opens the envelope first. It's one of aunt Vera's infamous homemade ones with a picture of a Robin Redbreast glued askew to the front (obviously cut out of one of last year's Christmas cards because it is wearing a Father Christmas hat and scarf). The cardboard itself looks as if it has been folded by shaky hands because the ends don't meet in a straight line. A flimsy piece of paper flies out and swizzles around before landing on the floor as she opens the card out. On the right, inside flap of the greeting card is a little homemade verse:

Robin Redbreast is a bird,
That in winter, I have heard,
Rests its head beneath its wing,
'Til new life comes in the Spring!

Forty years this year you'll be
No spring chicken, just like me!
And so this gift of shiny gold,
Will adorn you, brave and bold-

With colour, charm, and beauty,
Help you keep fresh and juicy:
Fit to enter your latter years
And keep away too many tears!

My God, Aunt Vera. I didn't know you had it in you! What else are you hiding behind your blue rinse and dentures! I like the fresh and juicy bit, and Sabina's chair shakes in appreciation of her deep-bellied laughter.

My dear Sabina,

Please forgive me for sending you this parcel so very early. I wish to apologise for the fact that I will not be able to come to your very special 40th birthday celebration in Luxembourg as I hoped I would. It's the rheumatism you know. Terrible thing. But, oh well, can't complain can I? I still have my mind and a nice new set of teeth from the dentist. I am sending your present early. I know how difficult it is for a woman to move into her prime and thought that these might just cheer you up a little before your big day.

I think it's marvellous how your husband is going out of his way to give you such a lovely birthday treat. He's a smasher. You're a lucky girl to have found such a devoted man. Give him my kindest regards and greet those grown-up sons of yours, too.

I will be thinking of you on your night—and drink a glass of Baileys at the midnight hour!

With much love,
Your auntie Vera

Cheers! Sabina calls out to the letter and raises an imaginary glass to her good-old Auntie who she believes has excelled herself beyond all imagining on this so very clear day.

The zipper of the patent gold leather toiletry bag is made of thick white plastic—large teeth which separate into a wide smile with ease as Sabina pulls on the tab, reminding her of her aunt Vera's broad, dentured grin. Out come the following:

—Several sachets of different coloured hair highlighter (sunshine blonde, copper red, mahogany, burned sienna brown, peach delight and—*what's this? Purple pleasure!*).
—Two tubes of 'extra-white-teeth' toothpaste and a glittery-stemmed toothbrush with bristles the colour of the rainbow.
—Red blusher with matching lipstick.
—A small box of *Mmmm my favourite* marzipan chocolates.
—And a (*auntie Vera, what on earth's got into you?*) pair of false eyelashes (*!!*)

This is the icing on the cake! she exclaims and puts Vera's letter and card into the bag, carries it upstairs to the bathroom, makes a mental note to write a thank-you letter, and places it next to her own one.

Sabina steps onto the last rung of the ladder and manoeuvres her body into a sitting position on the edge of the opening with great caution; placing one buttock after the other onto the firm wooden floorboard. As she rests before heaving herself inside, her legs, which are now dangling free in the air below, begin to feel heavier and heavier and she struggles to stop them pulling her down and making her fall the two and a half metres to the tiled floor of the bathroom. The vertigo attack subsides as soon as she turns her head away from the opening and focuses on the dust particles dancing in the beam of electric light. She heaves herself up and out of danger.

Her eyes squint and her head tilts backwards to see as far into the room as she can. The back part is still too dark to discern anything. The front part is full of boxes, books, rugs, pieces of furniture, Christmas decorations and bags of clothes. An old pram guards one of the supporting beams and Sabina looks at it lovingly. She has kept it (much to Adrian's disgust) secretly hoping that Jennifer would start a family. Jennifer may be too old to start a family now. There are a couple of bulging bin-liners stuffed with baby clothes and she goes over to them. One had a white label on it, stuck down with sticky tape: 'Baby clothes, 12–18 months.' She unties the string at the neck of the bag and sneezes violently as the smell of mothballs wafts into her face. She pulls a tissue from her pocket, blows her nose and, holding it in front of her face so as not to be affected by the smell again, delves into the bag. First she retrieves a hand-knitted sweater. Did she really knit that? It is beautiful. A pair of bright red and blue leather shoes plop onto the wooden floor as she pulls out a pair of dungarees. She digs deeper into the bag and finds the matching jacket. What an achievement! She made all those things: the dungarees, the matching jacket and the sweater. How proud she used to be of her sewing and knitting. What pleasure it used to give her! How could she have forgotten that? She pulls the trousers over her forearms, pushes her fingers into the tiny shoes as far as they will go and hops, skips and jumps along the bare floorboards, laughing as she watches the shoes dance in a merry way, as if a pair of toddler's feet were inside them.

Where did all that time go?

She smiles. She doesn't wish for that time again. It was a hard slog—especially as Adrian worked long hours in the office and went off mountain biking, or to football training at weekends. She regrets that he didn't play a more active role in the upbringing of his children. They missed him. And it's probably too late to build up a relationship with them now; they are strangers to him despite living under the same roof. She kicks the shoes off her hands, slides the trousers off her arms and admires her creations once more before folding them neatly and placing them back into the bag. How many hours did she work on that little suit? It gave her a wonderful feeling of satisfaction. She used to sew during Dominic's midday nap and into the night on days when Adrian was away on business or at a sport's event. The housework would be neglected on those occasions but she did not care: she had achieved something tangible—not like scrubbing the grime off the bath or scratching the urine crusts off the toilet bowl. Whenever someone admired the suit and asked her where she had bought it, her eyes would spark up and her voice would go up an octave or two as she sang her favourite song: 'Oh, I didn't buy it. I made it myself.' She would never give her creations away to a jumble sale. If her sister does not have children, she will save them for her children's children; and if they do not have children, she will keep them herself—dress her childhood teddies in them.

She puts the bag back and looks towards the far corner of the loft. It's still very dark; the electric light is too weak to reach that far. She grabs the torch that is hanging by a piece of string on a nail bashed into a beam in an attempt to encourage users to return it, and sets off on her quest. There are more boxes than she can count.

My university files!

She crouches down at a dusty box, pulls off the lid, takes out an A4 ring-binder and starts flicking through the hand-written pages: notes on computer programming languages. She finds a program she once wrote to parse a sentence and perform a word-count and reads through it. If x=0 then; else…She's surprised she can read it and, as if transported back to that student world and the day she wrote the program, she takes a biro out of her shirt pocket and corrects the mistake in it. *Well, better late that never!* she exclaims and blows her streaming nose. The dust! That's why she hates dusting; allergic to it. She switches the torch on again, points it at the farthest corner of the loft and cranes her neck to get a better view. A large silver-coloured trunk squats square in the sloped-roof corner looking as if it could be stuffed full with pirate's treasure. Sabina picks her way over some more boxes, past living-room shelves, and a dozen rolls of flowery wallpaper from the previous owners of the house. Cobwebs tickle her face as she wades her way to her destination and the air turns from cold to musty. There's a padlock on the trunk. She'd forgotten. *The key? Where's the key?* She can't remember. *Did I throw it away? Probably!* She never thought she would want to open it. Today she is determined that it will be opened if it's the last thing she does and she stumbles back to the loft entrance, down the ladder, through the bathroom, down the stairs and out into the garage. A large glass jar that used to contain pickled gherkins sits on a shelf in there crammed full with old keys, screws, drawing pins, rubber washers and out-dated coins. The contents of the jar clatter deafeningly onto the floor: large mortis keys, car keys, a key to bleed radiators. She grabs half a dozen that look like they could fit and hurries back to the loft. She forces one key after another into the padlock. None of them fit.

Then she remembers the crowbar Adrian keeps in the cellar and rushes to get it. With one confident jab, she forces the bent end of the crowbar into the millimetre gap between lid and bottom and pushes down. She keeps on jerking the tool down until there is a satisfying crunching sound as the lid is given a 2 cm buckle into which she cheerfully rams the tool. A loud crack announces the success of her operation. She slowly lifts the lid. A large bathrobe conceals the contents. She lifts it out tenderly and nuzzles into it.

Her perfume. I had forgotten that smell!

Her eyes become watery as she carefully places the robe on the floor beside the chest and peers back into it. Novels, various ornamental things, toiletry articles, clothes. She pulls all the items out one by one and places them in a neat pile beside her. And then she sees that the bottom of the chest is covered with countless black leather books: each one as thick as a thousand-page novel. Sabina selects one, strokes its cold cover and, after positioning herself on the bathrobe, opens it. On the first page are the lines:

'This diary belongs to Miss Veronica Hope:'

Underneath is written

'now Mrs Agarthy'

The statement has been signed and dated: 1st January 1955.

She turns the page and shines the torch on the entry for that day:

1st January 1955.

> 'I got married today. Oh, God, what have I done? I don't think it's right. I don't know why I did it. It's too late now. We slept together for the first time—after the ceremony, in the hotel. It hurt. I don't think that I will ever like sleeping with him. I hope he doesn't find this diary. I don't want him to know. It's so humiliating...'

Her heart is racing, her throat feels as though she has swallowed cotton wool and she snaps the book shut: *I shouldn't be doing this; it's not my property. I have no right to go through my mother's possessions.*

Yes, you do! a whispering voice tells her, *you have to.*

She continues to read:

> '...I always wanted to be an actor. Well, girl, this is your chance: you can now start acting out your own life.'

Sabina turns a few pages.

> 'I should have started my period by now. I think I'm pregnant. It must have been beginner's luck. A baby? What will I do with a baby?'

Sabina pages to December 3rd—her sister's birthday.

> 'She's arrived. She's beautiful. She's perfect. What a miracle it is to give birth! Painful, yes, but it's worth it. I know I'm going to love being a mum. I love it already and she's only a few hours old. I'm in love with her. I don't know how I could love anything stronger than I love her. Poor Richard. He doesn't know what to do with babies. He looks lost. I wish he would just relax and enjoy being a father.'

The moment when she first held Dominic in her arms comes rushing back to her. *Giving birth truly is a miracle!*

At the bottom of the page her mother has written something upside down. Sabina turns the book to read it:

> 'P.S. I'm glad that I won't have to have sex with him for a while!'

On and on she reads, learning how her mother struggled to breastfeed Jennifer and then finally gave up because of pressure from her husband: 'He blames all the crying on my milk.' Jennifer had colic and after four weeks of nothing but 'screaming, stress and Richard's accusations,' she bought a dozen bottles and a shelf-full of formula milk. She had countless questions about the raising of her baby but seemed to have no one to ask. Her mother and father lived miles away and she said she didn't want to discuss the difficulties she was experiencing on the phone, or in letters. 'They would interpret it as a sign that I'm failing at the most fundamental thing in a woman's life.' She wrote how much she was looking forward to Christmas when they would come over for the first time since Jennifer's birth.

Sabina flicks ahead to Christmas day:

> 'No snow today. I'm glad really. My parents would have probably blamed the snow on me too. They hate snow. This has been one of my saddest Christmases ever. My parents were supposed to stay on until the New Year, but they are leaving on Boxing Day. I was so looking forward to them being here, to celebrating a proper family Christmas with little Jennifer. I still have a stinking cold and was in bed with a temperature when they arrived on 23rd. So they're leaving because I had the audacity to be ill when they were coming to visit. I have spoiled their Christmas and I should have been more considerate! Why are they so cruel? Well, mother isn't I suppose. She just goes along with him. She lets him oppress her—and me. He always manages to have me in tears. He is so hurtful. Why? What did I do wrong? He has never shown any love or understanding. Unless you call slapping a child in the face, love. He used to slap me for no reason. I would just have to ask a simple question and he would fire back with an insult or a slap in the face. I used to run away and hide. Today I did too. I ran into the garden to hide the tears. I didn't want him to have the satisfaction of seeing them. Not now as a grown woman. I hate him and yet I'm still trying to prove to him what a good girl I am. Why can't he accept me—be nice to me—show that he cares?'

Sabina's cheeks are wet with tears and she holds the diary away from her body so as not to soak it before tearing a piece of cardboard off one of the boxes and marking the page. She peers back into the chest to count them: there are twenty-five.

One for each year of their marriage—until my father's death.

She knows what she will be doing from now until her birthday and promptly opens the next diary.

Frozen

"What did you do today?" Adrian asks as soon as he comes home from the office.

Oh, God. What did I do? Nothing. Well there was the walk, the sunshine, and the rock. I can't tell him that. He won't approve. Then there was the loft and the diaries—he'll just tell me I'm wasting my time getting lost in the past. I should have done some gardening, more cutting ready for spring. Maybe I could say that I was going to but someone called and wouldn't shut up…

"Sabina?"

"Yes?" she says and twitches.

"I asked you something!"

"Oh, yes. Um."

"Aren't you listening to me?"

"Oh, yes."

"What's wrong then?"

"Oh, nothing."

"You're not saying much."

If only you knew how much I was saying!

"No."

"Did you have a nice day?"

"Yes. I mean, it was okay. You know, the usual. A friend called and wouldn't shut up."

"Women! Always so much to say."

"Yes. Did you have a nice day, Adrian?"

"Stressful—nothing but rush, rush, rush. More pressing jobs. I'm going to have to stay extra hours tomorrow and do a few things tonight, too."

"You poor thing."

"Well, someone has to do it, don't they?"

Sabina is glad she didn't tell him about the walk or her discovery in the loft and goes upstairs to soak in the bath.

Later, Adrian is back in his usual position at the table, reading the newspaper as he always does, pretending to be oblivious to all who enter and exit. He's not, though. He's been secretly observing his wife and is becoming more and more suspicious of her. She breezes in looking as fresh as the morning due.

"Hello!" he greets, looking her up and down.

Her hair shines and bounces all the way over to the oven and then back over to the table.

"Hi Adrian," she says matter-of-factly and starts to dish out the Lasagne. He stares at her.

"What's the matter?" she asks as she feels his eyes on her.

"Oh, nothing," he says and bobs back behind his newspaper.

A few moments later his head pops up again.

"I like your new hair style," he comments. "It suits you,"—and he returns to his paper.

"Thank you, Adrian. I'm pleased with it too. What about the colour? Did you notice that I have a new colour?"

Adrian looks up again. *That's why it's so shiny and full of life. God, she has beautiful hair!*

He would have liked to stroke it, but feels embarrassed just thinking about it. He doesn't feel he has the right to go up and stroke her hair, her cheek.

"Yes, I did," he lies. "You should have had it done years ago."

Sabina doesn't comment. *As if my hair colour would have made any difference. How primitive men think sometimes!*

Sabina is feeling exceptionally attractive. She has turfed out most of her synthetic articles of clothing, takes care to apply her make-up in the way Madame Anastasia has shown her, and feels that she is beginning to hold herself like a ballet dancer—her back straight, head high. When she walks down the road like this, she really fells that she is flaunting her mature beauty in a positive way and has begun to savour the sensation of having male eyes watching her as she goes by.

Adrian hasn't slept well for a fortnight and is suffering a daytime loss of concentration. *What is Sabina up to? Where does she keep disappearing to?* Adrian doesn't like it one bit and, despite being proud of his plans, is beginning to dread the actual party.

"Oh, hi Dominic. I didn't hear you come in," Adrian says, peeping over his newspaper. He hasn't read a word and the delicious-smelling lasagne sits uninvitingly in front of him on the plate. Everything tastes bitter.

She's not poisoning me, is she?

Dominic plonks himself down on the chair next to Adrian, fingers the pile of newspaper and pulls out the sport's pages.

"Hi, Dominic," Sabina says, leaning over the table and pulling the newspaper out of his hands. "I would rather you didn't read at table. You have plenty of time to do that afterwards. I would like mealtimes to be a sociable event. Why not tell me about yesterday. Didn't you have a career interview at school?"

Dominic stares at her.

"What about Dad?"

"Pardon?" Adrian asks

"Dad's always reading at table. Why not tell him to stop."

"Your father is far too old to learn new tricks."

Adrian is shocked, annoyed, insulted.

Dominic and Adrian fold their papers in unison, lean forward with their elbows on the table and their heads resting in their cupped hands. Dominic explains that he doesn't feel like telling her about his career plans, wondering why she wants to talk about it over mealtime anyway.

Sabina explains that she would like him to let her know whether he needed any help in decision-making.

She has lost touch with him and his needs. She feels bad about it and reprimands herself for being a bad mother. It may be a little late to start changing that now, but it is better than giving up altogether. Dominic will soon have to decide which university course he would like to apply for and where he was going to study. She would like him to feel that he could come to her if he needed to—and not just with that sort of problem.

She finishes her meal, puts her plate in the dishwasher and hums her way upstairs. A few moments later she's back in the kitchen saying goodbye. All they hear is, 'to the cinema,' and did she say 'on my own'?

The front door slams shut. Dominic and Adrian erect their newspapers anew and continue staring at them.

When Dominic leaves the house to go to a disco, Adrian is still sitting at the table, newspaper in front of his eyes, thinking. All of a sudden he springs up, runs to the cupboard in the hall and pulls out the yellow pages for Luxembourg. He anxiously scans the index and flicks the book open at the appropriate page.

"Detectives Professionels," he says out loud and then glances round, half expecting someone to be there.

He reads several, his eyes resting for a long time on one with the largest advert and the most claims to discretion. He scribbles the number down on a bank note and puts it into his wallet.

Why he does what he does next, he can't really explain. It's not like him to pry into other people's private property, but before he can stop himself, he's in the bedroom, at Sabina's side of the bed, his right hand pulling the bedside table drawer open, his left hand jumping inside and searching through her things.

The hand finds the box of chocolates first, opens it and Adrian peeps inside. *Thought she was on a chocolate diet.* He sniffs a few and then tugs at the layers. What he's looking for, he's not entirely sure—a card? 'To darling Sabina from your lover.' What could he be called? Philippe? Pierre? He was bound to be French. If only he could find some hard evidence—something to hold against her, accuse her of? The jewellery box isn't locked and his right hand crawls up to the lid and lifts it with ease. It extracts: a heart pendant that looks like it came from a bubble-gum machine; various strings of colourful plastic beads; a few odd earrings and a couple of broken chains. Underneath it all, is a crumpled piece of pink-coloured paper. His fingers unfold it carefully. It looks as if there is an encoded message—written in magic ink—the kind that is barely visible and only becomes legible when a special chemical is put on it. He wonders whether this could be hard evidence—something for the private detective—if he makes an appointment, of course. He decides against it—too risky. She might notice it's been taken and would no doubt suspect him first. He digs a little more and finds another piece of paper. A blue-coloured sentence shines forth in a very provocative way and Adrian shudders. Punctuated by a red heart drawn flamboyantly in what looks and...Adrian's right hand shoves it under his nose...*smells like strawberry lipstick*...is the sentence:

I shall love and treat you like a precious object from now until forever

How childish and sloppy can a man get!

He throws it back in disgust and puts everything else neatly into place. Finally, he rubs the box with his hanky to remove the fingerprints. *You never know,* he tells himself, and goes back to the computer. The monitor remains stuck on the same website for half an hour. Adrian has been staring at it without really looking.

He was never sure they were doing the right thing when they got married. It all happened so fast. The tentative 'yes' to her question 'let's make a baby.' And then she was pregnant. Four weeks later she jumped into bed after completing the pregnancy test in the bathroom, lifted his pyjama top, nuzzled into his warm patch of chest hair and announced it. He couldn't see her face but knew she was beaming. He tried to inject enthusiasm into his voice but knew as soon as he uttered the words that he hadn't pulled it off. Sabina was the kind of woman who could see someone's life history in a split-second facial expression.

From then on, he began to despise her swollen belly. It was a solid mass between them. Touching it made him feel contemptuous—as if it already had a power of its own. There was a being in there that was getting all his wife's attention and it was not even born. What was it going to be like when it was born? How he wished he could just unbutton her stomach, remove the baby and have his wife back for a night, embrace her, make love to her, as he used to.

It wasn't just the physical closeness to his wife that Adrian missed; he missed his old Sabina: astute, lively, intellectual Sabina. The one who was concerned about current affairs; the one who read newspapers and discussed issues with him. With the baby inside her, she turned into the cliché in front of his eyes: a dumb, pregnant housewife. She didn't seem to notice or to care. Her nose was too busy buried in the 'Week by Week Guide to Pregnancy.' What about a 'Week by Week Guide to Destroying a Relationship'—that was how Adrian viewed it. He did not tell her, of course; not in her state. She would have become all emotional. Tears flowed freely at the best of times during her pregnancy. He didn't want to induce them; it was more than he could bear, seeing anyone cry. Sign of weakness, tears were. When you were crying, you had lost control.

When the boys leave, he muses, he will finally be alone with his wife and will be able to concentrate on the relationship again. As far as he is concerned, the relationship is still on hold whilst the kids grow up. He considered the family side of things a temporary situation—a mere eighteen years—after which he could return to normal.

He opens the e-mail program and finishes writing the directions to their house for friends who are coming to the party. After reading through the text one more time, he points the cursor at the send command and clicks with the left mouse button. The message promptly moves from the 'out' tray to the 'sent' tray and he smiles with satisfaction.

Why can't he communicate with Sabina anymore? he wonders. She's always shutting herself away in the bathroom whenever she's upset. He'll be damned if he's always the one who has to coax her out. He used to do that when he was a student: all she had to do was pout in that sexy way of hers and he was on his back like a puppy begging to be tickled. Arguments just never happened. They were students and they were happy with their lives. And now that they have been married for eighteen years, he has got into the habit of just carrying on with his own life, not bothering about hers, whether she is happy or sad.

Adrian finds the website he has bookmarked and peruses through its pages. The function hall which will be the venue for the party is featured on it—you can even go on a virtual tour of it. The bar, dance floor, stage, changing rooms. He has engaged a jazz band for the night, despite the extra cost. He got so carried away with the organisation of the event that he forgot about his main motivation for holding it in the hall as opposed to a fancy restaurant. There seemed to be a certain amount of pressure on him to offer a great night for his guests.

He's looking forward to all the praise his efforts will earn from friends and relatives when they come. He also can't wait to show off his sports car and large modern house. None of them have a turbo lawn-mower, a computerised light system for the garden or a lounge as big as a tennis court. And on the family front, many had only just married and were in the baby-burping stage.

He stretches his arms high over his head. What a good choice he made when he moved to Luxembourg, leaving that drab little life in London behind. When he thinks of that poky semi-detached house he wonders how he stood living in it for so long. He could never go back to that. Money has given him more freedom of choice and that feels good.

Dear Jennifer,

I would be glad to take up your kind offer of a place to stay whilst I'm at the conference in London. I don't think I'll feel like going out after the long day listening to boring speakers—If you wouldn't mind, I would prefer to stay in for dinner.

Love from
Adrian

Just before sending the e-mail, he remembers that she can't cook. Not wishing to embarrass her, or subject himself to one of her rotten meals, he adds:

Ps. We could get a take-away if you like. I love Chinese.

Birthing

January 1st 1960:

> 'Our 5th wedding anniversary. I'm feeling unattractive and heavy. How I hate being pregnant. I feel so ugly and undesirable. Richard doesn't like to look at me. He dislikes how I look—even though he hasn't said so. I can feel it. He avoids cuddling me. It is as if he sees me as a different being when I'm pregnant. He feels detached, and uninvolved. I wish he were more attentive to my needs. I wish he would order me to lie on the bed, massage my aching back and legs, make Jennifer some tea and put her to bed. But that's too much to ask, I know. Still, I do wish that he would come back from work a little earlier. Today, I thought about phoning him at work and telling him to come back. But I didn't have an excuse other than it's our wedding anniversary and I'm pregnant. He wouldn't understand. He would feel a fool in front of his colleagues. Besides, I'd rather him think of it himself and not wait to be told. Oh well, at least I've got my baby to look forward to. I can't wait to see what it looks like. I wonder whether it's a boy or a girl. When I close my eyes and feel the bump, I try to imagine how baby is lying. Sometimes when I breathe deeply into my stomach it starts to do a little jig. When I hold my breath, it stops again. I sometimes play little games with baby when it is active like that. When it pushes a limb up to form a hard protrusion on my stomach, I push it gently back in and the baby automatically moves it and protrudes it somewhere else. It's a primitive way of communicating, but it's fun.'

Sabina understands because she did the same and felt similar things in her pregnancies. Adrian was not as attentive to her needs as she would have liked. He did however make one token effort at reading a book on birth preparation even though he gave up after two pages. He would have preferred to stay home during the birth, too but social pressure got the better of him and he came: all his friends and colleagues and even the doctor expected it. She was glad that he stayed by her side because he was a born natural to it, spending six tedious hours massaging her back in a loving, but firm way that soothed and warmed her. The constant bodily contact reassured her and gave her a strong sense of solidarity with him. When the doctor made Sabina climb onto the bed and lie on her back, they felt like lost lambs. The doctor had said it was just a routine examination of the cervix and then shoved a huge needle in and sliced through half her birth canal. It happened so fast and unexpectedly that Sabina and Adrian were defenceless. The episiotomy was a success and the doctor had Sabina in his favourite birthing position: pinned on her back like a dying beetle with both legs fixed in stirrups. All contractions and willpower subsided and the birthing process came to an inexplicable halt. The doctor could not understand why Sabina no longer wanted to have her baby. 'Push, or I'll get the forceps,' the doctor announced importantly. She pushed. 'No! You're doing it all wrong. Push as though you are going to the toilet!' 'I don't usually go to the toilet in this position,' she shouted at the doctor's frowning face. He tutted loudly and stomped out of the room to fetch the forceps. With the doctor out, the midwife had the courage to take charge: 'You *can* do it. Don't let the doctor put you off. He had no right to treat you like that!' She hastily attached a drip to Sabina's arm and soon the contractions were back. By the time the doctor returned, she was feeling a strong urge to push. 'Don't push!' he cried. Sabina ignored him and with one almighty hot-ripping gush, the baby shot out of her womb and into the doctor's arms. Sabina reached out to receive the baby but was merely met with another disapproving look from the doctor. 'What's wrong?' she asked. No answer. She couldn't hear a baby's cry and strained to see him. The doctor had a tube down the infant's mouth and a revolting sucking sound was all she could hear. She grabbed Adrian's arm. 'It's okay,' he said. 'The doctor is just sucking out the mucous. He's healthy.' The doctor finally handed the baby over. He smelled good. He was perfect. Her joy at such a moment was rudely seized from her when the doctor started pummelling her sore stomach. 'If I don't get your placenta out I shall have to operate!' he snarled at her. No one had told her about this in the antenatal classes. She thought that the afterbirth would just slip out by itself—it shouldn't have to be kneaded out with a knuckle massage. 'Relax,' he ordered and pushed a terrifying-looking metal tool inside her and began scraping around. Sabina no longer had the energy to protest. After the disembowelling, he sewed up the enormous cut he had made a few hours previously. 'It hurts,' she cried. 'No it doesn't. You saw the needle—it's just psychological,' he accused and refused to give her a top up of anaesthetic.

Sabina is trembling. She is back at the will of the doctor again. God, how she would love to ram a brick up his backside and make him shit it out. She would cut half way up his anus first of course—to help him! She doesn't think she'll ever forgive him. Compared with the first birth, the second was a doddle. She changed doctors and this one, like a line prompter in the wings of a première, let her perform without interfering. Within four hours of arriving at hospital, Carl was born and Sabina walked back to her hospital bed, pushing her prize in front of her. Adrian was proud of her that day.

March 25th 1960

> 'Having babies is what I can do best. I should have a whole house full of them. How wonderful it would be to be swamped in your own creations. I love giving life. I am so glad that I can, and that I am a woman. It is an amazing feeling. I wish that my own life would always be like that—like the feeling I have when I give birth, without all the pain of course. I don't want my babies to suffer any pain in life like I did. I'll protect them from life. I want them to be the happiest children ever.
>
> I wish Richard wouldn't insist on calling this baby 'Sabina'. I know that his first love used to be called that. I know that he loved her more than me and that she let him down. I found a couple of letters from her. What can I do? I can't tell him that I know—that I was prying. I can't bear to call her by that name either. I'll think of something—at the moment she is just 'baby'.'

Sabina reads on and on, page after page, book after book. She's thirsty to learn all about her mother. By the time she hears Carl, he has already climbed up the ladder and is half way through the opening to the loft:

"Mum!"

"C-Carl. Why aren't you at school?"

"School finished over an hour ago!"

"Oh," she says and glances down at her watch. It's six. She's been in the loft all day.

"What are you doing up there?" he asks.

"Oh, just sorting things out," she says, hiding in her dark corner.

"Are you going to make some tea?"

"Yes, of course. Give me a few minutes—I'll be down."

Carl strains to see where she is. He can only see a dark shadow where she could be. Suddenly the torch slips her grasp, momentarily lighting up her face and he gasps in horror at a face, red and blotchy from hours of crying. Carl descends the ladder slowly and retreats to his room.

Sabina hangs the torch back on the nail and climbs out of the loft, clutching two of the diaries.

Carl observes her through the crack in his bedroom door. He would have liked to talk to her, comfort her, but he does not know how to approach her. He does not want to pry, or uncover details of his Mum and Dad's relationship that he would rather not know about. What if she broke down and asked him to stand up for her in front of Adrian? He cannot do that. He hardly knows Adrian. But he has known for a long time that something is wrong and he voiced his concern to his brother last week about it. Dominic refused to listen: he did not believe there was anything wrong. But then Dominic only saw his parents as functions; Dad bought him new bikes and told him all about football and Mum made his sandwiches and washed his sweaty T-shirts.

As Sabina disappears into the bathroom, Carl goes to stand outside the door for a while listening to the sound of water splashing. She was washing away the tear marks. *Why does she have to do that?* By the time Sabina emerges from the bathroom, Carl has settled back down on his bed with his headphones on. He's not listening to the music. He's thinking. He saw the books clamped under his mother's arm when she went into the bathroom and wonders whether they are still there. He unplugs one of his headphone so that he can listen out for when she goes downstairs. Then he tiptoes to the bathroom to look for the books. He finds them hidden behind a large pot-plant and takes them to his room to read.

'This book belongs to: Mrs Veronica Hope, now Veronica Agarthy.'

He knows that 'Agarthy' is his mother's maiden name and it does not take him long to work out who Veronica is.

January 1st 1980

> 'He's gone. I heard it on the news in the radio this morning over breakfast. He has left me—gone forever. He's DEAD. What am I going to do now? How am I going to carry on with life now? I don't want to look after Richard anymore. Why couldn't he have died instead.'

Carl stops reading and snaps the book shut. He should not be reading this. It's none of his business. But his curiosity burns furiously, begging him to open the book again and read more.

> 'I had to act normally today. I couldn't tell Richard. It's our wedding anniversary for God's sake. I had to be extra kind to him today and make him his favourite Shepherd's Pie and pamper him more than usual. I think I'm going to be sick.'

There is a gap in the writing at that point and it looks like she really did run off to be sick.

> 'My darling Frank. Why did you leave me? Why did you drive under that bridge? I loved you. I was going to spend the rest of my life with you. Now what am I going to do? I don't want Richard. I don't want to nurse him. But I have to. It's my duty and I feel sorry for him. The doctor's have given him three more months to live. If only it were I who only had three more months. I think I could stand to live three more months. If only someone would throw a brick into the windscreen of my car when I pass under one of the motorway bridges. Why did it have to be you? God! Thousands of cars drive under that bridge and yours had to be the one.'

Carl is fascinated, intrigued, excited. He feels guilty; yet thirsty, greedily thirsty for more. He imagines his grandmother sobbing uncontrollably as she wrote. He detects watermarks that could have been her tears and he lifts the page to his nose to sniff at it. It smells of lavender.

He reads the next pages and is fascinated, and at the same time horrified, to learn that she hated nursing Richard (his grandfather!) but did it to keep going and to relieve the 'terrible guilt' she kept on and on about (ten pages at least). Carl didn't find any passages in which she wrote anything kind about her own dying husband. She kept on repeating things like, 'spent and empty like a disposable battery,' adding on one occasion that she wished she could be 'disposed of'. Then there were pages of complaining about how she suffered and how responsible she felt towards her daughters and that she 'could hardly abandon them—leaving them with a dying man to look after.' She said she had 'to get on with it—see it through to the bitter end.' Towards the end of the book, 1980, her writing became more and more monotonous until she just wrote line after line of the same: 'If only Richard would go, then I'd be free to leave this world too.'

Not once in the pages did Carl find nice things said about his grandfather. She didn't write that she would miss him or that she loved him. She merely mocked how he called her his Florence Nightingale and literally shouted out of the paper: 'HE DOESN'T KNOW ME—NEVER HAS AND NEVER WILL!'

Carl felt deeply sorry for his dying grandfather and couldn't help himself despising his grandmother for writing such callous things about a suffering man.

She talked about being depressed and only 'going through the motions of living, getting up, washing him, reading the newspaper to him, listening to his moaning, feeding him, lifting him on to the toilet and wiping his bottom.'

Carl flicks through the book to the month of his death—it was in November, the same month his grandmother had died—he knows this, not because he was there, because he was only just born, but because for many years his mother used to retreat to her room at this time of year and come out with red-rimmed eyes. He knew she had been crying. Grieving.

November 5th 1980

> 'Ironic that it's bonfire night the day I bury my husband and I have no tears to put out the fire—or any energy to start the fireworks. I didn't cry at the funeral, or before, or now. I can't. I'm all dried up. Sucked dry by Frank's death and my husband's illness. If only Frank hadn't been killed—I would light a thousand Catherine Wheels and let off just as many rockets in celebration. He was the love of my life—my reason for living. I should end it all.'

Carl reads on. She tried an overdose—but woke up the next day 'feeling ghastly, but still alive.' She began to drink saying that it 'helps me to forget what a wretched life I have.' Her main wish now was that she would 'drink herself to death.' Nothing seemed to work and she moaned about 'interfering friends and neighbours who presume I am mourning the death of Richard and come up with ridiculous suggestions to try and console me. BLOODY MEETINGS FOR RECENT WIDOWS! GO AWAY AND LEAVE ME IN PEACE!' Carl noticed that she got more depressed after that outburst and the 'I am guilty—*mea ultima culpa*—it's all my fault!' went on for pages and pages again like it had at the beginning of the year. And at the end of that venting she wrote, 'I wish I could talk to someone about it.' Followed by, 'Where would I begin? With the tale of my wedding night? With my first extra-marital affair? No. The only person I could possibly talk to is myself, through my diary.'

Carl puts the book down. Tears have filled his eyes and the writing looks blurry. He doesn't want any to spill onto the book and smudge the ink—his mother may know he's read them. During the reading session he had been pinching his arm so hard to stop himself from getting emotional that there are red marks where his nails have dug into the skin on his forearm. He'll be called down to tea any moment and he doesn't want his mother questioning him. He hears the sound of the radio and the dishwasher being emptied and goes into the bathroom to put the books back and dab his face with a cold flannel.

Sabina is humming as she prepares the tea. A male voice on the English-speaking radio station is talking about St. Valentines Day. Sabina's not really interested and is about to switch it off to enjoy some peace and quiet when her attention is caught by a female voice announcing: 'Valentine trick—to win my lover's heart.' Sabina moves closer to the transistor. 'I got really fed up with my boyfriend because he never sent me a card, flowers or a single chocolate on Valentine's Day. So I rang him up on the Sunday and thanked him for a lovely box of chocolates in the shape of a giant red heart. You should've heard him on the phone, stuttering and grappling for words. And then he said that it was a pleasure and that he knew how I loved those large heart-shaped boxes and that he'd been everywhere to find one…he called it his romanticism coming out. I had to try really hard not to burst out laughing and ruin it. I didn't let on that there was no box of chocolates for a whole week. I let him stew in it. And, I tell you, it was worth it! He was the kindest, most romantic boyfriend that week—sending me a bouquet of flowers, a cuddly toy and—at the end of it he proposed!'

"Mum, is it ready?"

It's Dominic calling from the lounge.

"Yes," she shouts back and then adds, "Call Carl, would you?"

"I'm coming," Carl says as he enters the kitchen and makes his way to the table.

"I've made a delicious Greek salad!" Sabina exclaims with pride, wafting the delight under his nose.

It is a truly exceptional-looking salad, with sheep's cheese, juicy red tomatoes and an abundance of cucumber chunks. She places it in the centre of the table next to a cheese platter decorated with mice-shaped radishes whose thin tails all point towards a large slice of Brie de Meaux, the ripeness of which is oozing out like cream out of a slice of Victoria Sandwich cake when bitten into. The slithers of leftover radish now sit in the centre of some neatly sliced eggs around which petals have been drawn using a tube of mayonnaise. Even the bread, which usually looks as if it has been hacked off by an incompetent lumberjack and hurled into the basket from fifty metres, has been artistically arranged into the shape of a fan.

Sabina smiles as she invites Carl and Dominic to sit down at the tea table. Carl is confused at the contrast to half an hour ago when she had run, bloody-eyed into the bathroom.

"What's the occasion?" he asks cautiously.

"It's Tuesday."

"So? Why the fancy stuff?" Dominic says in a disapproving tone.

"Why not?" she replies in a merry voice. "It looks wonderful, it smells wonderful," and pointing her nose towards the table and breathing in the air above it, "and," pausing dramatically, dipping thumb and forefinger into the Greek salad, pulling out a tomato chunk, popping it into her mouth, "it tastes wonderful!"

Dominic looks at Carl, Carl looks at Dominic. Dominic shrugs and Carl frowns.

"But why the fancy decorating?" Dominic asks, unimpressed by his mother's efforts. Sabina is pleased that Adrian is away at a conference in London so that he can't chuck another bucket of cold water over her Tuesday surprise. Today she feels that she has achieved something worth celebrating. If only they could read her mind and know how important today has been to her. *But how could she even begin to explain?*

"Let's just enjoy it!" she says and tucks in. Her two boys follow suit.

The food tastes different. Better. Sabina's taste buds discover flavours that, before today, went undetected: the nutty flavour of the sesame and sunflower seeds in the bread, the exquisite creaminess of the cheese, the sharp but sweet flavour of the salad. Though simple, her tea feels like a feast.

Carl stares at her throughout the meal. He can't understand why she is behaving like the happiest person on earth. She should be depressed. He cannot remember the last time she had smiled so much, or expressed so much appreciation of her food. Maybe she has not read the diaries yet, he thinks; maybe she doesn't know about her mother.

Going Back Again

Sabina rushes through the front door and into the living room with great excitement. Madame Anastasia looks on with a broad smile, pleased that Sabina has returned. After her breakdown last time, she wondered whether she would come back at all; whether she would continue with the design of the dress; and whether she would even go to her own birthday party.

The dress design is coming along well—there is still much work to be donė, but there are six weeks left until the day, giving them enough time to successfully complete the project. Once the design details have been passed on to the 'craftsmen and women', as Madame Anastasia calls the seamstresses (*and taylors, I presume*), all the work except the hem and some of the embroidery can be done without Sabina's presence. Madame Anastasia has pinned the pattern pieces together and Sabina is allowing herself to be used as dressmaker's doll so that the size will be just right. Due to all the swimming and walking she has been doing, her body has tightened and toned up and a lot of the winter fat reserve has been running off her like melted butter. The first measurements taken are now completely invalid. Seeing as it will be a fitted bodice—to show off her 'beautiful full-bosomed figure'—Madame Anastasia has to postpone the actual sewing for another week, convinced that her boobs will lose another centimeter. Sabina is much more thrilled at the news than Madame Anastasia who had grown rather enthusiastic about the idea of a great-bosomed-design. She tells Sabina that she has learned to live with this kind of disappointment.

"As soon as my clients begin to like themselves," she laments, "they start looking after themselves and this inevitably leads to a loss of the extra pounds gained in their hate-myself years. The choice of fabric colour will also be influenced by the emergence of the new self. But I have not been disappointed by any one client's choice of material to date."

Even as a pinned-on paper pattern, the dress looks magnificent. Sabina can't wait to move on to the real material—she feels uncomfortable and chilly standing around in a pinned paper dress with nothing underneath but bra and knickers.

"Oh, my faithful Gerard. There you are!" Madame Anastasia exclaims and a pin jabs into Sabina's side as she swivels around to see whom on earth she is referring to. A man is walking across the room with more elegance and poise than a male ballet dancer. He is not a tall man, but he carries his height as if he were. Sabina is momentarily stunned. Not just by the man's looks, but by the fact he is there at all. *Where did he come from? Who is he? Is this Margot Fonteyn's Nureyev?*

Madame Anastasia reads Sabina's thoughts and offers:

"Sabina, meet my image therapist who claims to open the door to the unconscious."

"Oh, Ana, such big words. You'll scare your customers off!" he says smiling and offers Sabina a glove-covered hand.

She takes it. He bows before her and kisses her hand just like Prince Charming would have done before swirling Cinderella around the dance floor.

"I can wear fabulous clothes," he says "but if I walk into the room and you can't *feel* me, then who cares?"

"Too true, too true," applauds Madame Anastasia and for the first time Sabina notices a slight reddening of her face.

She's embarrassed—wow! I never thought she was capable of it.

Gerard sits on the arm of the other armchair in the room (Madame Anastasia has her sewing basket on the other) and takes out a pad and paper.

"So, tell me, Madame Connoisseur of Stitch and Cloth—which selection of fabric samples should I bring you this time? Midnight-Blue Velvets, Rainbow-Rouge Cashmeres, Peakock-Pride Silks, Black-Tempest Cottons, perhaps?"

"Blue is too cold for this lady's life—her life is hotting up, not cooling down."

"Ah well then, how about the Rainbow-Rouge selection?"

"Any new Rainbow-Rouges?"

"Yes! One that is a veritable colour explosion: a deep burgundy, through terracotta, orange, yellow and pink to white."

"Sounds wonderful!" shrieks Madame Anastasia and words begin to bubble out of her as she turns into the gesticulating artist with paintbrush in hand, mumbling under her breath and sweeps the imaginary brush up and down the air: "The darker tones could be used to hide those parts of the body that are not ready yet for the critical eye. And the lighter shades could grandly emphasise the parts the wearer is proud of."

Then all she hears is 'fire' and 'vitality' as she turns pirouettes and ushers Gerard out of the door, making Sabina's heart leap and twizzle with her.

The front door slams shut and the seamstress returns to her paper-covered model.

Sabina is bursting to tell her about the diaries and how she feels like she can breathe and live easily once more. As if on cue, Madame Anastasia says:

"How well you look!"

"Yes," Sabina replies "And I feel well. I feel relieved. I feel new. No, more than new. Oh, I can't describe how I feel, but it is wonderful. I have so many plans. I can't wait for this party. I never thought I would feel this way about it."

"I am pleased for you, Sabina."

Sabina enjoys hearing Madame Anastasia call her by her first name. It makes her feel much closer to her, less like the customer, more like an equal.

"Thank you. May I call you Anastasia?"

"Call me Ana. I hate long names. They are so awkward, don't you think?"

Sabina feels a surge of love for Ana and hopes they will become friends after the dressmaking is over. If it weren't for her, she would still be heading blindly towards her fortieth birthday with dread and negativity. As she slips back into her usual clothes, she begins.

"I found my mother's diaries in the loft."

Ana nods, prompting her to continue.

"I read them."

She nods again. Sabina sits down and continues. She tells her all she has learned from the diaries. Eventually, she quietens and, in a soft, compassionate voice recounts the story she has most wanted to tell.

"My mother came to Luxembourg on very few occasions. The last time was in November 1985. She stayed for a week, helping me with my son and cooking and stuff. The doctor had insisted I rest as much as possible because of the two miscarriages I'd had. My baby wasn't due for three months but I had been having some mild contractions. On the last day of her visit, she insisted on going into Luxembourg on her own—'to do some shopping,' she had told me. I interpreted it as a request to secretly buy some leaving presents for the family before catching the evening flight. I already had my jacket on, had locked up and was about to leave the house to pick her up and take her to the airport when the phone rang. It was already 6 p.m. and the flight was at 8.30 p.m. Thinking that it might be her, I answered it. Inspector Dubois from the Luxembourg police was on the phone. I thought he had a wrong number at first and grew impatient, knowing that time was ticking on and my mother had a plane to catch. I didn't understand his garbled French either. When he switched to English, I didn't understand much more at first either. Eventually, I began to understand what he was trying to tell me. My mother was a suicide victim—jumped off the Red Bridge into the Pétrusse valley below."

Madame Anastasia takes hold of one of Sabina's trembling hands. Sabina wants to go on.

"I nearly had another miscarriage that cold, misty November day. The doctor gave me an injection, a packet of homeopathic anti-stress pills and admitted me to hospital. Jennifer arrived on the next possible flight. It was the same aeroplane that would have come back to Luxembourg after taking my mother to Heathrow. She sat on the edge of my hospital bed and wept. When we felt able to speak, we talked about her, wondering what could have driven her life to its tragic end. We talked about our father who died of cancer in 1980, leaving our mother with a large and lonely house, a modest pension and two mangy black cats that she hated. We both agreed that she had bravely pieced her life back together after our father's death and was soon functioning normally again. Men started to take interest in her and she started dating again. Six months before she died, her boyfriend André decided to get back together with his ex-wife. I had talked to my mother on the phone about it—but she hadn't seemed disconcerted at all. Yet somehow I felt she wasn't being honest about it. Jennifer wished that Dad hadn't died so young saying that she must have been more heart-broken than we thought. I was worried about my baby. It hadn't stirred since I heard the news and I feared it had left me too.

Jennifer recounted loads of stories and memories from childhood. She talked about the times Mum used to play hide-and-seek with us. She would always hide in the utility room, behind the piles of un-ironed clothes and we would always know that she was there. We'd giggle so much that she'd come out to see what all the fun was about and then we'd all fall about laughing on the floor.

I was shocked by her directness when she suddenly asked me whether I loved Adrian as much as Mum loved Dad. I replied that I didn't think anyone could love her husband as much as Mum had loved Dad, adding that I would never kill myself if Adrian died. Jennifer also said that she couldn't imagine ever killing herself over a man. We've never talked since about anything in connection with the suicide.

Then we were silent for what seemed like hours. And suddenly, quite out of the blue, she said, 'Maybe somebody pushed her.' I reminded her that the police had already ruled that out. A while later she broke the silence again with, 'She could have slipped.' 'She would have had to be walking on top of the railing to have slipped,' I told her. 'Why would she be walking on the railing? She's hardly likely to climb up above a 50-metre drop unless she was intending to jump off it.' Jennifer burst into tears at that point and shouted at me that I didn't have to be so callous. She shrieked at me that it could have been an impulse, a crazy moment, like she used to have. And then she described the time Mum had balanced along a fallen tree in the woods. It must have been six metres above the leafed floor. She had shouted down to us that we must never copy her. It was much too dangerous. This anecdote reminded me of the impulse I had once had whilst I was hiking. As I walked along the edge of a cliff, I was suddenly possessed by an overpowering urge to jump off it. I had the choice: I could take one step forward or one step back. My feet twitched, daring me to do it. I had no reason whatsoever to take my life that day—but there was the offer, beckoning me, tempting me. As soon as I had taken the decisive step back, the impulse left me as quickly as it had come and I carried on my way. But I haven't dared to go any where near to the edge of cliffs ever since.

Jennifer asked if Mum had said anything to me about Dad's illness. I told her that she had said very little. Jennifer then told me of a time she'd overheard her speaking to herself. First she assumed she was on the phone, but after listening for a while, realised that she must be talking to herself. She said that she was pretending to argue with Dad, criticise him, and tell him off. She kept on repeating things like 'fluff up your pillows' and 'never get any appreciation for what I'm doing' and 'you always have to have the last word' and 'like a prisoner in my own house'. She said that she never told me because she was ashamed that she'd eavesdropped. Also, she'd never heard her speak in that particular tone of voice before and that had scared her. Sabina said that she remembered seeing her mother running out of their bedroom once, her eyes bloodshot. Later her eyes were still red and she commented about a terrible spate of hay fever.

We kept on puzzling over it. We wondered whether she was heart broken, but it didn't seem to fit. We concluded that she must have attempted to piece her life together after he died, but couldn't. The question that gnawed at us the most, though, was why she didn't ask for help. We guessed it must have been her pride and then cried some more about how beautiful and perfect a mother she was. Finally, we flung ourselves into an embrace and sobbed and sobbed.

My baby eventually started kicking inside me. It seemed to be saying, 'Don't worry, I'm still here, Mum.' It was a wonderful feeling amidst all the grief. I was elated and at the same time indefinably sad—thinking how ironic it was that there was a new human being inside me when one had just left the world.

On the anniversary of her death, I used to shut myself up in the attic of the house where no one looked for me and I would chew over the events and conversations prior to the suicide. I kept on thinking how inadequate I was as my mother's lifesaver and would tremble violently, incessantly. I reprimanded myself constantly, convinced that I could have saved her if I'd tried to find the truth behind her pallid complexion when I collected her from the airport. Her killing herself was so unlike the open, tender and loving person who was so compassionate and encouraging to us daughters.

But the diaries are revealing another side to my mother that I had never known. She regretted ever marrying my father but got pregnant straight away and got stuck. When Jennifer and I got older, she had several lovers and eventually fell in love with one of them. She was going to leave my father for him when he was killed in a car crash. I think she became so infested with the pain and grief from that tragedy she turned it on herself. On the outside, she was sociable and warm to the point of being extroverted; on the inside a raging sea of turmoil possessed her. My mother—a person who always had an open ear for other peoples' troubles and was the perfect therapist when it came to sorting out the kaleidoscopic problems of others, neglected her own needs. She let her vitality drain away. Gradually at first, but with ever increasing speed, I think a tide of turmoil caught her up and swept her over the bridge to her death.

Adrian was never very fond of my mother and, after a few days of mourning, was able to get on with his life again. I couldn't. Never have since. I have always resented Adrian for his ability to carry on with his life whilst I had to suffer. I wanted him to read my feelings, broach the subject, snap me out of my bereavement and stop my own self-destruction. He didn't. He couldn't and I probably wouldn't have let him if he'd tried.

I've often wondered how he'd have coped if it had been *his* mother. But then, as he said himself, his mother would never do it. She had a 'robust mind,' 'nerves of steel' and was 'strongly in control of her life.' Though my mother-in-law was sincerely sympathetic at the time, she did tend to bring up 'suicidal tendencies running in the family' more often than felt comfortable. I guess she was merely trying to protect him from the horror of waking up one day to find his wife dead on the lounge carpet with a bullet through her head and a farewell note on the mantelpiece. I tried to talk to her once or twice, but she's a lousy listener trying to better any problem, injury or illness as if fighting for gold in the sympathy and attention competition.

I still feel responsible for my mother's death. I wish I could have saved her—been there to pull her away!"

There's silence. Sabina can't remember ever speaking for such a long time in her life—and certainly not with someone listening to her, really listening.

Eventually, Ana says something.

"How long are you going to torture yourself with the blame, Sabina?"

Sabina's sobs prevent her from speaking for a while. When she can, the words come out in spasms.

"Do y-ou th-ink she w-ould h-ave k-illed h-erself in En-gland?"

"That's the question that has occupied you all these years, isn't it?"

"Yes."

"I think she would have found her way to a similar bridge regardless of where she was, don't you?"

"I don't know. I didn't think so until I read her diaries. I wasn't actually expecting to see it in writing."

"See what in writing?"

"That she wanted to kill herself. So you don't think that Luxembourg plays a role?"

"I don't think Luxembourg has anything to do with it other than her taking its offer of the Red Bridge."

"What if the atmosphere here just tipped her volatile balance? It seems too significant that it happened here—what with the high suicide rate and that bloody Red Bridge. It was the time before they erected the shields, you know."

"I know. But she came to Luxembourg for no other reason than to support you in the last weeks of pregnancy."

"Yes, but…?"

"Everyone chooses their path. She chose hers. She had lost faith in her ability to create goodness in her life. She had reached the limit of happiness and such was her fear to experience the fall that she preferred to go before it happened. Like an amateur gambler, she got scared, grabbed her winnings and got out before she lost it all again. She did it in style—Luxembourg her helping hand. She did it for herself—probably the first act she did for herself in her entire life. God bless her."

"Yes. G-od-bless–er," is all that Sabina manages, and then curls up in the chair and cries.

Cupid's Work

Adrian arrives at Jennifer's flat after the long conference, glad that he hasn't made dinner arrangements with the other delegates. He was pleasantly surprised by Jennifer's enthusiasm after he took up her offer to stay. He had thought that her Friday and Saturday nights were booked months in advance. At least, that was what Sabina tended to say whenever he asked about the possibility of staying at her sister's—*but that's typical of a woman to be jealous of other women.*

Though he wouldn't admit it, his acceptance of her invitation is not altogether without ulterior motive: he is hoping to rope her into helping him organise the party—at least for Sabina's side of the family. *What with all the time and energy I am forced to waste on Sabina ever since that day she came back from the swimming pool a different woman, I don't think I should have to do it all single handed!*

Jennifer is the only person he can think of who might be willing to offer a hand. Besides, she may just know a secret or two about Sabina and *if I could find that out, it's well worth sleeping on her uncomfortable designer furniture.* He rings the doorbell and is greeted by a fresh-faced, evening-dress-wearing, lean and lanky woman with black curls spilling over her face and shoulders as if they have just been poured fresh out of a bottle.

"Hi!"

"Come on in! Oh good, you managed to find the Chinese Takeaway," she says joyfully, grabbing the bulging white plastic bag from his right hand and holding the door open with the other. "How was the conference?"

"Fine. Tiring. I'll be glad when it's over."

"Oh, I meant to ask you—when will it be over?"

"Not until late tomorrow—I have to chair a discussion group after the official end. I don't suppose I'll be done before 8."

"I know—once people start on some topic, it's difficult to shut them up, isn't it. I've often been in discussion groups till midnight." She laughs and points to a cupboard. "You can hang your coat up in there." He looks at her blankly (he just slings his coat over the banister at home). She reaches inside, hands him a large wooden hanger and continues, "We could have an Indian tomorrow night then."

"Okay," he says with little enthusiasm. Takeaways were no longer his idea of good food—and no comparison to the kind of food Sabina had been feeding him lately. He wonders whether she's taking cookery lessons and makes a mental note to ask Jennifer. "What a lot of stuff!" he exclaims as he struggles to separate the stiff row of hangers holding female work suits, and a collection of Spring, Summer and Winter overcoats so that he can slot his in.

"Need it all for work," she explains. "Amazing how much space it takes!"

Adrian isn't interested in her excuses for her extravagance and just nods whilst moving towards the living room.

"Oh, you remember where my living room is!" she exclaims, trotting up behind him and he rolls his eyes before she catches up with him. Sabina's sister, he is reminded, has the annoying habit of being over-enthusiastic about everything—as if what other people say and do is so god-damned wonderfully profound! He finds it hard to deal with her exuberance—now more than ever and wonders whether it's a good idea to ask her for help. She pushes in front of him to open the door and show him in. The room is as neat as the day he last entered a year and a half ago. Not a single change—unless you count the movement of a chair two millimetres to the right and the addition or subtraction of a pot plant. The colours (modern pastels—greys, blues); the three pieces of stern-looking furniture and the large-but-practical stow-away-everything cupboard system, have remained stationary and just as unappealing as they always had been. He was secretly hoping that the couch on which he was going to have to sleep tonight and tomorrow might at least have earned an extra cushion or two over the past eighteen months. But no, it stood there just as unexciting and severe as it had last time. It may be okay for a skeleton but anyone with some flesh suffers all kinds of scrapes and bruises just by turning over in their sleep. By Sunday, he knows already, he'll be in desperate need of a deep body massage but hardly thinks Sabina will give him one this time—even if he dared ask her.

"Do sit down. And help yourself to a drink—you know where I keep all the lovely booze," she says and Adrian's eyes turn another circle at her as she does a pirouette-like movement with the carrier bag and bounces towards the kitchen with the Chinese food. The smell of Chop-Suey hangs in her wake like perfume from burning incense.

Adrian reaches for the bottle of whisky—a mature Scottish malt. 'Fifteen years old', he reads. *That'll do,* he mumbles to himself and pours the glass to the brim.

"Sabina been in touch lately?" he shouts in the direction of the kitchen.

"In touch?" comes the defensive reply.

"Oh, just wondering whether she'd mentioned anything about her new hobbies!"

"Hobbies?"

"Yes, it is. I mean…cooking or anything?"

"Cooking?"

Adrian feels exasperated already. *It's like getting blood out of a stone. Women really do stick together, don't they. Most suspicious.* He continues to probe.

"Cookery classes! Has she said she is doing lessons?"

"Cookery lessons?"

Can't she understand plain English?

"Yes! She's been making some fabulous meals lately and, well, I wondered…not that it's important. Probably a surprise for her…"—and the rest of the sentence dribbles down the side of the whisky glass.

Jennifer feels very hot and uncomfortable. The oven has reached temperature and is beeping loudly, demanding that she put the Chinese food inside to heat up. She wouldn't be surprised if her sister was taking secret cookery lessons just so that she could show off when she visited her a week before her Birthday—*just to rub it in that I'm a crap cook. I can just see her having a good laugh over my attempt at wining and dining her husband—getting him to pick up a takeaway on the way back from the conference. Rotten wife I'd make! Can't even pick up the food myself and at least make it look like I've put some effort into it.*

"Celebration!" he finally exclaims and Jennifer drops the porcelain dish she's holding. On hearing the sound of breaking crockery, he rolls his eyes again and wonders whether this kind of clumsiness runs in the family.

"Learning to cook for her birthday celebration—as a surprise," he announces like someone who has just come to a brilliant conclusion after hearing all kinds of facts.

Silence.

A sob?

"Jennifer?"

"Y-yes. Just brushing up the mess."

"Want a hand?"

"N-no," she says as cheerfully as she can muster from inside her broom cupboard and turns on the liquidiser to muffle the sound of her blowing her nose.

What's she doing with that Chinese? Mincing it?

"Um, I thought you were having caterers," she manages before another attack gets the better of her. This time she switches on the dishwasher.

"Yes, we are. But she's…"

He wants to say 'acting strange', or 'having an affair', but all that comes out is. "Forget it!"

Jennifer can't forget it now that it's been brought up. She'd been trying to forget all about her inability to cook and had been relieved when Adrian had suggested a takeaway and had been excited all week about spending the weekend with her brother-in-law and hearing news about her nephews and Sabina and the party preparations. She had hoped Adrian would ask her to help. She'd like very much to feel part of it all, feel useful, that she was contributing to her sister's important day in some way. She knew what a big day it was—the transition from 39 to 40.

"Okay," she mumbles behind a tray full of steaming rice, Sweet and Sour Pork and Chop Suey. "Here it is—your gourmet meal!" and sets it down on the large dining table in the living room with less control than she had hoped. The sound ricochets off the pastel walls and makes Adrian stand to attention.

"R-ready?" he stutters.

"Let's eat now."

"Okay. Got any wine?"

Shit. Another thing I forgot. She was in the habit of drinking bubbly—not always the good champagne, but always the sparkling stuff. She found it pepped her up when she was feeling flat and without energy.

"Champagne?"

"No, I mean red or white wine!" he says impatiently.

"No. I could go and get…"

"Don't bother! Give me some champagne," he demands a bit more forcefully than he had meant and she trots off to the kitchen, head bowed and mouth drooping as low as he had often seen Sabina's.

Such a wimpy family, he thinks and digs his fork into the Sweet and Sour.

"brrrrringgg, brrrrringgg, brrrrringgg."

Jennifer and Adrian are sound asleep. It's 9:00 a.m. on Sunday 14th February and Adrian is lying in a semi coma after devouring several platefuls of hot Vindaloo and the wine Jennifer had picked up from the local off-license after she ran out of champagne. The alcohol may have worked as anaesthetic and enabled him to fall asleep on the furniture made for dead people, but it was now banging like a thousand wild drummers inside his head. Jennifer is not helping matters by stomping into the living room, knocking into the couch on the way to the phone and slamming something down (*fists?*) on the sideboard before picking up the receiver.

"Sabina!" she exclaims, scowls, rolls her eyes, sighs and walks over to what she refers to as the 'sofa bed' to see if Adrian is awake. He's sitting bolt upright and holding out a hand ready for the phone.

"What on earth do you want so early?" he fires.

Sabina remains cheerful at the other end.

"They've just arrived and they're beautiful! I couldn't wait to phone and say Thank You."

Adrian is silent, waiting for more information.

Sabina offers it.

"And so thoughtful. Eighteen—one for every year of our marriage! I didn't know you had it in you anymore. But then you go and surprise me like this with the roses!"

"Well," he says nervously, then stops, unsure how to continue. She takes over:

"This is the first time since our marriage that you've thought to send me flowers."

"Hmmm," he mumbles, all the time wondering who the roses are from and how he's going to find out. He would have to take some out of the bunch without her knowing, take them to the private detective. Surely he could trace them back to the shop and find out who sent them. He suddenly realises that Sabina has been talking all the time. He just hears the last part of her sentence:

"...very first Valentine's Day in hall, remember?..."

Adrian remembers and can't help smiling as he does. Jennifer is staring at him, feeling left out and more jealous of their love than ever.

"And then I looked out of the window and all I could see was a pair of teeth with a rose clamped between them and a huge heart..."

He remembers sticking that heart on his forehead with Bluetack and stuffing a huge teddy bear down his training trousers. They were the only ones stretchy enough for it to fit. She had shrieked with fright and then opened the window to let him in. "Not enough room for the two of you in there," she had said, tugging at the bear with one hand and taking him in her other. Then they had toppled over onto the bed and made love for the rest of the day.

Adrian shifts his weight. He can feel a certain part of him moving towards the opening in his pyjamas and Jennifer is staring at him at exactly that place with a look of horror. He turns his back. Jennifer leaves the room.

"I still have that rose."

"What?" Adrian is jolted back to the topic of conversation. "Rose?" *What fucking rose?*

"You know, the one you had between your teeth. I've kept it in my jewellery box all these years. It's become a bit dismembered—most of the petals are crushed, but the stalk is intact. That's all I need to remember."

Silence

"Adrian, are you still there?"

"Remember," he says dreamily.

"I wish you were here now so that I could show you how much I appreciate this gesture."

Adrian suddenly feels anger again. He feels like blurting, *I didn't buy the bloody roses,* but thinks better of it. It's quite nice to be appreciated. Even if he didn't do it. Maybe he would now. He used to be very creative in the way he showed Sabina how much he cared for her. *No, Adrian, you fool—she's having an affair!*

"I'll be home in a couple of days," he says, curtly. "You'll be able to express it to me in person."

Before he hangs up, Sabina asks to talk to Jennifer.

The curls on the back of Jennifer's neck feel like they are turning into hard broom bristles when Sabina answers Jennifer's question, 'What kind of roses?' with 'Eighteen beautiful long-stemmed red ones.'

"How wonderful," she manages and then feels drained of all energy to continue the conversation.

"And you?...What did Rick get you?"

After a pause, she tells Sabina that it's still a bit too early in the day for a Sunday, reminds her that there is an hour difference between the UK and continental Europe, accepts her apology, tells her that she's in the middle of preparing breakfast for Adrian and that the toast will burn if she doesn't keep an eye on it and hangs up. When the hand-held receiver hits the main set, Adrian's body convulses on the sofa and he feels his chest to check whether he's broken a couple of ribs. By the time he manages to manoeuvre his body to flash a disapproving look at Jennifer, she's no longer there.

Jennifer sits down and spreads her hands wide on the kitchen table to stop them from shaking, or balling up into tight fists. She hasn't received so much as a birthday card from a lover in years. *And my bloody sister, married for eighteen years, is enjoying more romance than I have ever had. It just isn't fair. She has all the luck!* A *caring husband, a family to be proud of...*

The way she feels right now makes her wonder whether she'll cope with going to Luxembourg to celebrate her sister's fortieth. A lot of family will be there and she is bound to be exposed to yet another Aunt-Vera inquisition, and all the other relatives' critical comparisons to her successful sister. They love to judge and advise on matters concerning her marital status and childless life. The impending celebration suddenly feels like a sharp breeze prodding her cold-front clouds when a weather change has been forecast. And she had been so proud of how she'd managed to suppress the depression that had tried to move in on her since her own fortieth when she was stuck at home, boyfriend-less and party-less because no one organised anything for her. If the neighbour hadn't popped round to ask whether she would mind her cat whilst she was away for a few days, she may have put an end to her misery that very night. All this on top of the fact that a week ago, her latest boyfriend, Antonio from Italy, announced his intention to leave for the States only a day before he actually left. She hasn't heard from him since. But her friend Marge had sworn she had seen him in Oxford a couple of days ago, walking beside the river with his arm around a girl.

Her thoughts are interrupted by Adrian as he staggers into the kitchen and plonks first himself and then a glass down at the kitchen table. Though he detests the stuff, he has helped himself to some of her egg liqueur to ease the pain of the night and the rude awakening. He leans back in her torturous kitchen chair and sucks on the mouthful of thick, sickly liquid as if it were a bitter sweet. The warm sensation as it slips down his throat is the only pleasant thing about it. Jennifer watches in disgust, misinterpreting the look on his face as secret male smugness because of the romantic thing he did for his wife. Why else would he celebrate with a Sunday-morning drink?

She walks over to the sink to fill the kettle and, before boiling the water, pours some into a pot on the windowsill. The pot contains a limp-looking plant that had shed many blossoms overnight turning it into by far the most untidy thing in her apartment. 'Hyacinth bulbs—two of them,' her colleague had explained at work on the Monday after the Asperge-Argenteuil disaster, adding, 'a consolation prize,' as Jennifer took the cellophane-wrapped pot of earth with a look of puzzlement on her face. Her colleagues code-named the evening AA-disaster (*Alcoholics Anonymous, haw, haw, haw).* When the same joke was triggered every time one of them came into her office, cruelly reminding her of the reason why she no longer had Rick as a boyfriend (or colleague because he left shortly afterwards for a job in France), she had taken it home and put it on the windowsill. Adrian frowns at

Jennifer's back—*why does she bother giving that horrible dying plant water?* He says nothing. He feels so dreadful that if he opens his mouth, he thinks he'll either bark ferociously or vomit all over her prim little kitchen. Either way, he would end up scrubbing things clean for the rest of the day.

Back in Luxembourg, Sabina is jumping around her kitchen like a jack-in-the-box that has just been released, laughing out loud and chanting: *You naughty, naughty, girl. You naughty, naughty girl.* She did feel wicked but couldn't ignore how great she felt, too. It had been a spontaneous idea. She had woken early in the morning, heard the announcement on the radio that it was St. Valentines Day and, all of a sudden, she was tapping Jennifer's number into the phone. Now she wonders whether to go out and buy herself the eighteen red roses just for the hell of it and keep Adrian guessing for a while longer.

She jumps up, rushes to her bedside table in which she has placed a notebook to write down her 'raw feelings and emotions,' as Madame Anastasia had suggested on her last visit, and makes the first entry:

February 14th 2000

> 'I'm so excited. I've found a new kind of love. It's enthralling and stimulating and much stronger than anything else I've known before. The most wonderful thing about it, though, is that I don't think anyone or anything will ever manage to take it away from me this time; it feels solid and right. It's growing stronger and more right every day. There'll be fights and conflicts, no doubt, just like there have been in my marriage; yet I'm convinced that this love will grow rather than die because of it. I'll make sure it does. I'll nurture it.'

She puts the pen down and slots it back into the bedside drawer between the box of half-empty Belgian chocolates and her jewellery box. Feeling pleased for finally allowing herself to acknowledge her feelings, she decides that she deserves the eighteen red roses and sets off to the centre of town to buy them.

Her house is basking in winter sunshine when she backs up the driveway and onto the road. Sun accompanies her as far as the plateau *Kirchberg* ('Church Hill') where it disappears behind a thick layer of fog just before the Red Bridge. Such weather changes have been something she has begun to notice more and more since her experience in the forest. To her surprise, she has found that, for such a small country, and the short distances she travels from day-to-day, there seems to be a relatively high frequency of contrasting weather conditions from one place to another. This is the third time in a few weeks that she has left her house in sunshine and arrived at the bridge in dense fog. Each time it has very nearly caused a change of heart. Today as her car enters the murky, moist air, she is less sure about the purchase of flowers. *It's a cruel thing to do. Nothing to do with love. I don't deserve the roses and shouldn't be such a callous wife!*

The interplay between fog and sunshine is the most striking meteorological occurrence in Luxembourg and reminds Sabina once more of the correlation between the Golden Gate Bridge and it's younger brother, the Red Bridge. When she was working in San Francisco as waitress during the long university summer vacation, she was advised to ring a special 'Meteo Number' before heading off to visit the Golden Gate Bridge. Mist rolling in from the Pacific often shrouded it in the moisture-filled air for most of the day whilst the city centre was scorching in the sun. The sea is miles away from land-locked Luxembourg. *It must come up from the valley*, she muses and shudders.

Unhindered by the fog, she crosses, as she has several times on her way to Madame Anastasias over the past month. In fact, she feels so relaxed during today's crossing that she wonders whether she would soon dare venture down the stone steps into the Pétrusse valley. When she parks near to the flower shop, she takes the neatly folded piece of paper out of her handbag which accompanies her everywhere she goes, and writes:

5. Visit the Pétrusse valley

After buying the roses, the heavens open, soaking her hair and her wonderful bunch of roses as she dashes back to her car. She is about to set off when a large digger blocks her path. Her head shakes like a wet dog trying to get dry and her mind starts spinning all kinds of ridiculous thread-like thoughts. *Nonsense,* she says out loud, *the river demanding I go now! See if it's gone wild!* And as soon as the digger shifts out of her car's path, she turns the key in the ignition and sets off home before her frayed mind gets the better of her.

Road works were a typical sight in Luxembourg and she begins tutting at the hole in the ground on her left. Over the past decade, she has seen nearly every street in the city centre being pierced by a pneumatic drill or ripped open by another monster machine. Some of the trenches were made so deep that for a while she had seriously wondered whether archaeologists were searching for historical treasures beneath the city. She soon learned that there was no such exciting project going on. The government was merely desperate to add a sophisticated sewage system, and more computer, TV and telephone cables to cater for the influx of banking business which had gradually transformed the agricultural land into the second richest country in the world. This particular hole was on the road which ran snake-like around the rim of the valley and had been made by the water board.

As she drives across the bridge, homeward bound, she reflects on the flow of water in the city. After the downpour of rain, water was dripping off everything; off roofs onto pavements; off pavements into gutters; down gutters into drains; through drains into pipes, through pipes under roads; under roads and out of sight. In the city, water was seen as a hazard and the flow of it had to be controlled—it could otherwise impede traffic and pedestrians, get into houses, and office buildings. It didn't used to be like that. In modern-day Luxembourg, there's not the remotest chance of a street flooding; all water goes underground through well-maintained pipes and is whisked silently and invisibly away to distant streams and rivers where it can flow freely again along its course. Sabina suddenly feels inexplicably emotional about this. On arrival back home, she sees, to her horror, that tears have soaked her crotch. For the final five kilometres of her drive back, tears were dripping off the end of her chin, down her front, and landed in her lap, her centre.

Once the roses are in the large glass vase on top of the dresser in the bedroom, her wet patch has dried and she feels elated. If it weren't for the huge pile of un-ironed clothes next to the vase, the flowers would look stunning. *I really ought to do something about the ironing*, she thinks, and promptly fetches a large black bin liner from the cupboard under the sink in the kitchen, stuffs the pile of clothes into it like one stuffs a turkey (pushing everything to the bottom to fill all the space), opens the cellar door and throws it down the stairs. The bag bursts, spewing a crumpled mass of material down the narrow stairwell and hurtling the individual garments across the cellar floor in the direction of the back door. Sabina watches until the last piece of clothing has landed and then slams the door shut with great satisfaction.

The hyacinths hadn't been on Jennifer's mind quite so much over the few days running up to Adrian's visit and she had thought she was finally getting over the pain and embarrassment associated with that disastrous asparagus evening.

When she received them, they were like two Spanish red onions sitting prettily in the soil: flaky and burgundy coloured. A day later, a shocking green stem began to shoot out of the fragile-looking bulbs, heading skyward with a sense of strength and purpose. Around the stem were slender leaves curling protectively around a bunch of buds. Like a group of grapes all huddling together, the blossom buds were facing inwards, their backs hunched and striped: a greenish-yellow smear on top of a bruise blue back The following day, the bunch of buds had started to lean away from the stem, their tiny pointed tips indicating the direction of their intended growth and giving them the appearance of beetles—backs turned, legs drawn in, waiting to be woken up and crawl to the top of the plant. Another day and the bottommost of the bunch had burst open revealing yellow middles like many peeled purple bananas. For two days they stared at Jennifer as she worked at her desk in her office—full frontal and unabashed. Their smell began to pervade the office and, anyone entering her office would immediately comment on it, demanding her almost constant attention because people were in and out her office constantly. To some it was like a 'flower shop'; to others 'outdoors', or 'woods,' or 'it smelled like the start of spring?' On less optimistic days, the hyacinth scent reminded her of 'damp,' 'rot,' and 'the smell coming from her biological waste bin when it hadn't been emptied for a week. On positive days, the scent was 'rose,' or 'earthy,' 'the first rays of sunshine,' and the 'smell of childhood dreams and adult hope.' When the hyacinth plants reached their full height and all the buds exploded open to let the purple tongues emerge from their banana centres, the stems top heavy with flower and already leaning towards the light coming from the office window, were threatening to make the whole pot topple over and off the desk. A blaze of purple splendour greeted every visitor and filled Jennifer's office (and occasionally her heart) with scintillating colour and vitalising perfume. It was when they were in this stage of blossoming that Jennifer had packed the pot in a carrier bag and taken it home. Ten people had been into her office within the space of an hour and every conversation had been dominated by the hyacinths—'glorious colour!' 'You should support the stem or it'll topple!' 'If it weren't for the AA-disaster…' 'By the way, have you heard from Rick?' She had had enough of this plant's impertinence. At home, she threw the plastic bag in a corner where it remained until the Friday evening Adrian was due to arrive. When she took them out of their prison, they had changed. The stem had grown long and lanky, no longer able to support the blossoms that had exploded like bulrushes and were beginning to drop off through lack of water and attention.

After Adrian's visit, she had stuck a couple of chopsticks into the soil next to the two stems in a last-minute attempt to give them some hold. They had slid into the soil with ease and she had carefully lifted the stems and placed them over their nice new crutches. An hour later, both stems had hit their heavy heads on the hard stone of her windowsill—thud, thud—as if demanding she rush immediately to the local garden centre down the road and get more effective support. She knew that if the stems didn't get a support soon, they would snap in half, finishing them off entirely; yet she just sat there, motionless, staring at the plants. Though she wouldn't say she was a destructive person, she didn't feel like rescuing the hyacinths. What was it they were telling her? Or was it in her mind? (or her heart?): *Don't keep on patching things up*, and *stop trying to mend things,* and *don't smile when what you really want to do is curl up and cry.*

Looking at them this evening, a week after Adrian had been to stay, noting that there are no blossoms left, just two bulbs with leaves and part of the stem still intact, she feels quite a bit of remorse. The one on the left has become limp and is hanging over the side of the pot where it keeled over after the crutch broke under it's weight. The one on the right looks like a giant spider on the end of a stick.

Am I a long-suffering, self-hating, self-pitying mess?

When the convulsions from hours of incessant sobbing subside, she wonders whether she should give the hyacinths some water after all—a peace offering. A small, barely audible voice inside her say a definite 'yes.' *If you keep the bulbs in a dark, cool place, you could replant them next spring and they will shoot up and blossom once more.* She remembers her Dad doing that with the tulips.

In this moment of great hope, she decides that she will neither take time off work to stay with Sabina in Luxembourg a week before her birthday, nor will she go to the 40th party celebration. The cork of a magnum bottle of champagne makes a dent in her perfectly plastered ceiling. *Cheers,* she calls out to her reflection in the kitchen window and drinks a glassful down with one great big gulp.

Detective's Work

As he tries to slide the notebook back in place between the chocolates and the jewellery box, it falls open at the first page. '*February 14th 2000*', he reads and his eyes continue down, taking in the entire passage. A deep stabbing sensation—one he has been having at regular intervals ever since he slept over at Jennifers—now not only jabs him in the ribs, but continues into his heart and back out the other side and he vows to contact the detective's office first thing in the morning.

The secretary puts his call through to the detective's car phone after Adrian explains that it is an emergency, a matter of life and death. The voice on the end of the phone is friendly and arranges a rendezvous with Adrian that afternoon.

The detective's office is drab—a lifeless office in one of the hyper modern constructions in the centre of town. The building squats fatly on the site where a town villa used to be. Looking at it from a distance, you get the impression that it marched resolutely in and plonked itself down where it pleased, crushing the old building into rubble. Now, the entire *Boulevard Royal*, which once boasted a collection of the most luxurious villas in the country, is lined with one outlandish-looking office building after the other. Most have been built by banks. Adrian remembers when the last villa in the Boulevard was bulldozed down; he had felt for the pile of stones and bricks lying in a forlorn heap on the ground, dreading being scooped up and dumped out of town somewhere. *What a shame it was that the old buildings couldn't be kept.* Luxembourg hadn't learned from its neighbours, which, in times of expansion had also knocked their historical buildings down. How empty of character the Boulevard was. Not even the fancy reflective facades, brightly coloured window frames, or innovative architectural designs could recreate the atmosphere or majesty that the central street used to possess.

Adrian knocks lightly on the detective's door.

"*Entrez!*" comes the curt reply.

Adrian pushes the door open slowly and enters.

It's a small office, darker than Adrian expected, seeing as the building itself is bright and modern-looking, almost entirely of glass. The office, too, is not Adrian's idea of the 21st century paperless office that he's used to. There are piles of documents everywhere: half a metre's worth on the windowsill, another on the desk, and various sizes ranging between ten centimetres and half a metre on the cupboards and floor. The bits of floor that can be seen look decidedly fluffy, mouldy green and could have done with a good wipe over. The driving rain outside does nothing to improve the light conditions in the room, nor do the milky smoke-infested windows. Adrian counts at least five cups of forgotten, cold coffee together with just as many half-smoked cigars and wrinkles his nose as the stale smell invades his nostrils. There is not a computer in sight.

Adrian is used to Luxembourg's tendency to be a bit behind the times, but this was ridiculous. The most modern piece of equipment he can see is the mobile phone and even that is far from the latest model. The man sitting behind the desk looks like a cross between Val Doonican and the character Cannon from the American detective series. Val Doonican's mother has obviously not knitted this sweater, he thinks; it is too tight around the middle and too long in the arms. The detective peers over his enormous pile of papers through half-rimmed spectacles and extends a woolly arm to greet Adrian.

"*Monsieur Waldsmere*?" he asks.

The baggy sleeve of the detective's Christmas sweater dangles down into a mug full of old coffee and paints a brown line across a letter he has been signing. He notices his malheur and promptly withdraws his hand before Adrian can shake it.

"*Excusez-moi*," he mumbles, wringing his soggy sleeve out into the cup and gulping it down. He then holds out his hand once more for Adrian to shake. Adrian is reluctant to do so; he can't help being disgusted.

He wishes he could back out there and then, but he can't—not now that he was already in the office, face-to-face with him; he feels terribly ill at ease and foolish already. He shakes the hand and withdraws it hastily to wipe it on the back of his trousers.

"*Monsieur Trouve à votre service.*"

If the man had said *'Inspecteur Clouseau'*, Adrian would have believed him. He didn't think that this sort of person existed in real life.

Adrian takes the rose out of his briefcase, lies it on the table in front of him and begins to tell the story. He finds it difficult to talk about it at first, but soon gets going and is overwhelmed by certain sensations he starts to feel; like tiny electric shocks jabbing into his heart and zooming up and down his body.

The detective listens.

"This was the emergency?"

"Y-yes."

"What do you want me to do?"

"Find out where she got the roses from!" *Stupid man! Wasn't it obvious. What are detectives for anyway?*

"And what then?"

Arrest the bugger, tell him to piss off. I don't know—you're the detective.

"Monsieur Waldsmere?"

"Yes?"

"What exactly is your motivation for coming here with this 'emergency'?"

"Motivation?"

"Divorce, politics, money…shall I go on?"

"Um, I just want to know…" *whether she still loves me* "…so that I have something."

"Something?"

"Evidence."

"And what will you do with the evidence?"

What will I do with it? Isn't that your job?

"I don't know! Confront her with it."

"You mean give an ultimatum—him or you!"

"I s-suppose so."

"To be honest, Monsieur, I have a pile of very pressing jobs at present," arms swaying full-circle around him at the numerous piles of documents; "If you have time, which you do seem to have," he adds, looking at his wrist watch, "why not talk to your wife first."

"N-no."

"Why not?"

Why not? How would he like it if his wife was having an affair? The humiliation.

"I…"

"Well?"

"I can't just ask her directly."

"Why not?"

"I…"

"Can I suggest something?"

At last.

"Yes! That's what I'm paying you for!"

"Tell her how much you care. Acknowledge her."

"What?"

"Acknowledgement. Appreciation. Respect. That's all it often takes—that's my experience. Half the cases are solved that way. Works for both wives who think their husbands are being unfaithful and for husbands who think their wives are being unfaithful…"

That's all I need. A bloody moral teacher!

"…Tell her you love and care for her more than anything in the world and she'll probably drop the new guy like a hotcake."

"Huh? Why should I when she's the one having the affair?"

"Because she won't be expecting it!"

"And how does that help?"

"Most women take a lover to get what they don't get from their partner. If you can give her what she needs, she doesn't need the lover. Simple as that."

Adrian is feeling more and more irritated by this so-called detective. When is he finally going to make a serious proposal, draw up a contract and let him walk out of the office with confidence that the matter is in good, professional hands?

"Hmmm."

"Look. Why not speak to your wife? Tell her you're worried about the relationship. She might tell you everything you want to know."

Adrian is silent—pretending to be in deep thought—and eventually explains that he doesn't have the time, the patience or desire to do work which he thinks is a detective's work. He would rather it be done by a professional, discretely, and above all, quickly. He has to know before the birthday celebration on March 25th and that is only six weeks away. The detective assures him that this kind of work will take less than a week, advises him to start tomorrow and wishes him good luck.

Adrian leaves the office like an unwanted puppy leaves a family. His eyes are burning and heavy. He no longer feels like going back to the office.

He drives into a side road nearby and parks the car. A man approaches and taps on the car window. Adrian scowls at him, *God, not a lost tourist!* he thinks and reluctantly opens the window.

"*Monsieur, Vous parlez anglais*?"

Adrian nods and rolls his eyes.

Here we go—another complicated destination to explain.

But the man does not ask for directions; he holds out a ticket and says, "You can have my parking ticket if you like. There's still an hour left on it."

Adrian is feeling so hateful towards this rude intruder that he shouts "No thank you" and presses his automatic window winder. The stranger snatches his hand out at the last minute and scuttles back to his vehicle where his family is waiting for him.

"You'll never guess what happened," he pants.

"What?" his family choruses.

"Well, I just offered our ticket to that Luxembourger over there and he point-blank rejected it—as if I had insulted him. Funny lot these Luxembourgers are. I'm glad we're leaving. Get back to good old Britain. Not even the Queen would refuse a parking ticket there!"

Adrian buys a ticket for 60 minutes and sets off towards the main square. He gets himself a chicken-burger and sits down on a bench. Some pigeons gather around his feet pecking up the remains of someone else's snack on the ground. They coo loudly as they go about their feeding time and Adrian is annoyed further. He wants to concentrate, think, and the pigeons have the audacity to interrupt him. 'Town rats with wings,' he shouts at them, but they merely fly once around the square to return to the squashed sandwich next to his feet. Adrian refuses to be defeated and stays on the bench, trying to ignore the pests until the cold air penetrates his woollen suit jacket, his shirt, his underwear, his skin, his muscles and pours into his bones, making him shiver uncontrollably. He thinks about Sabina; their first meeting at the student's union, her announcement of the pregnancy. He remembers how proud he was walking around the campus with his arm around her; he remembers telling her he loved her for the first time and their passionate lovemaking in Paris. He remembers laughing with her, looking excitedly for houses in Luxembourg and planning their new life together. And then he stops. All his memories are from eighteen years ago. He can't remember much about Sabina after that. What came after that? His affairs. He thought about his affairs. Sabina only knew about one, but there had, in fact, been more. He confessed that first one to her because she had made him and, even though he had not wanted to tell her about it, he had actually felt relieved afterwards. It had been a weight off his mind that he no longer had to think up elaborate excuses. She knew and that made his unfaithful life more accessible, interesting and frequent. She hardly protested; she just became quieter. He told her that he would not leave her for another woman and she had nodded and not brought up the subject again. Adrian had not brought it up either. He had a free ticket to have a bit on the side and he was not going to question her reaction. That went on for many years. He had three different affairs. At the beginning they gave his life new meaning and made him feel young again. But as they went on and Sabina didn't protest, they became as banal as his marriage. He then gave them up in favour of sports.

By the time he's finished reflecting about Sabina and how to catch her lover, the cathedral bells are calling for six o'clock mass. He remembers his office and quickly taps the number on his mobile. The secretary is no longer there. The answering machine beeps loudly into his ear and he hangs up.

Adrian sets off, drives about 200 metres down the road and then turns off into a wooded lane, parks the car behind some bushes to conceal it from the road and waits. It's half an hour before he sees his wife's car coming up the road. He starts his, waits until she is out of sight again, and sets off after her. It's not easy keeping out of sight and still seeing where she is going. He knows that if she catches one glimpse of him in her rear-view mirror, she will immediately recognise him and his plan will be ruined.

Sabina's car leads him over the Red Bridge, into town and along the Pétrusse valley road. She parks in a side road, gets out of the car and then disappears.

He's sweating, his heart is pounding and the skin on his cheeks feels tight and hot as he gets out of his car and sneaks towards hers. He thinks she must have run behind the hedge lining the pavement and walks along it, looking for an entrance. He reaches an iron gate and hesitates. His mind wills him to go on and his hands obey, pushing the gate open, slowly at first, and then with a quick motion because he thinks it might creak loudly and draw unwanted attention. He starts down the path, uneasy about the fact that he can't see where it ends and unsure if this is even where his wife has gone. As he gets half way, he notices that he is walking towards the Pétrusse valley and feels inexplicably odd about it. One slip, and you could fall into it. He has never been scared of heights or edges, unlike his wife, but in that brief, unguarded moment, his heart flutters and his knees wobble.

He hurries towards the red front door and stops to read the plaque:

Residence Avoir

There's no clue in the name and there are no windows low enough for him to see into the villa, so he places his ear to the door and tries to hear something through it. When he hears footsteps, he jumps away and darts behind a bush.

The door opens and a man with dark hair steps out onto the path, pulls the door shut and walks nonchalantly to the gate. Adrian waits.

It's 11:30 when the man returns with his arms loaded with rolls of what look like red velvet wallpaper wrapped in plastic. He balances the rolls on one arm, reaches into his coat pocket with the other, unlocks the door and disappears behind it.

That's him! Just the kind of ponce to draw a heart with lipstick.

Adrian is fed up, annoyed, not only with Sabina, but also with the detective whose work he is forced to do.

"I think I may have just seen your husband," Gerard states and comes over to sit on the arm of Sabina's chair as Ana often does.

Sabina's not surprised. She thought she had caught sight of him this morning as she set off.

"He thinks I'm having an affair," she says and can't suppress a giggle. "I sent myself some roses when he was away in London and then phoned him to thank him for them. Now he obviously wants to find out who they are from. I was going to tell him when he came back, but got a bit carried away, enjoying being wicked. I feel like getting him back for all the pain he's caused me and this idea just happened along quite unexpectedly."

Both are smiling, looking very pleased with themselves.

"Do you want him to find you?"

"No."

"Okay." Ana looks at Gerard, Gerard looks at Ana. Both nod in unison and announce, as if they have practised this many times before.

"What you need is the secret passageway!"

Ana and Gerard usher her down some stairs and into the cellar. Ana pushes a firedoor open and points at the passageway. Sabina knows that it is the only way but is hesitant to take it. She hates being unkind to Adrian. He doesn't deserve the same suffering that she's been through; no-one does. She feels a sudden fear—that she is going the wrong way about it. Was this not tit for tat? Ana puts her great hands on Sabina's shoulders and presses down reassuringly.

"You have to be cruel to be kind," she says.

"If only my mother could have met you," Sabina laments and takes her coat, scarf and gloves from Gerard. Ana speaks again:

"If you wish to continue your life together with him, you must help him to let go of you and who you have been for him throughout the marriage. You have changed, Sabina. There is no way back into the old life now; being and doing for him, for others."

Ana releases the pressure from Sabina's shoulders and energy pours into her as though it has been injected it into her through Ana's hands. The weight she felt she was carrying becomes immediately lighter and her legs propel her forwards and through the doorway with ease.

The first twenty metres are lit with small spotlights. Ana switched them on from a switch in her cellar. 'They function on a timer,' she had explained, 'and will go off in about ten minutes at which point you will have to rely on the torch I have given you.'

Click. The lights go out. Sabina is thrown into complete darkness and her heart plops into her belly as if splashing into a well. The switch on the torch is stiff with newness and she rips a fingernail whilst pushing it up.

The beam from the torch lights the tunnel splendidly; she can now see at least twenty metres ahead. *This must be the straight bit Ana told me about*, she thinks and starts towards the end of the light. The sandstone rock shines a warm orange and she reflects about what she knows about the tunnel. It connects to many more tunnels called 'Casemates' that were hewn by hundreds of men over centuries. A network of about twenty kilometres of passageways was the result of years of hand chiselling underneath the city of Luxembourg. It made the city into an unconquerable force; troops could be manoeuvred swiftly without the enemy suspecting a thing.

There are many tunnels branching off from the main one and Sabina has to concentrate hard not to mistakenly go down one. Ana gave her instructions to follow the main tunnel until she gets to a junction where three tunnels come together. At that point, she was to head down the one on her right. About ten metres down, she was to shine the torch upwards to find a white arrow on the ceiling. This arrow would help her find a trap door on the floor nearby. She was to find the door, pull it open using the large metal ring and climb down the metal ladder to another tunnel. This lower tunnel would lead her through the Pétrusse valley, underneath the man-made riverbed and up to the other side. 'The tunnel at the other side of the valley which leads onto the *Place de la Constitution* is open to the public, but not until after Easter,' Ana had explained. 'Here are two keys: one for the door leading out from the tunnels to the town square in the *Ville Haute;* the other for this cellar. You can enter and exit the villa via the secret passageway whenever you suspect you are being followed.'

Sabina walks slowly, surprised by her calmness. She feels protected by the tunnels. Alone; yet without fear. She knows now that she has made the right decision to follow Ana's guidance.

Adrian waits.

By 14:00 she still hasn't returned to her car and there has been no other movement in or outside the house. He feels cold, nauseous and angry. He has no choice but to leave. The day has been wasted—and all because the stupid detective refused to do his job!

Adrian gets back into his car and accelerates down the road and across the Red Bridge to the Church Hill plateau to get back to work in time for a meeting at 3 p.m.

BOOK THREE

Writing it Down...

When Sabina gets home, she sits down and writes:

> 'If only everybody in Luxembourg, no, in the world, knew about the love I have found. What a place this would be. We could teach our children early on in life not to become dependent on a source of love from outside—from other people, places, objects—a love that they can never regulate and never be satisfied with, but to depend on the love they have within themselves. This is a teaching I have always expected to come from religion and I am sure this is one of the intentions of it; yet, there have been no teachers in my life who have been able to reach me. The words never meant that to me. All 'religious' people I have had contact with have not convinced me of this kind of love because they have always used the word God and I couldn't believe in God. A belief in God starts with a belief in yourself. I am beginning to realise that now. You have to acknowledge yourself, listen to your inner thoughts, nurture them and then you can achieve a love that can lead you to God and guide you through life.'

Sabina runs into the kitchen and hastily makes a cup of tea before speeding back to her desk with it to continue writing.

> 'My mother's life was tragic and I have great sympathy for her. Like me, she let life get on top of her. She married a man who she thought she loved, but really he was a substitute for the kind of father she wished she had had. It was a mistake, and she recognised that on the night of her wedding. If she hadn't become pregnant that night, she might have had the courage to admit her mistake and re-marry. But she was fertile (like me) and nine months after con-

summating the marriage, had Jennifer, my older sister. The baby gave her a great sense of achievement and filled her with love. Even so, she felt abandoned by her family and husband, who did not offer a helping hand. She refused to admit to her parents that she could not cope with the baby and so did not ask for their help. Her father would have made her feel inadequate and she did not want to feel any more inadequate than she was already feeling. So she kept silent. She got on with it and started to despise my father for his neglect. He was so busy working that she said that we daughters would have probably screamed and run away as if from a stranger if he had come home to give us a good night kiss. He was away to work before breakfast and returned after we were tucked up in bed. We only ever saw him briefly at weekends.

Her own mother had been the same and her mother's mother as well probably. Over generations, this type of behaviour had turned into something like a genetic disorder. Her father was an abusive, controlling man. I think his way of treating her stemmed from bitterness, from un-lived desires. He recognised a vitality in her that had long died in himself. He could not express his feelings in any other way than to try to oppress her—keep her pinned down so that he, at least, felt some sort of power. He had to do that or he would not have survived. No one was allowed to voice an opinion in her household that went against his own. If she hadn't met my father and left her parents to live with him at the other end of the country, she would have wilted and died much earlier than she actually did. The problem when she met my father was that she had been so used to keeping her feelings and opinions to herself that she continued to do so throughout her marriage, making herself miserable in her silent suffering world. My father was not a perceptive man. Things had to be spelled out for him to acknowledge them. She was unhappy and he didn't realise it. My mother thought he did realise it and chose to ignore it. She thought that he was not in love with her, but with the Sabina he named me after—the one he proposed to and who turned him down. She didn't want to complain: that would be showing weakness. She wanted to prove her strength and show how she could suffer like a martyr for him. She carried on day to day, toiling away, looking after his children, the house, and the garden. She was superwoman. But every day she felt regret, remorse, and bitterness that he wasn't doing anything about her situation. She wanted him to read her thoughts and come to her rescue. She didn't dare call him home from work early to help her, or to take the children off her hands for an afternoon. She never told him that she didn't enjoy sex with him or that she was having affairs with the neighbours. She never told him how she struggled to make ends meet or how she hated having to sew the children's clothes and knit their sweaters. She just acted on, pretending everything was okay, eking out her life. Her own father had conditioned her so well that it was near to impossible for her to kick the habit. She was addicted to wallowing in her own self-pity and didn't want to get up and fight. It would have been too much of an effort for her to communicate all her feelings, opinions, regrets. She was mute; my father dumb and there was nothing to break the communication stalemate. But the feelings, the remorse, the bitterness didn't go away. She filled up with it until she was so full that she could find no other solution than to fling herself off the bridge.'

Sabina pauses for a moment to gather her thoughts before continuing. None of it was her mother's fault. How was her mother supposed to have made Sabina into a strong person? That had not been her task. What her mother had given her could not be taken away and was worth more than words could express: her fairytale childhood.

She was not proud of how she had acted over the years—of her own self-pitying, her give-up attitude. She was shocked that she could have allowed herself to go so far and cross with herself for blaming it all on the hormones, on her husband and on her mother…

She continues:

> 'As a child I grew up believing that girls were made of sugar and spice and boys of slugs and snails. I could easily believe it because I felt that I was good. I was a good little girl. I hated being bad. I learned to not speak loudly, not to rough and tumble, not to swear or fight. Along the way I also learned to feel guilty for the wrongdoings of others and to keep all my feelings locked up. No-one taught me these things. I just picked them up at home, at school, at the shops, sports clubs. You name it, there was plenty of material hanging around waiting for me to pick up and add to my collection until I did not act how my emotions wanted me to act, but how I thought a girl should.
>
> As a student, equality reigned. I didn't wear a bra (hence the sagging breasts now). I threw away all my make-up and let my legs grow hairy. Men were to love me in the raw, if at all. Feminine was out, girlie was a definite no no and I drifted from one fad to the next without really knowing with whom and with what image to identify myself. I felt I had to find the right niche for me—somewhere to belong. All along, there was a woman inside me trying to get out and yet I was suppressing her. I wanted to belong to the modern girls, the ones that were as good at men's things as men were and who liked doing them. So, I learned how to perform an oil change, pretended I was good at orienteering, signed up for Judo and volleyball. I began a life of activities that I did not even like because I did not want to admit that I was really a woman. I would have loved to have danced, continued a ballet career that began at the age of four and ended abruptly at eighteen. Pretending to like the things that you do not really like and to be a person that you are not became quite a habit and was one of the reasons for my discontent. I was ashamed of being a woman because all the things I liked were sneered at for being typical female, or girlie, or old-fashioned or cliché. I systematically denied myself all typical female traits in favour of the ones I thought men would want me to

have as a modern woman and in that way lost respect for myself and most women.

When I had my first child, I was overwhelmed by the power of the female hormone and retreated into its arms. I realised that I was a good mother and used that as the basis for my existence—the meaning of my life. I hid behind my 'Mummy' title like a scared rabbit and used it as an excuse for my insufficiencies and inadequacies in other areas. And there I hid and hid and hid for almost seventeen years. Hiding, pretending, acting. I did my job, I gave my all and it was a professional, qualified job I did, even if it was not recognised as such at the time (either from me, my children, or my husband). I did not expect it because I did not think I had earned it. I knew I was copping out of life.'

Continuation

The jasmine-scented candles cast crystal light into her beer glass, which sits half-filled in front of her. Outside, she hears the steady drip drop of spring rain on the grass. She feels as if she's out there—in the drenched garden—rather than in the dry and promising atmosphere inside.

Questions. Stop the questions, her mind screams. *State the truth and things will become clear. Words and wisdoms; my mind is full of them. Yet I still quest for that which is proving so difficult to find: my voice. My real, accepted, truthful voice.*

It's late. She's drunk four bottles of beer. Adrian is away on business and she has spent the evening writing, reading, and Internet surfing. She feels she can't sleep until she's achieved something great; yet she doesn't think she would recognise greatness even if it had an enormous neon sign attached to it.

She is getting so sick of lamenting that it gives her hope that she may be driving it away. Write, write, write and eventually it will come out, this slimy monster of self-destruction, self-hate and pity.

She reads a story on the Internet about a woman of thirty who has only a few months to live. She is dying of a rare cancer and worries about telling her children when the time comes. They are four and seven. She wonders whether to write a letter, make a video and put together an album documenting her life. Each time she thinks about it, she stops herself. She worries about those she is leaving behind. How can children bear to see a video of their Mummy when they can't cuddle and kiss her? How will they be able to understand that she has gone and will never be able to hold them again?

The Internet story touches Sabina and she vows to write the story: theirs and her own. It will be her most valuable gift. In this way, greatness could be achieved. Not through literary excellence, the most polished prose or researched article, but through the basic, honest wish to pass on valid and life-giving stories.

The smell of jasmine pervades the air in her dry, ordered indoors. It's an artificial smell from the candle and doesn't compare with the smell of the blossoming jasmine tree in the drenched garden.

Sabina takes her new fountain pen out of its black leather box and writes:

Letters to My Children

> I was sitting in the living room when I heard a commotion coming from outside. It sounded like a flock of irate birds, crows or similar. I listened a little longer and then knew what the sound was. I ran outside and looked up. Sure enough, there they were, high up in the sky and flying in formation; the wild geese were returning home to have their young.
>
> I immediately felt a sense of great joy and well-being as I watched the geese high above my head and, in that moment, I was with them, soaring across the sky; free, alive and heading into spring.
>
> How can you feel like that always? I asked myself. Why can't there be joy in your heart on dull days when things go wrong and you're feeling sad. After I said this to myself, another voice in me answered. 'You can,' it said, 'Every single one of us has the capacity to feel joy so deeply and strongly that it has the power to carry you up high into the sky to fly with the wild geese.' This can't be achieved by loving another person or having a beautiful house or modern computer technology. It can't be achieved by pleasing or helping others, eating a healthy diet or taking vitamin tablets. It can't be achieved by eating chocolate, treating yourself to lovely clothes or a trip abroad.
>
> These things may please you, give you a brief taste of what it could be like to be happy. But that is all. You get a glimpse and then what? You are left feeling emptier than ever when they are taken away from you again.
>
> No, the way to experience great joy and happiness is by knowing, being and loving who you are.
>
> You achieve this and then you can jump, fly, soar and dance higher than you ever imagined possible.
>
> So, how do you know who you are? You don't at first. This is what life is all about; it is a journey of discovery. Life is a mystery and we are all here to participate in it. There is no right or wrong way for you to go; there is simply your way. You listen, you watch, you experience and then, you know.
>
> Of course, a lot of who we are can be influenced by our parents and our parents' parents, and our parents', parents' parents. This has to be looked at in order to become your true self. Some call it unlearning. I call it letting go of the past to enter life in the present.

If you want to live life in the present as who you really are, you have to live now; you can't live yesterday, or tomorrow. Yesterday holds the past and tomorrow the future—the past can haunt you and the future can make you fear what is to come. The only safe place is the present time; it is now.

You may not understand what I mean. That doesn't matter. One day you may and then this letter may be helpful. If you do, remember this. If it helps you, it is because you let it. If it doesn't, it's because you let it. The choice is always yours. You are always responsible for your life.

I have spent many painful years unravelling who I am, starting from my childhood. In the following pages, I will tell you what I found out. I hope that this information will spare you having to find out who your mother was before your journey can begin like I had to do before mine could.

Sabina has the entire evening to write. In-between the letter, she suddenly has inspiration to write something else and turns to a blank page in her book:

Why I Write—by Sabina Waldsmere

I write because it takes me
to a place I didn't know existed;
my own unique story within
of a thirsty traveller
trudging on and on
in search of a well
through tunnels
of sandstone
to arrive
expectedly
a guest
anticipated
to drink the gift
of writing
to leave
expectedly
to continue
making tracks
to the next well

through more tunnels
of sandstone
to arrive
expectedly
to continue

Beginnings:

I arrived three weeks overdue; shot out in an hour and landed on my parent's double bed whilst my father was on the phone to the midwife. Home births were encouraged in those days—especially for the second or subsequent births. I was number 2. My mother, shocked by the speed of the birth, threw a blanket over me and, before passing out, shouted down to my father to tell the midwife that it was another girl.

She had desperately wanted a son and she couldn't hide her disappointment when I arrived. The midwife came shortly afterwards to cut the umbilical cord and offer my mother a cup of tea. My mother quietly remarked that a bottle of brandy would be more appropriate and then fell into an exhausted sleep.

'There's a baby in the basket,' my sister Jennifer shouted excitedly through the house next morning. My grandmother, who was staying in the house to help my mother out during the last weeks of pregnancy, tried to calm Jennifer by explaining that the midwife would be coming to put the baby in the basket today (it was going to be an induced birth), and that she would have to be patient for a little while longer. My grandmother was oblivious to the flash birth that happened during the night.

So, my birth was sudden; with no help from anyone and it even happened without waking the other sleeping people in the house. That birth says a lot about the kind of person I was destined to become: someone who does things alone and unaided by anyone or anything.

I was born with so much hair that my mother had to give me a haircut when I was two days old so that she could tie the bib around my neck when she fed me. My nails were a few millimetres too long as well and had to be cut so that I didn't scratch my eyes out. I was definitely ready when I gushed out of her womb. Perhaps a little over-cooked!

My grandmother thought I was an odd-looking thing and didn't tell any of her friends about her second granddaughter until I was about a year old and no longer looked quite so strange. Maybe she wondered, as I did myself, whether I had the same father as my older sister. Thank God for my father's distinctive nose which I inherited or I may have continued to wonder all my life!

Some of the first memories I have of me as a child are around the age of four. Everything before that has come from stories my Mum has told, or from old photographs.

My mother used to call me Bee, which I find ironic now that I am trying to 'be' who I am rather that who she and other people thought I was. My hair was kept short because it was so thick and unmanageable when allowed to grow. Even when I was wearing a flowery summer dress, people used to think I was a boy; it wasn't customary for little girls to have such short hair in the sixties.

I loved dancing and passed all the ballet grades with honours. I wasn't a girlie kind of girl, though. I hated dolls and mainly played with building bricks or outside on the swing or in the bushes around our house.

Jennifer and I used to go off on adventures through the bushes, pretending we were kids from a lost Amazon tribe, gallivanting through as much dirt as possible to look authentic. Our mother was probably not quite as pleased as we were with the results, but I don't remember her ever telling us off for having soiled our clothes.

My mother made most of my dresses and knitted all the cardigans, pullovers and socks. When she was sewing, she wore glasses that were shaped like cats eyes, with pointy ends. My sister and I called them her 'cross glasses'. Whenever she had them on, she was in a bad mood—especially if we disturbed her.

I used to wish for a brother more than anything in the world, until I was about ten and was chased home nearly every day by a gang of boys. I began to hate and fear little boys and so you can imagine my initial apprehension when my first-born was a boy. Don't worry, Dominic, I quickly learned that my picture of boys had been terribly distorted by those horrid specimens from childhood and soon experienced how wonderful male children can be.

At ten I was proud of my house, my Mum, and my best friend Samantha who lived up the road in a huge property that was later transformed into an old-people's home. Samantha and I spent hours playing hide and seek in her huge house. In one of the disused rooms stood a giant antique wardrobe and I used to imagine I could step into the wardrobe and out into a fantasy world. I know now that the fantasy world is my inner world of dreams where I can be who I am.

I used to ride to and from Samantha's house on a blue and silver bike. Her house was at the end of a row of other large properties that had been built at the turn of the century out of sandstone from the Yorkshire countryside. They were all set back from the road with long tree-lined drives. As I hadn't passed my cycling proficiency test, my mother advised me to ride on the pavement. One day, when I was riding along, past the large properties, a car zoomed up the drive and was suddenly right in front of my speeding bicycle. My reaction was to jump for my life, so I did and fell hard on the gravel pavement. My bike skidded on its side and slid right under the car. All I remember is looking helplessly at my mangled bicycle and then being frightened by the faces staring at me through the car windows. An irate woman came out and reprimanded me for giving her and her baby a deathly fright. The woman's husband marched out, pulled my broken bike out from under his car, flung it on the floor in front of me, and drove away with his family. I was left staring forlornly at my bent handlebars and pedals jammed into the frame. My elbows were bleeding and my knees had deep gashes, speckled with pieces of grit from the pavement. A van stopped beside me, and its owner came over. 'I saw what happened,' he said. 'Come on, I'll give you a lift home.' I said, 'No thank you. I don't accept lifts from strangers,' and limped all the way back, dragging the remnants of my bike behind me. A builder working on our house at the time straightened the bike with sheer muscle power. He became my friend but I hardly ever used the bike again. After a while, the lovely silver paint flaked off the handlebars to reveal a rusty underneath. I tried various kinds of silver polish from my mother's selection of detergents from the cupboard below the sink in the utility room, but I never managed to shine it up again.

My family was not very well off, Samantha's was. I often found two-penny pieces around her house when playing there. They were lying everywhere; under the cupboards, in drawers, in the unused rooms, attic and downstairs loo. I would show them to her and she would shrug and say 'keep them.' I was thrilled to bits. The other great thing about being at her house was that you were allowed to help yourself to as many chocolate biscuits, fizzy pop and crisps as you liked. My mother never bought things like that; she said they were too expensive.

I think I always sensed we had little money without actually knowing it; my mother never told my sister or me that she and Dad were struggling to feed and clothe us. I had a strong intuition right from the start I think but spent most of my life not listening to it. Now I have learned to trust it as a kind of guide. Without it I could easily get lost!

I think my parents were ashamed and embarrassed to talk about our financial situation because they didn't want us to suffer the stigma of it. They'd rather struggle to pay for a house they couldn't really afford than have us grow up thinking we were poor. I accepted the lie despite sensing the truth because I believed what my parent's said like every obedient child would do. The price for that obedience, however, has been a few decades of searching for the real truth.

My parents were constantly living lies, especially my mother. This is not a reproach. I don't think it was intentional (or conscious). It has to do with who we really are and who we think we are, or should be. One is the true self, and is what I think can lead to happiness. The other is what others and society at large thinks of us and is what can lead down the path of sadness, despair, and suicide.

When I was in junior school, I sat next to Samantha in the classroom and cheated at spelling tests. At the end of term there was always a small examination on all the spellings learned so far and the prize was a triangular-shaped golden pencil. I had written all the spellings in my neatest writing on a piece of paper and trapped it under our legs between our chairs; her left thigh pressing down on the left side of the paper and my right thigh pressing down on the right side of it. We won the spelling competition and a golden pencil each. We got away with it—and a lifetime of mis-spelled words.

In another year at the same school, I was on 'Top Table' with Samantha and we continued to cheat. I let her copy my answers every time she didn't know them herself until the day I was smacked three times across my bare legs. It was a spinster teacher who did it and then, after being reprimanded by the head for the physical abuse of pupils, sent naughty children out of the class to eat grass on the playing fields until they learned to behave properly! My cheating went underground after that—I didn't get caught and I didn't even admit to myself that I was doing it. I would come into the classroom early to copy the answers down from the teacher's answer book so that I could put them in place when needed in lesson time.

I became very good at deception. I never counted the amount of detentions I had in first year secondary, but it must have amounted to over fifty; that's several a week! I explained my late arrival at home by saying I had joined the chess club, the Rounders team, gymnastics club and any other activity that met after school hours. My parents believed me and probably felt proud to have such an active and motivated daughter. Active and motivated I certainly was, but not necessarily in the things they would have approved of. I got found out of course; the teachers told them every single detail of my bad behaviour at parent's evening. My mother sighed deeply and heavily before finding enough breath to speak to me: 'At your school today, the teachers told me about a girl I didn't recognise. I kept protesting, telling them that they must have the wrong notes. My little Bee was not like that; they must be making a mistake. Finally, after I had been to every single one of your teachers and heard tales of behaviour I could have never associated with you, I had to start believing it. It was so embarrassing. I am so disappointed and shocked that I don't know what to say to you.' She left the room then and we never spoke about it again. I felt a void and dropped into it, vowing to never, ever be a disappointment or embarrassment again. I blamed my bad behaviour at school on the classmates and my mother helped me move to a different class where they couldn't have that effect on me any longer. I spent the rest of my school-years disassociating from my previous friends, including Samantha, and going against my free-spirited nature to squeeze myself into a tight glove of conformity with a capital C. Occasionally, the other self, the Bee, would get out of the glove and buzz wildly around for a while. It left me feeling guilty and more determined to tighten the locks on that part of me, crushing it even more.

I led a secretive puberty—hiding my experiences and questions away; I would be evasive and non-committal in my comment or simply say nothing at all. I avoided conflict at all costs which meant that I had to keep up with the art of lying; at least this was a challenge in my life—a small pay-off against the dullness of living in a tight glove.

I never seemed to have much money of my own, which could be a reflection of my parents' shortage of it, or that I squandered it on sweets and crisps at the corner shop in the village. The school tuck shop also sold me five packets of cheese quavers for ten pence which I bought and consumed at break time.

My name caused people to make fun of me. They called me Ribena, or currant and many other stupid things they associated with my name. Later, they called me Ani which I put up with until I went to university. I have often wondered why people find it necessary to re-christen you with different names. It's as if they find it difficult to accept you as you are.

The teachers at school also had nicknames. There was 'Mona-Lisa', the longhaired English teacher, 'Erco', the history teacher who looked and acted like one of the monkeys from 'Planet of the Apes' and there was 'Spitfire', the French teacher who found it hard to speak French without spitting. One time, he bent forwards to pick up a piece of chalk and all his pens fell with a loud clattering noise out of his suit pocket onto his desk. In an attempt to save face after this clumsy act, he spat out *'une cascade de stylos'* and soaked the entire front row of pupils. The class soon took revenge. There is a saying in the north of England which is a code for telling someone that their front trouser zipper is open; it's 'you've got egg on your chin.' Spitfire came into the classroom with some-such problem and we shouted to him: 'Sir, you've got egg on your chin!' Spitfire thanked us kindly, pulled an enormous hanky out of his pocket, covered it in spit and rubbed his chin with great vigour. No-one could control themselves in that moment. The entire class guffawed and shrieked with delight. Spitfire got angry and sent the loudest out to explain to the headmaster why they had to laugh so much over such nonsense as egg on someone's chin. Two of them jumped at the chance and came back triumphant, headmaster in tow. The headmaster whispered in the teacher's ear and the two of them stepped out of the classroom for a moment. When he returned, he was zipped up and purple-faced.

I hated reading. Somehow I got away with not reading a book until I went to university. Even for 'O' level English, I didn't read the set book, *Great Expectations* by Charles Dickens. I read some literary criticisms about it, went to see the film, listened closely to the 'important' passages the teacher read out and passed the exam with an A. The first book I read cover-to-cover was the *World According to Garp.*

Sabina puts her pen down and closes her notebook and, instead of placing it in her bedside drawer, decides to take it up into the loft and hide it in her mother's silver chest. She knows that Adrian has been in her drawer and does not want to give the game away by letting him read her writing. She takes herself to bed and falls into a satisfying sleep.

Dream Colours

Sabina gets out her diary and writes:

'I am wild with rage. He blinds me and keeps me raging! He treats me like a two-year old and never forgives. Never. I hate it when he makes me feel this way. "Shame on you," he says. "Shame on you for leaving the Internet running for so long unattended. It won't do, Sabina. Grow up, Sabina."

I felt like shouting, protesting that I am responsible enough to suffer the consequences of my mistakes. I don't need him to reprimand me. I don't want your discipline. I refuse to listen to your preaching and I won't accept your authority, superiority and dictator tone. I would learn from my mistakes if you let me. I would set a timer so that the connection to the Internet automatically cuts off after a few minutes inactivity. You don't let me. You have damned me. You despise and ridicule me because you won't admit that you don't love me.

I love you but don't want to live under those conditions. I would rather muddle through on my own, take the responsibility on single-handed. I can't handle your attitude, your disciplinary blows. You treat me as if I were your teenage daughter who has to be trained in the way to live.

I want to be autonomous and I have the right to strive for it, mistakes and all. I know it's wrong to connect to the Internet when I haven't actually got the time. Let me make that mistake. Give me my pride and my honour. Forgive me, don't damn me!

You don't want to. You want me to beg and walk at your heel. I won't. I'll romp through the woods and muddy our living-room carpet until you respect me for being human and a woman. Until you step off your pedestal and call yourself by the same name as we all have: a weak human.

> You are driving me away. I love you, because you are not perfect. Neither am I, neither are our children.
>
> Through your eyes, I am crumbling and am the catastrophe you are desperate to see in someone else; the imperfection you can't see in yourself. I am the weak female you distrust and despise.'

As she is about to leave the house, she catches a glimpse of next door's Golden Retriever taking toilet position on her front lawn. Without hesitating for a minute, she runs to the neighbours and rings the bell. When the lady opens the door, Sabina politely but forcefully tells her to go and pick the dog's shit up from her garden at once. The lady looks at her somewhat surprised and does as she's told.

An hour later, Sabina is sitting on a cold metal chair on platform 3AB waiting for the Luxembourg to Brussels Intercity via Namur. A Tannoy announces in French, German and Luxembourgish that the train will be ten to fifteen minutes late and so she has time to write:

How perfect! Everything has it's time and place.

There's a spring in her step; it's her spirit rejoicing. After Adrian's outbreak at breakfast because she left the Internet running all night, and her consequent writing session (her mirror-soliloquy days are coming to an end!), things have become much clearer to her than before. Adrian reluctantly brought her to the station, said goodbye through gritted teeth, and seethed as she skipped away and out of sight. She is now aglow about taking herself on this trip to the capital city of Belgium to fetch the material for her dress. Gerard and Ana were too busy, and Sabina was happy to oblige.

She writes in her notebook that she is on a voyage of discovery—to find her true colours and is pleased with the connection between the colours of the materials for her dress and her emerging persona.

When Adrian asked at breakfast what she was going to do there, she simply replied that she would see where the trip takes her and continued to dig the soft orange centre out of her egg with a piece of toast.

The terracotta-coloured chair in the Intercity train compartment to Brussels-Midi station feels like a feathered cushion to her backside after the hard one on the platform and she sinks gratefully into it. The journey will last three hours. She should be in the middle of Brussels at Midday; carried straight and true through the hilly Ardennes to the heart of European Unification, her marriage and her self.

A week ago, she unpacked the slides and projector from their box where they have remained unwanted for years, and laid tray after tray onto the projector arm.

Adrian came over to her after a while and the projector arm gently led them down many dusty paths covering almost two decades of togetherness. Some of the dust on those paths was dull; some multi-coloured; and some golden. Some of the gold dust landed on them that evening—and afterwards in bed.

The day is cloudless; yet hazy. The horizon has the colour of a glass where milk once was: a white smudge has been left for the washer up to clear up. If the sunrays reach far enough to wipe the milk remains off the new morning sky, the afternoon will be clear. Sabina wonders what the Ardennes will have to say about it. They may send down a few clouds for the sun to deal with. The wind too will play its part: it may blow more clouds in the sun's path, or westward to await sunset. The sun will decide the outcome of the day: it will determine whether the wisps of cloud will turn into a thick blanket cover or be evaporated into a translucent blue.

After the roses trick, Adrian had surprised her with a romantic idea: 'Let's take the bikes and a bottle of wine and ride out into the hills to watch the sunset,' he offered. She nearly toppled over at his suggestion; despite being worried about the frost, her heart beat furiously with delight. He said to give him half an hour to finish his job (he was tiling the front-doorstep ready for her birthday!) and then he would be ready. She made herself a cup of tea and waited. One and three-quarter hours later, they set off: he had underestimated the time he needed for the tiling job. 'Each tile has to be measured and hand cut before it can be fixed into place,' he later lamented. 'It is a long and tricky job and the amount of time needed can't be predicted.' Sabina thought about the way he approaches their relationship and could understand why they ended up racing on the bikes to catch a glimpse of the sun before it was gobbled up by the wooded hills of the valley. He is a tiler covering the front door step; cutting, trimming and polishing the tiles, spending large amounts of time, patience and energy to get them into perfect place. He takes so much pride in his work and precision, his calculations, predictions and organisation, getting it all to fit, that he neglects the interior. Because of this, he makes them chase a setting sun and prevents them from experiencing the full glory.

The train reaches the hills. The sky is heavy with grey contemplative cloud: shall we rain now or later? The rain does not come, but Sabina knows they are full-to-bursting. 'Are they enjoying the tension of the atmosphere?' she ponders.

Anticipation and fear hang over the hilltops, turning the spring morning into a menacing brew which makes her wonder what it must feel like in the transitional period between life and death.

There is much green from evergreens in the valleys—the deciduous trees are late in receiving leaf cover. The only sign of spring is the white-speckled hawthorn blossoms flashing at her menacingly on the side of the track as the train speeds past.

Sabina feels safe inside the empty train compartment: she does not have to expose herself to the atmospheric tension outside, but can look at it and consider its potential for ruining her day whilst remaining inside where it's dry and quiet.

The sun touches her shoulder: a compassionate pat of encouragement, reminiscent of Ana.

The train has travelled through the highest peaks of the Ardennes out into the foothills and the sky is clearing. Houses appear and with them more variation in vegetation and colour. She's back with the human touch: Forsythia splashes yellow here and there like spilled paint. Her husband would say it was an imperfection of nature and salivate at the thought of cutting the branches back.

Brussels will be new to Sabina. Despite living a mere two-hour drive away, she has never been: it was where her husband betrayed her. Today she's on a mission and his infidelity is far from her mind. Instead she's looking forward to seeing, watching and listening to what the city has to say to her.

Through her writing, she is learning to trust her way of learning and growing and each time clarity comes, she is surprised by its richness. *When growth is not forced, but experienced*, she muses, *it is pure: it is, in fact, the truth.*

Each time she looks out of the window, more and more blue sky is revealed to her; it is undressing for her, clouds cast to the horizon to float like negligées in an azure sea, reminding her of her lavender-oil bath.

Cows are lying down in the fields—a sign that the threat of rain has not yet subsided. The silver birch are shining like armour in the sun and the leaves are so new that the greenness looks artificial.

The train moves briskly on towards the city. Graffiti greets new arrivals in the station entrance; an encoded message known only by the owner of the spray can. Pigeons flap and displace themselves, a lazy metre. The train has just arrived in Brussels-Nord, or Brussel-Noord as the next sign announces, and is running behind schedule. Sabina doesn't mind. And a tongue of white cloud is all she sees before she plunges into the darkness of a tunnel. All there is now is the regular flashing of brightness as the tunnel lights whiz past the window. She feels as if she's on familiar ground here, pleased at the contrast after travelling over the surface all these kilometres.

Brussel-Sud, Brussel-Zuid, signs loom up and shock her out of thought. She has just travelled under the city from North to South, she presumes, and it will next head for the centre, Brussels-Midi. The centre is where she needs to be to collect the material.

She remains seated, holding on to its terracotta comfort, looking out of the window and wondering when the train is going to jerk into motion again. A conductor comes into her compartment.

"The train ends here," she announces, "You have to get off!"

Sabina is confused. "You mean it's not going on to the central station, Brussels-Midi?" she asks with some urgency. The woman smiles: "This is Midi, Madame," she says.

"But it says 'Sud,'" Sabina protests.

"'Sud' is 'Midi', Madame," she laughs

Sabina is embarrassed and as she climbs off the train, remembers one of Spitfire's drier French phrases, 'Midi de la France,' meaning the South of France.

Out of the station, she wanders onto the main road, looking at the street map Gerard gave her; but she's useless with maps and gives up, preferring to ask someone to point her in the direction of the central square known as the Grande Place.

Sabina follows the train tracks round as she was instructed to do. The large avenue is empty. Midday, she thinks to herself, the people will be having lunch. She is self-conscious walking down the large avenue alone, in a strange city, so quickens her pace and adds dark glasses to her face. The route into the city from the station takes her through an Arab quarter and she notices more and more groups of Arab men on the streets, chatting, sitting in cafes, standing at street corners. She wonders if it is a wise choice to be walking into the centre.

Her eyes search around for something familiar. She spots two young girls on the opposite side of the avenue wearing pedal pushers and modern haircuts. 'Students,' she thinks and crosses over to follow them. They eventually take a right turn and disappear into a building. Sabina continues. An empty square is all that greets her at the end of the avenue—she was expecting to be in the middle of a busy shopping street, but when she glances around at the shops, notices that they are all closed.

She looks up and sees the Mercedes star emblem on a high-rise she'd seen from the train near to *Gare du Nord*. She didn't want to end up there and miss the centre altogether! She moves diagonally across the square, continues straight on and then takes a right. The first thing she sees is a souvenir shop. She never thought she would welcome that sight—she usually avoided such places. Now she is thankful because it indicates that she is near to her goal. As she walks past, she peers in at Belgian lace, the peeing fountain boy, star-studded European Institution flags, cups with 'I love Brussels' printed on, little models of Belgian houses, waffles, seafood—and many other items that are being sold under the name 'souvenir'—to remember.

Sabina moves briskly on, arrives by coincidence at a tourist office and runs merrily inside. The man behind the counter gives her instructions and she sets off. She must have headed in the wrong direction because she ends up on *Place des Herbes* (Herb Square) and not *Rue de la Bourse* (Stock Exchange Street) as he had said she would and forlornly sits next to the fountain in the middle of the square and lets droplets of water shower her back. She looks at the street map once more but it's hopeless. She throws the map into her handbag with disgust and decides to retrace her steps, hoping to get back to the tourist office and start again.

She walks through some back streets, a labyrinth of tiny pedestrian pathways, and begins to relax, enjoying the atmosphere of the bustling city at lunchtime, and watching people pause in front of artistic displays of seafood which beckon them to eat in the restaurant. She doesn't care any more whether she finds her way immediately. She has all day and carries on exploring. When she finally looks at one of the street names, she is amazed to read *Rue de la Bourse*. Soon afterwards, she sees the Metro sign the man at the tourist office had told her about. It looks like the underground, he had said, but it is actually a tram stop. She climbs down the steps and asks for a return ticket to *Place E. Flagey* on the No. 81 tram. He gives her two tickets and sends her down another flight of steps to the tram platform. There is only one platform at the bottom of the steps: she was expecting two—one in each direction. Before she has time to do anything about the second thoughts she's having, the tram has arrived and she climbs on. After a couple of underground stops, the tram rises up to the noisy streets. It is full. She asks the man sitting opposite whether he knows *Place E. Flagey*. He doesn't. But he says that the stations are marked and she's sure not to miss it. It's beyond Brussels-Midi he says and then gets off himself in Brussels-Midi. Good, she thinks, if I am on the wrong tram and don't find the shop, at least I will be able to get back to the station for my return journey.

A black man sits opposite her. She nudges him accidentally with her leg when the tram shakes into motion again. *'Excusez-moi'* she says and he nods. 'I'll ask him,' she thinks. He has to extract earphones from his ears when she speaks. He smiles. *'Je vais montrer,'* he announces. I'll show you. 'Oh dear,' she thinks, 'have I made a mistake? I don't know if I want him to show me!' He smiles again when she catches his eye. Is it a shy or sly smile? 'What if he tells me where to get off and I do and it isn't *Place E. Flagey* but somewhere near his home and he grabs me and takes me there and…'

The tram stops at a square. She reads the name: *Bethlehem*. The black man stirs. He looks at her and shows her a pink palm, fingers spread wide. '*Encore 5 arrêtes*,' he says—another five stops. She begins to calm down. 'How kind!' she thinks, 'He has noticed my anxiety and has taken the trouble to calculate the number of stops,' and decides to trust him after all. She looks around her, more relaxed; the next stop is '*La Maison Blanche*' (the White House). It makes her laugh—she is searching for her material, her true colours via Bethlehem, and the White House.

Place E. Flagey arrives. There is no mistaking it. As she descends the steep tram steps, she looks around for signs of the shop. There are none. When she turns around, she comes face to face with the black man from the tram. 'You not know where you are going?' he asks in broken English. She shakes her head, turns away and heads up a hill. The black man stays at a street corner, watching. She turns left and looks at the road name: '*Sans Souci*' (carefree). 'This can't be right!' she exclaims and tries to get back to the main road. She takes a right down a road called '*Viaduc*' and at the end, sees the shop window loom up in front of her: *Dream Colours*.

She's arrived! Sabina walks past rows of different materials to a shelf at the far end of the shop like one reverently moves past pews in a church to the altar. She knows which material is hers immediately: it is made of the most incredible array of red she has ever seen in her life.

The assistant comes to greet her straight away: "You must be Sabina," he says politely and bows. "Welcome to Dream Colours." She smiles and hands him the letter from Gerard. "What a fiery material you have," he chuckles, pulls the roll of material from the shelf, places it into Sabina's arms like a baby and wishes her a wonderful birthday. Before she leaves, she asks him how to get back to *Place E. Flagey*—the direct route. He tells her to go out of the shop, turn left and then descend: '*toujours descendre, toujours descendre*' and you'll get there. She thanks him and knows he is absolutely right. It is downhill from now on.

Going Home

"It's for you," Adrian shouts at the bathroom door. Sabina opens it and takes the phone out of Adrian's hand.

"Hello, Ani?" the voice says.

"Yes—who…?"

"It's—antha, c-alling ab-your p-arty" is all Sabina manages to hear before the person's voice is muffled by what sounds like a sob. Sabina had recognised who it was when she had said 'Ani' but is unsure how to react. Had Samantha been invited? Adrian wrote all the invitations. Did she put Samantha on the list she made hastily all that time ago? Samantha continues to sob into the phone.

"Mother," she says, and then breaks off again.

"Sorry?" Sabina begins.

Samantha eventually manages to control her emotions long enough to explain that her mother has died.and she won't be able to come to Sabina's 40th birthday celebration. She died of cancer and will be buried in the village church tomorrow. A whole chunk of Sabina's childhood flashes through her mind in that moment and she wishes she could transport herself instantaneously down the phone to be with her friend. "Can I come?" is all she says and Samantha starts crying again: "I'd love you to."

Sabina feels elation more than dread as she settles down on her allocated seat in the Eurojet plane from Luxembourg to Manchester. *I'm going home,* she repeats to herself for the umpteenth time. It was twenty-three years ago when she was just embarking on her university course, full of a new lease for life that she felt similar to the way she is feeling now. She is flying to the place of her first independent footsteps and is filled with hope and love. Her child is there with her, unchained and holding the pen in her hand:

> 'Thank you, oh child, for you are wiser than life itself. You are life embodied in a beautiful adult. Sweet child. Where did you go to? I am sorry for the pain I caused you all these years. Come play with me again. I meant you no harm. I just didn't know you. I love you for who you are. I promise not to judge you, oppress you or chain you up again. I will feed you, take you out and comfort you. I will accept and nourish you and always love you. You are me and I am you. You are part of me and I am part of you. We belong together. Our marriage is meant for a lifetime. It must be. We cannot divorce. If we do, neither of us could live life as who we really are. We are inseparable. We are strong.'

She thinks of her achievements over the many years. Her degree course, graduation with a first, and a job in London for a renowned company. Falling in love, marriage, move to Luxembourg and birth of son Dominic. Another new adventure, country, way of life: culture, language. The birth of a second son. Devotion to being housewife and childraiser, involvement in many circles and clubs, charities and voluntary library work for the school. How successful I have been, she concedes. *Well done, Sabina,* she tells herself and smiles at her reflection in the aeroplane window. *You did it! You finally did it. You recognised your achievements without letting negativity come in and spoil everything.*

The plane takes off with the pulse of life throbbing inside her. Pure excitement fills her veins, her flesh all tingly like after the first orgasm.

It lands on time but the hired car is not ready and so she is a few minutes late for the funeral. She hears music coming from the church as she approaches it and her feet hurry her along and through the door. This is the first time since her mother died that she has stepped inside this church. Inside, it is warm with a scent of oak wood and polish. She is conscious of the noise her coat makes as she sits down in the back row. A conductor's arms are poised high in the air and the audience is waiting for the first notes of the male voice choir. With a forward gesture, the conductor seems to draw out sound from the men's open mouths; a soft 'p' comes first followed by 'eeeee' and then the soft 'ssss' which resounds around the church, touching everyone in it with its gentle power. She recognises the song; 'Peace to my Soul' from *Finlandia* by Sibelius—her father's favourite.

Her eyes drink the music and overflow with joy. A woman's voice interrupts her. She is sitting very close and whispers, 'Aye, its a moving piece in't it, duck?' Sabina nods and looks beyond the woman to the rest of the congregation; everyone is wiping tears away. Sabina feels immense warmth and comfort. She knows immediately that she has come to the right place.

When the service finishes, Sabina goes over to embrace Samantha. The two women seem to communicate half a lifetime through their bodies. Eventually, they release their hold. Sabina says that she'll see her later at the reception and goes out of the church to the graveyard.

It takes her a long time to find the grave; it is so overgrown that she hardly recognises it. When she was here for her mother's funeral, there were only a few gravestones on this particular plot—at the far right underneath a cherry blossom. High grass and climbing weeds have covered the stone. Sabina parts the long grass like hair and scratches with her fingertips to find the inscription. She fails to see anything but green lichen splattered in a messy pattern all over the gritty stone. She pulls at the grass and weeds, tearing them, ripping them. The grass comes away easily and soon she has created a clearing in which she discovers a couple of green shoots pushing through the soil. They are hyacinths. She's sure of it. There are some snowdrops, too. Sabina caresses the bulge that will become a hyacinth and holds her palm out under the snowdrops and lets them tickle her palms. She pulls a candle from her bag and lights it. She remembers how her mother used to love candles and would close the curtains in summer, blocking out all rays so that she could have tea by candlelight. She now kneels down in front of the stone and begins:

'I forgive you, Mum.'

'I love you, Mum.'

'I now recognise the strength and wisdom that you have given me. I will always carry you with me in my heart.'

She leaves the candle burning in the jar, rises slowly and turns to leave. A sound catches her attention. She stops still like a startled deer and listens again; leaves are rustling. She turns around and sees a figure darting behind the tree. It unnerves her and she hurries towards the path.

'You must be Veronica's daughter,' the tree says.

Sabina walks around the tree. He is a tall man, bushy white hair, a wide bullfrog mouth and two glossy eyes like precious stones (azure and emerald) which twinkle sea-green in the weak spring light. The eyes dazzle her for a moment and she is unsure how to react. The moment of hesitation must have been less than three seconds and yet Sabina felt frozen to the spot, turned to stone by his voice and eyes. He moves towards her. Three grand strides and he's there, shaking her hand and introducing himself.

"I'm André—your mother and I were dating before her death."

"Oh."

"I come here every Sunday just to talk to her."

"Oh." Sabina finds herself thinking, rather unkindly, that he hasn't bothered to tend the grave and this thought niggles her. She is not quite sure whether to believe the man.

There is a moment of silence. Both look at the floor as if looking for words. He is the one to break the silence.

"I haven't been gardening," he says, pointing to the grave. "I didn't feel I have a right. It's not my property."

"Oh." Sabina manages to look up again.

"I have always dreaded meeting a relative, but never have till today."

"I live in Luxembourg."

"I know. She talked a great deal about you and your sister Janet."

"Jennifer."

"Oh, yes. Sorry. Jennifer."

Silence.

He coughs. "Well, um. Must be getting on." He turns to leave.

Sabina feels panic rising up and a strong urge to grab onto this man, squeeze him for information, answers, the truth.

"Wait!" she shouts at his back and runs towards him, surprised at the force of her voice and the great strides her legs make. He stops and turns.

"Um. Well, I mean. Don't go. I would love to chat with you—about her. You know, find some answers?"

His eyes send out a ray of light—a blue sunbeam "Sure. I would love to. We can have tea and cakes in the next village."

Sabina and André order scones with plenty of strawberry jam and clotted cream at a small café a few kilometers away from the church. She feels at ease with him already and knows they are going to become great friends. André tells Sabina that leaving her mother to go back to his ex-wife had been the biggest mistake he had ever made in his life and he has suffered all these years because of it. He is no longer with his wife. He has no partner at all and thinks that he deserves having the punishment for not recognising an angel when he was sent one. Sabina instantly thinks of Madame Anastasia and how she would like this man. He accepts an invitation to her birthday party and Sabina leaves for Samantha's house with a tender feeling in her heart about seeing him again in a couple of weeks.

Samantha's house is packed full of guests eating sandwiches and drinking sherry. Sabina has always wondered how people can eat at funerals; after her mother's funeral, she struggled to get down a cup of tea, let alone anything solid. The two women finally manage to retreat for a few moments and sit on Samantha's double bed. The tears soon dry as they recount some of the mischief they used to get up to in their school days. Samantha begins to laugh uncontrollably as she remembers the day she hid in a row of lockers at the back the class during an English lesson:

'Do you remember, Sabina?'

'How could I forget?'

She had written the story in her notebook:

> 'At the back of the classroom were columns of lockers—four down, twenty across. Each one was big enough to fit a stack of about five A4 ring binders; and one of the columns, we discovered, could fit a pupil in because the locker 'floors' had been knocked out. Samantha thought this was a fantastic discovery and immediately volunteered to try it out. She squeezed herself into place and I closed all four doors. It was like a magician's box. You could open different doors to see different parts of her body. One for her head and shoulders, one for her chest and abdomen, one for her thighs and knees, one for her shins and feet.
>
> A gang of us sat at the back row in front to the locker wall and tried to make Samantha laugh so that different doors would burst open when her body shook. We were testing all our jokes to see which part of her body was most amused by them. Then the teacher arrived and she was still in the locker. We couldn't warn her, we just stopped telling the jokes. Samantha caught on and didn't dare come out. She kept on whispering through the metal door, asking us what we were doing, where the teacher was and trying to get us to laugh by telling rude stories about him.
>
> Our English teacher wasn't stupid. He knew there was something going on at the back of the class; he probably knew about the column of lockers that Samantha was contained in. Whether he knew or not, he decided to change the class around: i.e. the back row becomes the front row, the front row becomes the back row and he stands in front of the row of lockers to teach the rest of the lesson. My attempts at warning Samantha failed. She was still telling us a dirty story about Mona Lisa and Rembrandt.
>
> On and on Samantha went finding inspiration in her locker for the most disgustingly imaginative piece of prose you've ever heard. The real Mona Lisa stood in front of the lockers listening. Luckily for us, our Mona Lisa teacher was a sincere man who adored children and the challenge of teaching. He believed in children's goodness and appreciated their timeless humour.
>
> The entire class roared with laughter as the teacher opened the top locker door to reveal a very hot and pink face.'

On the Edge

Before driving to the airport and flying back to Luxembourg, Sabina feels compelled to visit a spot in the countryside she loved as a child. She leaves her hotel in sunshine and arrives at the car park for hikers in dense fog.

A new placard has been erected at the foot of the path leading up to the ridge. Sabina reads:

'Hello and welcome to the N. Lees Estate owned by the Peak District National Park Authority. The landscape you are standing in is a constantly changing one…'

Good, this is just what I like

'People have had an immense impact on how the landscape looks…'

Too right!

'…The landscape is changing still. These changes in the landscape are managed to conserve the fine scenery, rich wildlife, cultural and archaeological heritage and to provide opportunities for you to enjoy this special place.'

Well, that's exactly what I am here for!

She takes out her notebook.

March 20th 2000

> 'Here I am on Stanage Edge. For the first time in my entire life I have taken myself out into the countryside to walk by myself. I looked in the mirror this morning and I said to myself. 'You need to go on a good walk on Stanage Edge.' And my voice replied, 'But what about my vertigo?' The person in the mirror told me that I no longer had to fear it. It was gone.' 'Yes,' I said and

> began to cry. Finally, after years of striving to overcome it, I knew it was over. Thank you for loving and caring enough for me to make me see that. I would love to go to Stanage Edge. How simple. How profound.'

As Sabina sets off, she is calm and full of anticipation. She remembers the place from her childhood. She had not only been there many times with her Mum and Dad, but also with friends and their families. It was a popular place for hikers, hunters and, above all, mountain climbers from amateur to professional. The Edge provides every level of difficulty in a concentrated space and can be easily reached from the large cities nearby.

What always struck her most about the Edge was the beautiful view it afforded. Even on dull days, it was magnificent and she is excited about seeing it again, drinking in nature, and replenishing her soul. Yet, fog shrouded the place in a milky coat so thick that she can hardly see the car park, let alone the edge itself. At first she is despondent, unsure of herself.

What if I'm up there and fall off because I can't see? Vertigo cured or not; that could happen.

The more she thinks about the fog, the edge and her strong impulse to come here, the more she realises how significant it is. All she can see is fog and a path leading through. All she has to do is walk and sets off, muttering: *'Walk and find what it is you are looking for. Just keep on walking.'*

She is relieved that there are no distractions due to the fog: no other people, no views begging to be admired, no forking paths demanding to be explored—just one path leading towards her goal: the edge. Nothing to complicate things. No choices. The path is there, solid, undemanding. When she reaches the top, Madame Anastasia's words dance with greater fervor in her head:

"The path beckons because it has something to tell you. Find that experience. Don't be afraid. The path cannot bite. It is not alive. You are. The path will go on with or without you—that is what it is there for. You can choose it, or not choose it. Either way, it is about you and not about the path. Trust yourself. Love yourself. Love life."

Sabina sits on a rock and takes pen and notebook out of her pocket once more:

> 'Yes! It is about me. It's not the path, the vertigo. I could be anywhere in the entire world, on a muddy track with bracken growing all round and the occasional inquisitive sheep. Why, I could even be in Luxembourg. The place doesn't matter at all. It's what's inside me that matters. Who I am.'

She then mounts the rock, stands tall, moist air hitting her face and turns towards the wind.

Before setting off on her hike along the ridge, she collects a few loose rocks and makes them into a mini pyramid of stones as she has often seen out in the countryside in Luxembourg. This way she feels more confident that she will find the path again that will take her back down to her car.

> 'I am here now, on a good path, with a wonderful person. I don't feel alone with myself anymore. I'm not afraid of being alone with myself. I am many people, all with a right to be here with me, everyone has something to contribute to who I am. All are worthy of existence in and through me: my child, Sabina, the housewife, Sabina the student, Sabina the computer scientist, Sabina the wife, Sabina the mother, Sabina the writer.'

Writing this down, acknowledging it, makes her feel great. Things are finally making sense. For many, many years she felt like there was another person inside her wanting to come out; one who wanted to jump, turn cartwheels, run, skip and use up tons of energy. She held that person at bay and, in doing so, used up all her vitality.

> 'I suppose I have always been scared of exhausting the source of energy. I was sipping a little at a time, dosing it so that the source wouldn't run dry, making myself be adult about it; I thought I had to behave sensibly and not enjoy myself all the time. Now and again, I did get fed up of this meager diet and would gulp down liters of the stuff. Choke, splutter, burp, Yum. Wow, that made me feel good. Better go sparingly with that or I won't have enough for a lifetime. I didn't realise that I was in charge of the source. I could create more—as much as I wanted. Every day, every hour, every minute; I can always tap into it and refill it; it is like the magic porridge pot.'

When Sabina's flight takes off with her safely on board, the captain announces that a strong southerly breeze will get them back to Luxembourg earlier than expected.

She does not bother ringing Adrian to come and pick her up but decides to take a taxi back home. On her way, she asks the driver to wait for her whilst she pops into the supermarket. Sabina lets her child decide what she wants to buy. She fills the basket up with jelly, ice-cream, marshmallows, crisps and sponge fingers.

In her kitchen at home she merrily prepares the tea for her family. Adrian is the last to arrive; he sees the flicker of candlelight through the shutters on the window and is mentally rubbing his hands together at the thought of one of Sabina's feasts like she has been preparing regularly for a number of weeks. He thinks it's because she is secretly going to a cookery class in town (like the make-up, hair-do and fashion classes he presumes she has also been participating in); he often sees her on the *Place de la Constitution* with a cookery book under her arm and posh bag from exclusive boutiques in her hands.

When he enters the kitchen, sees the children's party food on the table and the ridiculous grin on his wife's face, he is disgusted.

"What a stupid, no, insane thing to do!" he exclaims. "Are you out of your mind? How do you explain this preposterous behaviour?" and he flicks the party hat off Dominic's head. It floats gracefully down onto the floor and crumples delicately in front of his left foot. Dominic follows the hat with his eyes, struck by the slowness of its flight down, marveling at the motion and agility. He has been getting quite into his new Mum and her 'estranged' behaviour. Of course, he thinks that this kid's party tea thing is a bit over the top; but he does so love jelly and ice-cream, and those biscuits with marshmallow on the top sprinkled with coconut, are just out of this world. As a twenty-first century punk rocker, you don't get the opportunity to eat (or admit to having eaten) those very often. Yes, the idea of a wacky mum appeals to him—a refreshing contrast to the stuck up, boring old fart he had been used to for most of his life.

Sabina replies with composure to Adrian's outburst.

"Oh, Adrian. All I did was take a child out to play and listened to what it would like for tea."

"Which child? That brat from across the road, I'll bet."

"No, dear. A new one. One you don't know yet." She pauses and then adds in a near whisper, "Although she lives in this house."

"What do you mean 'lives in this house'? You haven't adopted one, have you? Why would we want more children? You can't even deal with the ones we've got!"

"No dear, of course I haven't adopted one. You just can't see this child yet. You will in time. Here, have some strawberry jelly."

"Bloody hell, Sabina. What the hell's going on? Child. No child. Invisible child. I give up with you." He huffs and throws his serviette across the table at her. "I think you should go and see a psychiatrist!" And before slamming the door behind him, he swipes the pack of sponge fingers from the kitchen sideboard. "If there isn't anything sensible to eat around here, I shall have to eat these and it'll be your fault if I put on weight!"

Sabina merely smiles, excavates a large chunk of marshmallow off her biscuit with her spoon and pops it into her mouth. "Hmm, delicious," she rejoices.

Carl and Dominic observe—speechless, the pair of them. 'Our parents really do have problems,' they both think in unison. That is the first time for ages they have exactly the same view of the situation.

Wishful Thinking

Adrian eats one sponge finger after another in front of the computer screen and feels miserable. He has lost all motivation to work on the paper he's brought back from the office.

He looks in the e-mail box: all guests except Jennifer have RSVPed to the invitation, but he is certain she of all people will be coming to the party. He marvels for a second about the ease of communication between family and friends since the Internet. There were only two guests who are not connected and they were his parents. Just as he was thinking about this, the phone rings and he snatches it up.

"Waldsmere!" he fires

"Adrian?"

"Oh, hi Mum. Everything okay?"

"Yes, fine dear. And you?"

"Great."

"Good. All prepared for the party?"

"Of course. You know me. All planned to the final detail."

"Good. Listen, we still haven't got Sabina a present. I have no idea what she might like. Do you?"

There is a pause whilst Adrian pretends to think.

"I know she has everything really. But we can't come without a gift, can we?"

Adrian pauses again. He has been wondering about this himself. He's ordered her present but still could decide not to pick it up next week.

"Hello, hello. Adrian?"

Adrian is shocked into saying something

"What?" is all that comes out

"Is there something wrong with your phone? I don't think ours is faulty."

"I don't know, I mean, maybe. Yes, probably."

"Well, tell me quickly then—before we get cut off. She does have a wish list, doesn't she?"

"Um, well, no."

His Mum's voice suddenly changes, as if she's just eaten some chalk.

"Well, then, she can't need anything!" she screeches and hangs up.

Adrian doesn't really know what to think of that. His Mum has never put the phone down on him before. Maybe her phone was faulty after all. He should ring her back, he thinks, but couldn't be bothered with it now.

He decides to go downstairs and confront Sabina with it.

Sabina is still sitting at the table with a party hat on, sipping red-wine from a party cup with a straw and looking decidedly drunk.

"Sabina," he shouts. "Ring my Mum, would you—she wants to know what your birthday wishes are."

"No."

"What?"

"No, you ring her and tell her."

"But, I don't know!"

"Don't ring her then!"

It's no use talking to her in this state, he concludes, and scurries back upstairs and throws himself back into his chair in front of the computer.

'Ah, an e-mail from Jennifer—at least there's someone I can rely on,' he mumbles to the screen and clicks on the message.

> Dear Sabina and Adrian,
>
> After my news last week that I couldn't come a week before the do as planned, I now regret to inform you that I won't be able to come to the party on 25th March at all. Enjoy yourselves without me.
>
> Love,
> Jennifer

"Sod the whole family!" he exclaims and hurls a balled-up piece of paper at the computer screen.

Sabina stays at the table awhile thinking about the last time her mother-in-law asked what her wishes were.

* * * *

It was only August, but her mother-in-law insisted that Christmas was already on its way: "What do you and the lads want?" she rang to ask on the day before they were due to leave on a two-week summer vacation in the Mediterranean. Sabina was in a panic about the washing and the packing and didn't understand the urgency of the matter.

"Haven't you made a list?" her mother-in-law pestered

"No!"

"Well, I need to know soon. There are only 120 shopping days left until Christmas, you know. Couldn't you write a few ideas in your postcard from holiday?"

'No I bloody well couldn't,' she thought but said she would try and was glad to put the phone down and try to get back into the mood for the summer vacation. But she found it difficult after that. Her mother-in-law always managed to get her back up. 'Just when I was looking forward to switching off from the world of commercialisation and responsibility,' she lamented to her half-filled suitcase.

The day she got back, before she had even unpacked the dirty washing from the cases, mother-in-law phoned again.

"What do you want for Christmas?" she asked. "You must know by now. You've had all summer to think about it. Oh, how was it, by the way? We haven't received your postcard yet."

"No?" Sabina said in her best 'concerned' voice. "I hope it didn't get lost in the post."

"So, tell me!"

"I don't know, I don't know," Sabina said wearily

"Well, then, you can't need anything!" Mother-in-law replied and hung up.

Sabina thought long and hard about it afterwards. 'Perhaps I don't need anything like she said. After all, we are well off. I always have enough cash to go out and get myself the things I need: a new pair of knickers, a toothbrush, socks, scarf, creams and perfumes. I can go to the shops if I please and buy without a care. Some may call me a rich bitch. Got it all: house, car, turbo lawn mower, *Brie de Meaux* in the fridge and *Grand Premier Cru* in the cellar. It's all relative, of course. I am not rich enough to buy a house without worrying about the finances, or a car or any big thing for that matter. But I am rich enough not to worry about the grocery bill, or eating out, or buying the kids more than one pair of good, high-quality shoes a year. I am not rich and indulgent, though. Although some might imagine I am—because I can afford to be. The funny thing about being able to buy something is that it takes away the pleasure. In the end, you don't buy it, not because you can't, but because you could. You become rich and stingy, not rich and indulgent. Especially when it comes to yourself. So, what could someone like me possibly want for Christmas? I am not in the habit of making lists for relatives to pick over: 'Have you seen what she's written on her list? All luxury items, I'd say. Spoiled, she is, and the lads. And they have enough money themselves to get those things. They have everything anyway. The lads have so much stuff they don't know what to do with it!'

* * * *

Sabina never did send a list. Her mother-in-law put her name down for a collective present with her son.

Sabina blows her nose on a serviette and locks herself in the bathroom to wash her face. She no longer cares; she does not need anything. And if she did, she could buy it herself. Yet a voice inside her head keeps on: *I don't want to tell her what I want, for Christ Sake. I want her to know—take note. Get me anything small. A tiny packet of homemade biscuits. A used lottery ticket, just for luck. A hand-painted flowerpot. An old calendar picture cut out and framed. A dried flower. It's simple, really. Of course I want something for my Birthday. I want a sign—however small—that you care about me!*

Adrian sneaks into the kitchen and is delighted to see there is still some strawberry jelly left in the bowl. He takes a ladle and plops a large dollop onto a party plate. He sticks a straw into the wine bottle and sucks the rest up and then sits down in front of the jelly, spoon raised a centimetre above the plate as if suspended there. As if caught by a sudden change of heart, he throws the spoon down, lowers his head and sucks the jelly up with one big slurp.

Carl is standing in front of the bathroom door when Sabina comes out. He looks directly at her eyes. She lowers them.

"Need the bathroom?" she ventures.

"No. I want to talk to you."

Sabina feels a nervous shudder creeping up her legs and tries to stop it reaching her upper torso and giving her away.

"Will you come into my room for a minute?"

She follows sheepishly behind wondering what he wants to talk to her about.

He shuts the door, invites her to sit on his bed and then begins.

"I've been in the loft."

She gulps

"I know I shouldn't pry but I just couldn't help myself. I guess I owe you an apology for it but I'm not sorry I did it. I read your Mum's diaries. I know all about it."

Sabina is relieved. She was wondering when she was going to tell them or show them the letter—she'd been thinking about putting the entire silver chest in her will.

"I've also read your writing," he adds and looks at her with his large, puppy-dog eyes.

"Carl!"

"I know. I shouldn't. But I've done it now and can't pretend I didn't. I thought I had better let you know before it's too late."

"What do you mean?"

"Well, I took some of it to school and showed it to my English teacher."

"What?" she says angrily and glares at him, unsure whether she's going to hit him or storm out of the room or do both.

As if he reads her mind he adds:

"Please don't lash out at me. I know it was terribly wrong for me to do it. That's why I'm telling you. Please forgive me."

Sabina's temper settles and she takes his hand.

"You know I will, Carl. It doesn't make me any less angry about it, though. That's personal, private stuff. You have no right…"

He cuts her off, "I know! But it's also very good. Mr Toking thinks so, too. Good enough to publish!"

Sabina is shocked. The thought of publishing simply had not crossed her mind.

"That was my idea when I read it. I hadn't got you a present and wanted to give you something special and personal and so took the writing. I wanted to have it published for you as a birthday gift."

Sabina is touched and angry all at once—quite a lethal emotional cocktail on top of the red wine.

"Anyway, Mr Toking said he wouldn't go ahead with it without your consent and he was right. He urged me to tell you and I'm glad I did." He finishes and leans across the bed to hug his Mum.

"I love you Mum. I now know you better from the writing and it makes me love you all the more for it."

She returns his hug.
"I really think you should think about it though."
"Think about what?"
"Publishing, of course. I can arrange a meeting with my teacher, if you like."

Coming Out

Sabina hears Adrian's voice and follows the sound to the kitchen. The door is slightly ajar and she can see him standing on one of the kitchen chairs, waving his arms wildly above his head.

"I have to drone, drone, drone on—no-one else is as capable. No-one is as efficient. If only they would pull their weight—all of them, the lads included. Then we could become more efficient. It's all a question of planning and organisation. It won't happen if you just stand there staring at it. You have to get organised. Do it. Can't you see how inefficient and useless you all are compared to me? Can't you? Well?...

"...Look where I am! And look where all you are. Now get off your chairs and come up to me. This is where you should be. This is your goal. Are you too stupid to see it? What are you doing wasting your time giggling and eating fucking jelly and ice-cream and other such childish things? Who's going to sort out the broken toilet? Who's going to order drinks for the party? Who's going to mend the leaking taps? Who's going to sweep the leaves from the driveway and unblock the drain? Who's going to sort out all the office papers? Who's going to get us connected to better communication systems and make sure we move properly through the new millennium? Who? Me, that's who! Because you are all too busy enjoying yourselves."

"Adrian, what on earth are you doing on top of that chair? You look as though you're conducting an imaginary orchestra!"

"Too right! You've hit the nail on the head. I am conducting an imaginary orchestra. I'm a one-man show!"

"Is anything wrong? You seem quite perplexed."

"No, nothing's wrong. I'm fine. You just run along to your cookery class, or make-up lessons, or whatever it is tonight and I shall carry on with real life like a responsible adult."

"Okay," she replies and leaves.

"I don't believe it!" he fumes and marches out to find the lawn mower. Mowing the lawn when it has hardly grown more than a millimeter yet—well, someone has to do it, he huffs. And he trudges behind the mower, grass cuttings flying behind him, sneezing violently at the freshly cut grass.

Sabina drives into town and parks her car outside Madame Anastasia's villa. She rings the bell and, although she has not rung to tell her she's coming, Ana lets her in as if she's been expecting her. Sabina tells her all about her visit to England, the funeral, the grave, and André. Ana listens and laughs and cries with her.

Ana takes Sabina by the hand and goes down into the cellar. She opens the door to the Casemates and flicks the light switch. "Come and see this," she says and beckons Sabina over to a tiny alcove which is concealed by a long curtain.

"This is where I keep my good wines," she announces and points to rows and rows of bottles crammed up to the sandstone wall.

"You can choose one if you like," she says lovingly and lets Sabina come closer to the collection. Sabina pulls one out; a *Grand Premier Cru Classé*—eighteen years old.

"This one," she says and hands it to Ana.

Ana explains about how the temperature in the Casemate tunnel is ideal for storing wine and that she has been collecting them ever since she came to the villa.

Sabina tells Ana about the party tea and the writing and Adrian.

'What's the use?' she laments to Ana. 'If I can't produce writing for publishing, why produce at all?'

"Sabina," Ana's swaddling voice begins, "I think it's perfectly normal to feel lame when considering going out in the world with your voice and it may be too early. It's only just recently that you have found the courage to write. Faced with the challenge of submitting work, you're bound to feel uneasy. Think of yourself as a toddler taking your first steps. You still need a hold and landing points. Thoughts about publishing now are bound to feel like insurmountable obstacles for you. Perseverance…"

Sabina takes that word and spits it back at Ana as if it were poison.

"Perseverance! I don't have any."

"You're forgetting the chest stuffed with your work, Sabina. Enough to fill a book already! Where did that come from if not from perseverance!" she reprimands.

"But it's hidden away in the dark where no one can see it. Like that it may eat my heart out again like a plump and juicy slug on my flowers in the garden!"

"The day you started writing was the day you declared war on the slugs and you know it. Your writing is like anti-slug pellets; it's turning the thick creatures into a dissolving and disintegrating mass of slime over the fertile soil of your garden. Your skin, like the slugs skins, is dissolving. You're shedding an old life, Sabina. It's hardly surprising that you feel lost in the new one. The writing has triggered a process and there is a trail of goo in your wake!"

Sabina loves Ana's way of helping her disentangle her mind. She feels better already and plucks up the courage to pose a question that she has wanted to do for a long time.

"How come you have a key to the tunnels?"

Ana smiles and says that it it's a long story but, if she has time to listen, she will gladly tell it. Sabina nods.

"My mother was living in this house when World War II broke out. She grew up here with her father, an only child, too, and hadn't yet found a husband so that she could flee the nest. With the war starting, and all young men away, she worried whether she ever would find one.

"There were sometimes bomb scares in Luxembourg and the city finally found a good use for the Casemates. Whenever the sirens rang, they ushered the townsfolk down into the passageways where they were safe until the danger passed. My mother and her father were lucky to have direct access into the Casemates; it meant that they didn't have to expose themselves to danger on their way there, like most of the inhabitants of the city did.

"The people would huddle together in the long tunnels, trying to keep calm and warm. There were several kitchens to provide hot soup and cubicles with buckets of sand as toilets. It was mostly women, children and the elderly who were in there as most of the men had gone off to fight in the war.

"My mother hated going in and would delay as much as possible, staying in the cellar until her father grabbed her and forced her to come with him. One day, he pulled her so hard that she fell across the stone floor and gashed herself so badly that he had to take her to one of the nurses.

"It was in the medical section of the tunnel that she met my father.

"He came into the tunnels whenever there was an air-raid because he was the only one it seemed who knew his way around the network. He used to play down there as a child until a nasty accident blinded him and forced him to live a limited life as a handicap. The air-raids gave his life new meaning as he was promoted to 'Casemate Deputy' in charge of moving people in and around the city through the tunnels.

"He led my mother to another medical station nearer to the main exit through unlit passageways she never knew existed. He held her hand as he led her and she immediately fell in love with him. After that, they met in the Casemates even when there were no air-raids and made passionate love on the cool sandy floor."

She pauses, looks at Sabina with a slight blush and says proudly, "I was conceived in the Casemates, you know."

Sabina is enthralled. Ana goes on:

"So, my mother did find a husband after all and the Casemates became their courting ground. He took her on adventures through passageways that took them to every corner of the city. They especially liked the idea of slipping below the Pétrusse river and up the other side of the valley like you have been doing. She told me how enraged she was when the red bridge was built; the foundations were cut deep into the rock, blocking an entire section of the Casemates off to them. They felt like they owned the underground passages of the city.

"When I arrived, my mother and father left the house, and Luxembourg, to live in Paris. I don't think they ever recovered from that move. They both died in a tragic car accident shortly before my eighteenth birthday and all I was left with was their inheritance: this villa. I didn't come back but rented the house out to bank directors and civil servants. That paid for my dressmaking school and other studies in psychology and philosophy. In the summer vacation, I came to Luxembourg and worked in the Casemates as tourist guide. Even though I had never been in them myself until then, I knew all about them—my mother taught me and explained the network using the many drawings she had made.

"The job as tourist guide didn't pay very well, but that isn't why I did it. I didn't have financial problems; I just needed to be in the tunnels, where I had been conceived, to get through the grief at losing my parents.

"I didn't come to Luxembourg until a few years ago. As a student, I had found the people narrow-minded and stifling. It was no place for young people or a woman with ambitions to become a dressmaker with a difference. I stayed in Paris most of the time, travelling to New York and London to get ideas for my clothes. This is where I met my husband."

"So he was English?"

"Yes, I fell in love with his gentleness only to be disappointed by it later. He had always taken great interest in the clothes I designed and I guess this swept me off my feet. Not having parents to be proud of my achievements, I hadn't realised what I had missed until he showered me with praise. What neither of us knew when we married was that his interest in women's clothes went beyond mere aesthetics.

"He used to come to Luxembourg to sort out matters in connection with the villa—rent, repairs and the like. I discovered later that he always took one of my designs with him and went into the gay bars. Shortly after we moved into the villa and he began working at the European Institutions, he fell in love with a bank director and left for California. I've never been to see him, but our son visits him once a year."

Sabina is stunned. "You have a son?"

"Yes, Gerard!"

After she has let this news sink in, she asks,

"Don't you miss not having a husband or partner?"

"To be perfectly honest with you—yes, I do! I believe that I am more complete with a man at my side, if you know what I mean."

Sabina is not so sure she does, but does not say so. Before leaving the villa, she hesitates before saying:

"Will you come to my birthday party? I think I'll need your support!"

"Of course I will. Can I bring Gerard?"

"Yes."

She kisses Ana for the first time and the two of them part.

Adrian stands in front of the bathroom mirror scrutinising his face. There is a deep frown between his bushy eyebrows that he hasn't noticed before. He wonders why it has suddenly appeared and then thinks of Sabina. *She's making me age before my time.*

It's late and Sabina is still not back. He is livid that she can be so blatant about her affair; he hasn't caught the guy yet, but he knows he will. He has decided to go there tonight and claim her back.

What has he done to deserve such cruel treatment? he wonders. He's always supported her financially, making sure she has a roof over her head and a good car. He feels like an idiot for organising a party for her on top of everything else he does for her.

Well, he announces to the wise old man in the mirror, *she's not getting a present from me no matter how much she's desperate for it.*

His car is cold; there's been a frost already and he hadn't bothered to drive it into the garage; he'd been waiting for Sabina to return so they could drive both of their cars in together.

He remembers the address and has no trouble finding the entrance. Ana lets him in. He's embarrassed that a woman opens the door to him but she has such a soothing effect on him that he enters without a word. She spends the rest of the night swaddling him with some of her well-practised wisdoms and when dawn comes, he feels a confused, yet changed man.

Swimming

Sabina is back at the swimming pool café after a number of days absence. It's shortly after midday. Dominic finishes football training at half past and she has arranged to pick him up. She has twenty minutes to write. Before she met Ana, she wouldn't have dreamed of slipping into a cafe and writing an essay like one slips into a shop to pick up a litre of milk. She wouldn't have thought this enough time. She has learned that she does have the time if she lets herself take it. Those twenty minutes could make the difference between a day without writing and a day with writing. She may have some insights; she may just exercise her wrist.

A sixties song is playing. 'Say that you will. say that you love me...that you need me...Yeah, yeah, I want to know you been good to me baby.' *That's the cry of my writer's heart,* she muses. The music is blaring out so loudly that she wonders whether it's always as noisy as this at the cafe.

She told Adrian that she has started writing at the swimming pool. He couldn't see that it was conducive. No, it isn't really and yes, it is. It's both loud and silent, depending on what you want to listen to. She can watch the swimmers, divers and the clock; a large face on the far opposite wall. When she writes here, the hands go round slower. A second seems like the time it takes a swimmer to complete a length of the 50-metre pool. She can dip into the water with him and write a page in that time. *Look, it's not yet half past,* she tells herself. *Another ten minutes and I may have an analogy I could use for my book.*

She is so startled by her own thought that she nearly drops off her chair. *Am I really writing a book?*

> 'Samantha told me that her husband was on a spiritual journey. When she started hers, he had progressed far. She delved into his books and things began to move fast for her. He got scared she would overtake him. She began to hide her progress, suppressing it so as not to hurt him. She found it hard to keep this up and thought of this analogy: we all set off on our spiritual journeys at different times. We are heading towards the same goal. She sees this goal as God. Her image of God is a large sun; a fireball of light. We are all moving towards the light, she said. If you look at the sun, you will see there are million upon million of rays being sent to earth. Some long, some short, some crooked, some straight, some hazy, some clear. She imagines that on every single ray is a person travelling. No two persons are on the same ray; that is how different our paths are. Sometimes they may converge and that will be like a miracle when it does. But the span of time between moments of convergence can be infinite. This is how she sees her and her husband's paths now: very different, sometimes miles apart but always heading towards the same goal—the light.'

Sabina wishes that Adrian would embark on a spiritual journey with her. Over the past weeks, she has yearned for his company and understanding. Her friend's experience indicates that this wish won't be fulfilled.

> 'We journey alone. His path is not my path. It will be his and his alone. It may pull us apart for many years, or together. I need to surrender to this. Let go of the will to make things different. Things are not different, or the same, they just are and if I accept this, they will come and be experienced and move on and grow. This way I will step into the flow of things and grow too, as nature intended all along. The power of nature is a tool to help show us the way and, all too often, we go against it, digging in with our nails, scratching down into darkness rather than letting ourselves move towards the light as we are destined to do.'

She looks at the clock. It's exactly twenty past and she leaves the café to fetch Dominic.

Carl is in his room when they get back and Sabina doesn't even bother to take her coat off before going to knock at his door. He calls to her that she can come in and she feels like his daughter with a request for a favour as she stands in front of him, twiddling the toggles of her coat between her fingers.

"Carl?"

"Yeah?"

"You know this teacher of yours?"

"Yeah!"

"Do you think he'll still be interested in my work?"

"Mum! Brilliant! So you've decided to try and have it published?"

He jumps off his bed and almost leaps onto her with excitement.

He gives her his telephone number, the private one he gave to Carl 'in case she changes her mind' and urges her to call straight away.

Adrian is not at home yet and so she does decide to call straight away before her mood changes.

"Mr Toking?"

"'Tis the very same!"

She likes the sound of him already.

"Sabina Waldsmere. My son…"

"Ah, Carl's gone and talked you into it, has he! I knew he was a great diplomat the very first day I met him."

Sabina feels pleasantly at ease with this man and her heart leaps for the entire duration of the conversation.

They arrange to meet at his apartment in the part of town called 'Verlorenkost' the next evening and Sabina can hardly sleep all night and counts the minutes all the following day.

She is unsure whether she has met him before; Adrian goes to most of the parent evenings 'to give them a piece of his mind,' which he didn't think Sabina was capable of doing and so she has only met the odd one. Her stomach has been churning around so much that she has lost her appetite and it is now empty. For courage, which she thinks she may need, she downs half a glass of champagne; Adrian has opened a 'test' bottle for the celebration next weekend. She hasn't told Adrian where she's really going, but he's so distracted with last-minute preparations that he didn't question her lie about going out for a meal with some friends from a new writing group she has joined.

Being unfamiliar with this part of town, Sabina has to stop a number of times to study the map before she finds his road. He lives on the second floor and she is nearly out of breath when she rings his doorbell after climbing the two flights of stairs. She knows it has nothing to do with lack of fitness.

He opens the door and she nearly faints at the sight of him; he is a gorgeous man with olive-coloured skin and a stunning mass of black curly hair.

She coughs to clear her throat and moistens her mouth with her tongue so that she can speak. It does not matter that she cannot get a word out because he has already taken her arm and is escorting her graciously into his abode.

He has cooked but she declines with the shake of a head and he links an arm in hers once more and moves her into another room.

Walking into his living room is like gliding into a sunrise and she lets the breezy mood carry her like a feather and set her softly down onto the sofa.

She feels like she has just entered a waking dream.

He talks about how impressed he is with her writing, about his contacts in the publishing business, and some technical details like the size of the font to use when typing it up and the amount of space between the lines. She is not listening. She is gazing at the smooth skin of his thigh through a rip in his jeans, just above the knee. He has not finished all he wishes to say when, quite without thinking, her voice finds itself again:

"You're gorgeous," it says.

He gets up, walks to the sofa in front of her, kneels on the floor and carefully wraps his hands around her face like two giant tulip petals and draws her face to his lips. Sensation zooms through them flinging them and their clothes from one end of the room to another in a lovemaking frenzy.

At six in the morning, Sabina drags herself away from his sunrise apartment and drives dreamily back home.

She slips into her side of the bed and lies awake for another two hours remembering his beautiful face and smile. It makes her feel very horny but she decides that she does not want to give any of it to Adrian.

March 24th 2000

> 'Do I really want to start something like this? Is it fair on him? It's not fair on either of them; this lover is free and hopeful. I am tied and safe. It's a tough situation for a relationship to be in. Do I want to become open about it, tell Adrian and get him to fight for me—to really feel that he's losing me? I don't know what I am doing other than following some instincts and seeing where they lead me. No matter what, I must make a contract with myself to not let it stand in the way of my writing. I can't stop thinking about that man and all the pleasure we gave each other; it was like making poetry with our bodies. I think we need to do some more composing together, I really do. I wonder if I can see him again before my birthday celebration. I could tell Adrian that I have another appointment—with the school for Dominic's career, perhaps. That would give me from about 8 p.m. to midnight. Four hours! I feel desperately greedy. I don't just want four hours. I want much more than that. I'm already calculating in weeks, months, years! I know this is another side effect of unblocking. My child is out and wants to play. It could be dangerous. The child could steal all my energy and put it to bad use. Okay, deliciously bad use! I haven't felt this strong an attraction to a man since I met Adrian twenty years ago; it's suffocating. And, what's more dangerous and tempting about it

is that he is unattached: free and easily accessible. Funny how life throws temptation in your path like that…'

Stranger from a Book
A day, a dream;
vision moving past
for remembering…
Red, burning desire
for you
receptive artist:
We
make poetry
-not a masterpiece-
with body words
in passionate harmony.
Our secret
Smooth pleasure
from my page
You came
I came, too.
We lived one night
Alive.

by Sabina Waldsmere

The End of the Beginning

On the morning of the party, Sabina is up early. She has had a restless night. Now, she can't sleep any more so she opens her notebook and writes:

March 25th 2000

> 'When I walked into the kitchen this morning, I was greeted with a warm welcome from outside; the horizon was ablaze with the same colours as the dress I will be wearing later today. The cocktail of colour streamed in through the window, painting the white tiles. This, I thought, was a good start to the day. It is the beginning of spring (officially now, according to the papers) and the trees at the end of the garden are starting to sprout tiny leaves. The trees loom up behind the house like wispy black ghosts in front of the sunrise. Every morning I come into the kitchen and look out at those trees, and then beyond them, to a small stream, fields and a smattering of houses that is our village. In summer, the view disappears when the full leaf cover is on them. I love having the trees there. Adrian has many times said that he would like to raise them to the ground so that nothing mars his view of the valley. He likes to see far, he complains, 'All the time!' That's where we differ, Adrian and I. I see the detail of the trees, their changing faces and moods; the wildlife they attract and their variety of charm according to the season. I love change. I love surprises.
>
> My heart tells me that I need a separation; I need to withdraw from him like an alcoholic needs to withdraw from alcohol. My dependency on him has been like an addiction. I have been drunk, behaving like someone I am not, doing things that I don't want to do and feeling guilty whenever I did things

> for myself. Now I want to kick this habit, and to do that I have to keep away from that which I am addicted to: Adrian.
>
> That is what my heart is saying. My head tells me: you must try, you can't be defeated, you must prove that a marriage can work despite the odds. Communication is the key. You can't throw away eighteen years of relationship! You'll regret it. You'll be taking a father away from his children. You are bad.... On and on the voice goes whilst my heart tells me the truth. The simple truth.
>
> Writing will sort it out. I have faith in that. I also know I can fall in love again.
>
> Last night Adrian found everything so complex; my new way of seeing things, my philosophy. He thought I was trying too hard to change and was driving myself mad. No, my heart said, he is wrong. I am not mad. I know the truth—the heart never lies. If I deny that fact, I die; love dies.'

Sabina has just closed the book when Adrian comes into the kitchen, yawning and rubbing his eyes.

"Oh, I wondered where you were?" he says in the middle of a yawn. "Can I join you?"

"Sure," she says and pulls obligingly at the chair next to her.

He comes over and shuffles his chair up close. She is unsure what to think of it.

"Happy Birthday, darling." he says, putting an arm around her shoulders and dropping a little velvet box into her lap. "For you on your 40th," he says.

Sabina is speechless. She has not been expecting to get so much as a birthday kiss from him.

"Aren't you going to open it?" he asks

Her fingers tremble as she lifts the lid. She is worried about how she will react. Will she burst into tears of joy or hate?

It's a magnificent ruby ring.

Tears well up and she runs to the downstairs loo.

Adrian runs after her.

He doesn't ask whether she loves him, because part of him has already decided that she doesn't. In a voice that is barely audible through the closed door, he simple says:

"Do you like me just a little bit?"

Sabina does not answer.

Preparations are in full swing for the party and Adrian has no time to run after Sabina any more. She has an appointment at the hairdressers anyway until five and then she is going to the hotel where Samantha is staying to get changed into her dress. Why women have to make such a fuss about the clothes they wear, he does not know. He is actually glad to have her from under his feet because he needs all the energy he can muster to carry this celebration through as he has planned and she has been draining him of much of it these past few days.

The band strikes up at eight on the dot and Adrian is over-the-moon with his precision planning. All guests are gathered and eagerly awaiting the grand entrance of the birthday girl. He has arranged it so that she can enter from a side door and walk onto the stage where the band is playing with musical accompaniment—'My Baby Just Cares For Me' by Nina Simone.

Sabina has decided to go along with it because she cannot think of an alternative at this stage and reckons that she may as well let him have the satisfaction of one small triumph on her birthday in view of the fact that she rejected his gift.

She glides through the door in her sunrise costume and the audience gasps in wonder. The band continues to the end of the piece and then leaves the microphone free for her. She thanks the guests for coming such long distances for her 40th, for all their presents and compliments. Then, she announces that she would like to thank a very special person and invites Ana onto the stage with her.

Ana bounds up, taking the steps three at a time. Breathlessly she gasps her thanks as well and says that it all wouldn't have been possible without another very special person and she invites him to join her on the stage.

Adrian comes rushing up and everyone applauds.

Sabina disappears un-noticed via the same side-door through which she had entered. As she walks out of the hall, down the main road and past the European school on the Church Hill plateau, she hears children's singing voices. The sound carries over to where she is walking and accompanies her all the way to her car, and beyond, as she descends the irregular sandstone steps into the Pétrusse Valley:

Doe a deer, a female deer. Ray, a drop of golden sun. Me, a name I call myself. Far, a long, long way to run. Sew, a needle pulling thread, La, a note to follow sew. Tea, a drink with jam and bread. That will bring you back to doe, doe, doe, doe…Doe, a deer, a female deer…

Ad Nauseum

THE END

Curtain Up

Sabina's office window has shutters. They're rolled up neat and tight around a metal pole inside a shutterbox. A cord is attached so that she can let them down, or pull them up. Outside, there is a gap between the window frame and the shutterbox which has made it possible for a pair of blue tits to get in and build a nest. For weeks, she has watched them come with moss, twigs and fur. Now they bring delicacies such as live caterpillars, flies and other bugs. She can't tell male and female apart; both carry food in. She also has no idea how many baby birds there are. There could be up to fourteen, according to her bird book.

She has been admiring the birds' teamwork and dedication to the task of feeding their babies. She has also wondered when the parents manage to feed themselves, or rest. She decides that they must do it in true bird style, 'on the wing'! It's not important for them right now. What's important is that the chicks receive nourishment and grow strong enough to leave the nest when the time comes.

When the shutters are up, light floods into her room and the birds can get into their nest through the gap. When the shutters are down, the room is dark and the gap is closed. Shutters up, the birds live, shutters down, they perish.

This morning, she let the shutters sit at half-mast, slats open, letting in rectangular-shaped light. The sun shines through the slits and dances on the desk, seducing her to write page after page of prose. She feels joyful and creative—a sun without ferocity—safe and warm. The pages are her chicks and, like the blue tits, she is feeding them with plenty of nourishing words. She wants them nice and fat so they grow strong enough to fly out into the world.

Then she hears a tapping noise at the window. All she sees is a blur of blue and yellow; one of the tits is bobbing up and down, flapping his little wings frantically at the windowpane. To her horror, she realises what is wrong: when the shutters are at half-mast, the gap is closed, just as it is when the shutters are fully down.

The parent birds cannot get in to feed the chicks and the chicks cannot leave the nest.

Writing with the shutters at half-mast means that she starts but does not finish. She goes far, but not far enough. She may feed her chicks but does not let them leave the nest and live independent lives. At the beginning, she is like the dedicated parent birds, but after a while, she closes the gap and bars the way for her writing to leave the nest. It cannot go out when the shutters are at half-mast; yet she finds it easiest to write in the tantalising dancing light it creates.

She realises that she has only let her writing experience the safe, warm, dancing light and not the full glory. For that to change, she must lift the shutters up and let the light dazzle and frazzle her. Only then will her chicks be free to flee their nest and go out into the world. The same is true of her marriage, she concludes, and writes the final paragraph of her fairy tale about the Kingdom of Luxusberg:

> *Pinderess finished sewing the unique suit for the man and he put it on before walking onto the stage in front of family and friends who had gathered to celebrate the day with him. Applause was to be heard all the way to the king's castle and he knew at once that yet another of his subjects had been cured of Luxusitis. He smiled with great joy and relief and knew that there was still hope that the kingdom of Luxusberg would be saved from its doom.*

Sabina opens the magazine for the English-speaking community in Luxembourg at the 'Books' section and reads the following review by her editor, Mr Toking:

> **Marrying it All**
> —by Sabina Waldsmere
>
> This first-time novelist has created a delightful and profound cocktail of fantasy and reality. What at first appears to be a clichéd story of a mid-life crisis, turns out to be a deep and wise tale of universal proportions. Set in the wealthy country of Luxembourg, it asks the question: what is the price tag attached to wealth; not just for the individual but for the whole of the Western world? In a country with banks, European Institutions and one of the highest suicide rates, the author paints a tragicomic picture of the place, showing where our wealth can lead us and how simple it may be to stop this process (if only we would choose to).
>
> You'll catch yourself laughing, crying, in a rage and jumping for joy as the story whisks you off on an emotional journey with its heroine and leaves you feeling heady and strange. You're not quite sure why, but you know some-

thing is about to change...you are standing on the threshold of your own spiritual journey!

I highly recommend you take a close look at this work.

It is now available in translation for the following languages: Danish, Dutch, Finnish, French, German, Greek, Luxembourgish, Portuguese, Spanish and Swedish.

About the Author

Born in Great Britain, Diana Button's career began in the world of translation and computing but changed course when she began writing. Writing is now an integral part of her life together with painting, teaching creativity and free-style jazz dance. She currently lives in Luxembourg with her husband and two children.

0-595-29156-2

Printed in the United Kingdom
by Lightning Source UK Ltd.
9735500001BA/70-204

9 780595 291564